Tomorrow's Hope

A Journey of Exploration and Hope

Three Ravens Publishing
Chickamauga GA USA

Table of Contents

Science Fiction: *Hard* or *Hardly?* A Conversation

By: Arlan Andrews, Sr.

I have a confession to make to you readers. Ye Editor (pbuh) asked me to write advice for budding authors of "hard science fiction" but I don't really know what that is, or how I earned a reputation for writing it. Maybe because my career as an engineer, working with rockets and nukes and computers and virtual reality and biotech and all meant that my fiction was *hard?* Maybe it was because I had written several dozen short stories and a few articles for *Analog Science Fiction and Fact Magazine*, which itself has the reputation of being home to hard science fiction?

Could be, but to me, I just write stories, hopefully entertaining ones, and I write the kind of stuff I like to read, which is mostly science fictional. It turned out that a lot of them have to do with *kinda*-believable futures and technologies, so I guess that makes them "hard". Again, *maybe.*

My own definition is this: *Hard* science fiction just means *believable.* No math equations need solving, no physicists need apply. And it means no really stupid stuff, like a writer I once met whose characters landed on a planet in winter. Apparently, the whole *planet* was in winter, with no explanation? Don't do that. Or another published novel where alien invaders arrived "in Earth's orbit". *Where* in that orbit? Close by or on the other side of the sun? Don't do that; it's not believable, it disrespects the reader and ruins the story. It can't be hard SF.

But be warned if you're expecting my stuff to include starships, interstellar wars, or robot sidekicks: my own fabulations are set closer to Earth and range from (hopefully!) humorous or thoughtful short stories about people interacting with new technologies, about alien encounters and invasions, Cherokee magic, avatar-based warfare, alternate Civil War history, zombies, vampires, New Age spiritualism, and much more. My full-length novels are tales about Native American spiritual phenomena and a lost civilization in New Mexico, nanotech warfare and a catastrophic nanophage epidemic, time travelers during a future Mexican civil war, and the adventures of little emu-riding warriors after the next Ice Age. Though I will never have a spot in the pantheon of immortal science fictioneers, one thing I *can* claim is that each of my stories is different from all others, unique unto itself. (Except for the current *Thaw Trilogy* from Baen Books, which are really just one long story spread over three e-books.)

In case you're wondering, I prefer science fiction that is unique, new, novel, thought-provoking—*different*. I'm hoping that you do, too, because I hope to read it.

What Do *You* Have to Do to Write Hard SF??

As far as writing hard science fiction, I'll say right here: I don't give advice, I only relate experiences. Some of them may be applicable or suggestive or even helpful. Some may be the opposite. Your life is different, and the mileage may vary. But to be a science fiction writer, at first you must *write*. A lot. If you work harder than I did and write a lot more, you will do better than I.

I *can* pass on the advice that Jerry Pournelle, one of the Masters of Hard Science Fiction (well, other than the takeoffs on Dante's *Inferno*), once told me: "If a person has at least average intelligence, a grasp of English language and grammar, that person can just sit down and write stream-of-consciousness thoughts, whatever comes to mind, page after page, and eventually that person will find their own voice and begin to produce real writing. It may take writing a million words, but that person *will* write."

Don't give up! It doesn't take everybody that long. I was able to sell speculative non-fiction articles almost continuously beginning at age 29, but publishing my scarce and casual science fiction output was harder. After about a dozen rejections over a ten year period, at age 39 I finally sold short pieces to *Omni, Analog,* and *Asimov's* in the same year. Over the decades since I have sold about 100 short stories in a few dozen places, plus another 100 speculative articles on technology and space, over 200 more on paranormal and UFO subjects, and another few hundred in various periodic columns, including politics, humor, and some flash fiction.

So, how do *you* write the hard stuff? Well, whatever your strange, unusual, or weird situation, setting, technology, or future is, make it seem only as believable as necessary. No more. No unnecessary technical details. You're not writing to educate the reader, you're telling a story. *Only* a story.

Write the fictional story you'd like to read, not a textbook. Base it on your own thoughts, your own life, your own dreams, your own nightmares, but make it *yours*, a child of your mind, an intimate eruption from *you*.

But be warned: writing's an addiction. If you do succumb to its temptations, at least try to make sure you get paid for it. (And *that* is another story altogether.)

How Do *You* Get Here?

I discovered at an early age that I liked adventures set in other times and places—*Treasure Island, Tarzan*, some Jules Verne, even Zane Grey and westerns. They all were grist for the mill of my mind. But eventually, comic books about space and monsters led to Heinlein's *Red Planet*, H.G. Wells's *War of the Worlds*, and then the (allegedly) hard SF to be had in *Astounding Science Fiction and Fact Magazine*, the original name of *Analog*. I found immediately that the kind of stories—and movies!—that I liked had to do with adventures in the future, with rockets and space, with alien creatures, and with how people in those stories lived with their different cultures and technologies—what those differences were, how they affected people for good or bad, and how people coped with those new and novel situations. Superheroes and fantasy were fun for a while, too, but *believability* was always key—I wanted to think that maybe I myself could be there, *do* those things. Rockets I might could do; dragons and spells, no way.

That love of science fiction and space travel led to my career choice in engineering. (I wanted to *be* the scientist played by Gene Barry in the first *War of the Worlds* movie.) Your own career will be different, your own experiences maybe wildly so, but those can influence your writing, *should* influence your stories, because only *you* were there, only *you* know the first-hand details. Science fiction can allow you safely to satirize the disappointments, memorialize the accomplishments, trash the fools and idiots, praise the good folks, and send the others to Hell—all in good fiction, of course, providing unique opportunities for your own stories.

What is *Believability* Then?

It's what sets science fiction apart from fantasy but has no definition beyond that. *Science fantasy* stories may blend the boundaries, authors may interleave realities as they wish, but few of us have difficulty distinguishing spaceships from selkies, aliens from apparitions, or dragons from dreadnoughts.

To me, *hard* science fiction too often means stories hard for me to read. When I see page after page of explanation of the physics of revolutionary starship drives or the complex mathematics of orbital calculations or detailed comparisons of the capabilities of exotic weapons, (or the cultivation of potatoes on Mars...), my eyes tend to glaze over, skipping ahead to the next action verb or the next bit of dialogue. Most often, casual references to devices or effects or events can portray an equal amount of background knowledge in only a few words. Check out your favorite authors and see how they do it. (Heinlein was the first and possibly the best at this: "The door dilated.")

Don't do the stupid things I mentioned earlier; at least try to make your settings, and hand-waving technologies and fantastic cosmic events *seem* real, your characters even more so. (Quite frankly, that is all up to you. I haven't a clue; I've always just made up whatever I needed for the story, or more often merely watched what the characters were doing and tried to describe it in text.) Again, read your favorite authors, your favorite stories, and try to get a feel for it. Just a feel; don't copy, be yourself.

Summarizing, I define *believability* to mean it might could actually happen; I might be able to see it or even *do* it. This is how I summarized my own feelings, in a filk song about Robert Heinlein that I wrote and published on the ancient *Usenet* the day he died in 1988:

Requiem; The Day That SF Died
Long, long time ago
I can still remember
How his stories used to make me dream
And I thought if I read enough
I could learn of Space and stuff
And bring about the future he'd foreseen...

And that is why I became an engineer.

Any Other Non-Advice on Writing Hard SF?

Again, this is only personal experience and preference, nothing universally applicable, but to me an early attraction of hard (believable) science fiction was *novelty*, escapism, things wondrous and new, different from the mundane cares and concerns of daily life. I loved stories that took me to new worlds, other civilizations, other times and places, where through the characters I experienced new beings and planets and cultures and challenges and even threats and dangers, sometimes even overcome or defeated, but always carrying on with skill, hope, and determination.

But in succeeding decades, I have noticed too many SF stories are simple riffs on the themes of two of the most successful media properties—*Star Trek* and *Star Wars*. Re-doing those great stories over and over again, but with new names, is very much doing the same as the old "space operas"—the re-telling of American Western tales set in Space instead of Dodge City, substituting blasters for six-shooters. Please don't do that. Be original.

If you're a new writer, would you *please* create new and inspiring tropes, astounding novelties, fantastic events, a whole new spectrum of types of aliens, future technologies, alternate universes, new cultures, different ways of seeing the Universe—and *not* inject current political or sociological conflicts into them, things that date your story and might turn off half your readers?

I want to find new delights in the unknown futures and unimaginable worlds that only science fiction can provide. I look forward to reading your stuff.

A Matter of Perspective

By Les Johnson

Last year, I participated in a writer's retreat near Palmer, Alaska and spent two weeks sequestered with three other writers in two bucolic cabins nestled among the magnificent snow-covered mountains that characterize that part of Alaska. It was a heady time of learning more about the craft of writing from authors I had just met, trading ideas with them, getting feedback on story ideas as we wrote, talking about writing, eating communal meals, and making new friendships. After the retreat ended, I had a full day to tour Anchorage before my scheduled flight for home. I, of course, stopped in an Anchorage bookstore and then the nearby Barnes and Noble.

For reasons I still don't completely understand, science fiction and fantasy books are usually grouped together in a bookstore. (What does a novel about our first interstellar voyage have to do with a parallel world inhabited by dwarfs and goblins? It makes about as much sense as bookstores grouping together westerns with romance novels, which I have never seen. But that's an aside.) In this Barnes and Noble, however, they placed science fiction and fantasy in distinctly separate sections and created a third section called, "dystopian." I was stunned. I knew dystopian fiction was popular, but an entire section of the bookstore devoted to the end of the world?

I should not have been surprised. The media these days is filled with doom and gloom. Social media companies have discovered that clicks lead to advertisement dollars; and thanks to human psychology, negative news almost always garners more clicks than positive news. This feedback loop creates a constant stream of negative stories being brought to our attention on Facebook, Instagram, Twitter, and other platforms. Worse, the doom and gloom stories are coupled with our known political dispositions, providing constant unconscious confirmation bias about how bad 'the other side' is, regardless of which side you are on.

If you see a story about the acceleration of climate change and click on it, then you will get more stories about how bad the climate crisis is becoming. If you see and read an article about a politician you voted against doing something reprehensible, then you will begin seeing a constant stream of articles showing how badly all the people on the other side are misbehaving. Worried about inflation? No problem, you will begin getting stories about how people in this or that city are missing car payments because they had to buy dinner for their kids. Not that these stories are not true (they may or may not be), but in a nation of 350 million people, just about anything is bound to be happening to someone, somewhere. In a world of more than seven billion people, there are too many sad stories to even count, and they will begin to get even more numerous in our tailored news sources.

There is concern about war in Europe, war with China, and war in the Middle East. We just got through the first major outbreak of a lethal, contagious disease in the lifetimes of most people alive today, and there is already talk of the next one. Cities are burned after a seemingly endless series of police incidents. It seems like there is a mass shooting every week, and no one has a clue what to do to stop them.

Polling reflects our overall cultural negativity. In the late 1990s, polls showed that 71% of Americans believed their children would have a better standard of living than themselves. Today, the number who believe that is down to 42% [1]. A recent Harvard University poll found that two-thirds of young people, those aged 18 – 29, have little or no hope for the future of democracy in America [2].

The effects of this negative view of the future are real. Suicides are up. Couples are deciding to not have children for fear of the terrible future world their offspring might inherit. If this were the only news I saw and I didn't have a historical context into which this news could be considered, then I would also be in a state of total depression!

Young adults (primarily) are deluged with negative news, and thanks to the poor quality of history education in schools, they don't have sufficient perspective to interpret it. The Covid pandemic is a good example. I often hear young people say that the Covid pandemic was/is "unprecedented." Do they not know that smallpox killed over 500 million people in the 20th century alone before it was made extinct with a universal vaccine? Or that polio killed or paralyzed over half a million people each year for much of the 1930s, 40s, and 50s until a vaccine was developed? And then, of course, there was the infamous Spanish Flu pandemic of 1918, which killed about 50 million people worldwide. Covid was bad but hardly unprecedented.

My perspective on the current world situation is informed by my background. My parents were born before the Great Depression and experienced their teenage years amidst the worst economic crisis the USA and the world have ever seen. They witnessed the rise of the national socialism (Nazism) in Germany, communism in Russia and China, and militarism in Japan, leading to World War II. My mother recounted a childhood with hungry people knocking on their kitchen door asking for food; of not being able to go swimming for fear of catching polio; of her parents worrying every time she got sick, fearing a resurgence of the Spanish Flu that killed millions in the three years before her birth; and of her brother dying of Type 1 diabetes because her town in Eastern Kentucky did not yet have access to the recently discovered insulin needed to keep diabetic patients alive. My father enlisted in the Army like most other young men at the time, and he went on to fight in North Africa and Italy. Together, my parents then lived through the Cold War with the constant fear of tens of thousands of nuclear bombs falling on their heads. I was born just before the Cuban Missile crisis, and they wondered if I would live to see my second birthday.

As a youth, I watched America's defeat in Vietnam, race riots in major US cities, prolonged inflation coupled with low economic growth, and the sad state of crime and violence that at that time plagued nearly every major American city. (The portrayal by Charles Bronson in the movie, *Death Wish* was not far from the truth)

Yet I and many in my generation did not give up and fear the future. We did not decide to remain childless. We moved forward with the expectation that tomorrow would be another day. But then again, we didn't devour books that nurtured our fears about tomorrow and the day after. Instead, we looked at what our parents accomplished and dreamed of a better world. In the history books, I read about how the USA went from being in the Great Depression to being an industrial powerhouse that served as the 'arsenal of democracy' in the fight against political tyranny. I watched the legacy of Dr. Martin Luther King transform race relations with his admonition that we should "judge people by the quality of their character and not the color of their skin." I saw how we could use medical science to make smallpox extinct and polio nearly so. I watched with amazement as we developed computers and built machines that took people to the moon. I cheered when the Berlin Wall unexpectedly came down, the USSR collapsed, and the Cold War ended.

Consider these little-known facts:

Globally, the rates of extreme poverty have dropped faster than ever before over the last two decades — from 29.5% of the world's population in 1997 to just 9.1% in 2017 (Figure 1).

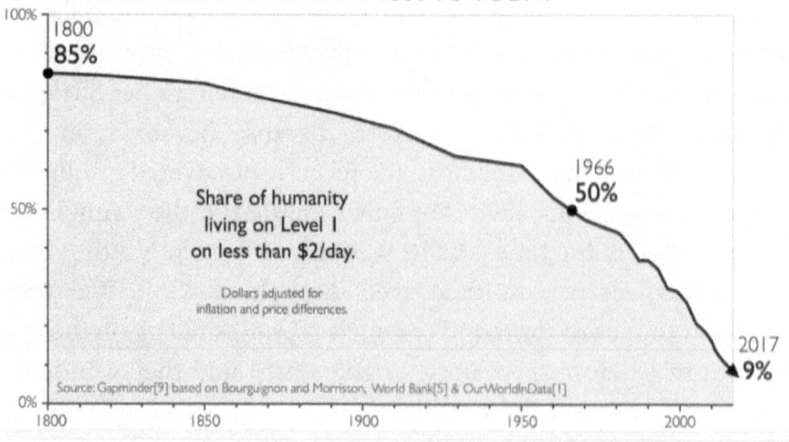

Figure 1. Image courtesy of Gapminder (https://www.gapminder.org/about/)

Life expectancies have risen every year until Covid, and most experts believe they will continue to rise as the pandemic subsides (Figure 2).

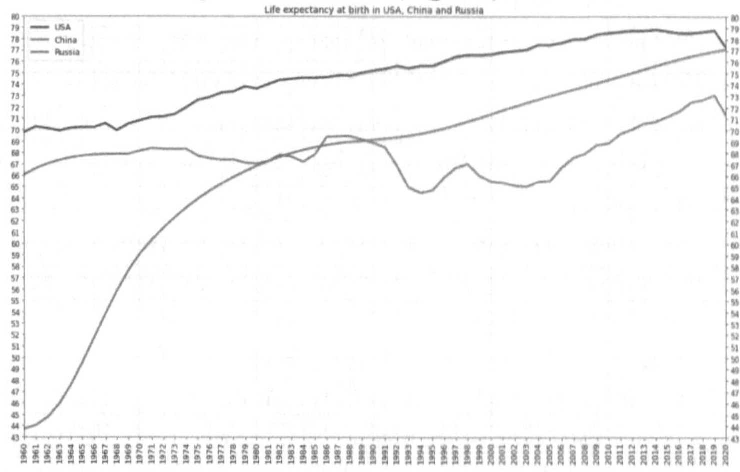

Figure 2. Image courtesy of Lady3mlnm (This file is made available under the Creative Commons CC0 1.0 Universal Public Domain Dedication)

Readers and authors take note: Worldwide, literacy has continued to increase and now exceeds 85% of the population (Figure 3).

Source: Our World in Data based on OECD and UNESCO (2016)   OurWorldInData.org/literacy • CC BY

You get the idea. The evidence is overwhelming: quality and quantity of life is increasing worldwide. We should be rejoicing and shouting this news from the rooftops.

It is true that we face many challenges today. Yes, climate change is real, and we are not doing enough to prevent it from getting worse. But I categorically reject the prevailing view that in order to save the planet we need to live in a world of zero growth, diminished standards of living, little or no travel, and, more generally, in a world of low expectations "for the good of the planet." Yes, we should become better stewards of the Earth by consuming less, recycling more, and transitioning to more renewable energy sources as they become economically viable. But we should also embrace developing fusion power systems and beaming clean electrical energy to the Earth from space, particularly in areas of the planet not already well-served by a reliable power infrastructure. Yes, we should consider the impact on the environment when we make personal, corporate, and governmental decisions, but we should also consider ways to improve the standard of living for everyone by mining asteroids for rare earth metals instead of strip-mining the planet and by embracing human creativity, ingenuity, and personal freedom instead of restricting it 'for the good of all.'

All this leads me back to the role of science fiction in shaping the future we all want to see: a prosperous and verdant future free from want, government tyranny, and war for all of Earth's citizens. Good science fiction involves heroes and heroines overcoming seemingly insurmountable obstacles to solve some problem or perform some quest, and they accomplish their goals in a way that entertains the reader and leaves them with a sense of optimism and hope. *Star Trek*, the original series, did not become a success by postulating a dystopian future. Instead, Gene Roddenberry set its story in a future where many of the problems we face today have been successfully overcome, with diverse peoples working together to better understand our universe and promote the ideals of freedom. Many fans of the show went on to study math, science, and engineering. Some were motivated to come to NASA or work in the space industry to help enable that *Star Trek* future. Others had the same goal but instead went into medicine (so they could build a tricorder to diagnose diseases), communications (Siri and Alexa owe their existence to the Enterprise's female computer), politics (to create Starfleet Academy in an organization known as the International Space University), etc. They saw the problems of their world, a fictional and inspiring future in which those problems had been solved and then decided to work on ways to make that future their future. I am one of them.

At age 7, I watched Neil Armstrong walk on the Moon and then began reading everything science fiction I could find in my school library and the local bookstore. When I was 12, I decided I wanted to become a physicist and work for NASA. I had no idea what a physicist was, only that they did 'science' and that NASA hired them. I attended Transylvania University as an undergraduate and graduate student at Vanderbilt University where I studied, you guessed it, physics. Upon completing my degree, I applied for a job at NASA and was not selected. However, I kept trying and three years later I landed my dream job at NASA's Marshall Space Flight Center where I still work today. I've been reading science fiction all the while. In the early 2000's, I raised my hand in a meeting to volunteer for a temporary assignment, which led me toward managing NASA's Interstellar Propulsion Technology Project, which then transitioned me into being one of NASA's experts in solar and laser sails — a technology that will one day allow us to send spacecraft to another star. I am now leading two interplanetary solar sail projects: Near-Earth Asteroid Scout, which launched into space in November 2022, and Solar Cruiser, which will fly in 2028. In addition to flying missions that will pave the way to the stars, I am writing books that I hope will inspire the next generation of space scientists, engineers, and creative thinkers who will carry on after I am gone.

And I am not alone. Many of my NASA colleagues were similarly inspired by *Star Trek*, *Star Wars*, the written works of Arthur C. Clark, Robert Heinlein, Isaac Asimov, and more. Others went on to make fortunes in the business world and then returned to their first love by founding companies like SpaceX, Blue Origin, Virgin Galactic, and others.

Negative news gets clicks, but it doesn't inspire or contribute to solving problems.

Being depressed about possible dystopian futures doesn't stop those futures from happening, but rolling up your sleeves and getting involved just might. Friends don't let friends read dystopian literature!

Tomorrow can be better than today, and it is pretty much up to us writers and readers of science fiction to posit positive futures and inspire the next generation to help make them a reality.

REFERENCES

[1]   https://news.gallup.com/poll/403760/americans-less-optimistic-next-generation-future.aspx)

[2]   https://iop.harvard.edu/about/newsletter-press-release/nearly-two-thirds-young-americans-fearful-about-future-democracy

Editor's Note

By Bart Kemper

Engineering is about problem solving. Science is about discovery. Traditionally, hard science fiction has been about one or both, with a "what if we make this one change to reality" and the hypothesized human (usually) response to the "what if." It seems like a simple formula. Like many things, it is simple in concept, but the real world is messy. In general, today's science fiction incorporates some degree of that mess.

Les Johnson makes excellent points about how well humanity has improved, but despite this a deluge of negativity forms many people's opinion. He cites how the COVID-19 pandemic was repeatedly called "unprecedented," yet even a quick internet search shows how smallpox, polio, and Spanish Flu killed far more. Les also points to measures of quality of life and how objectively humanity is living longer and better.

Arlan Andrews goes to the heart of science fiction to give a first-rate coaching session. He was born in 1940 and has seen science fiction grow from an obscure literary niche (perhaps the kindest way to express how it was seen) to a juggernaut driving much of the best-selling media across all platforms. He distills all of this into how your writing career will be different than anyone else's because you should draw from your own life to create good, original fiction.

In broad strokes, I share a similar professional background with our two essayists. My primary occupation is engineering but like my parents, I joined the military. Over the course of three and half decades, Active and Reserve, enlisted and officer, I saw how horrible things can get on a large scale. I've seen the infrastructure failure after Hurricane Katrina breached the levees. I saw how authoritarian regimes used the promise of basic water, power, and sanitation as a carrot and the consequences of decades of withholding those services. I've also worked with teams who learn from these situations and develop solutions, such as the changes to procedures that created the improved response during 2008's Hurricane Gustav, where a 100% evacuation happened in a timely, safe manner.

After I earned board-certification as a forensic engineer, the work brought the misery down to individuals and families. It can be a worker burned from an explosion or a grieving family fighting a corporation is trying to cover their driver's tracks and avoid liability. It makes it easy to assume the worst of organizations because these are when the system fails. On the other hand, working as a consulting engineer and doing the training to go into facilities, putting on the protective equipment, and having the safety representative stay on top of us reminds me of how many injuries are prevented by following the systems and continuously improving them.

In popular depictions, home computers, smart phones, and the internet are tools we had hoped would save labor, connect us, and provide information to uplift is popularly portrayed as ways to sabotage infrastructure, isolate ourselves, and steal money and even identities. All of the positive aspects of those tools exist, but it's not what many people choose to see. You have to look for the benign use of technology, all in the background where it works like it supposed to, to realize how much people simply expects everything to work for them.

Misery sells, unfortunately. It's easier to focus on how someone or something is "the worst ever." Not only has marketing cashed in on this, our political and social leaders appear to have a vested interest in wiping out all progress by society to sell "it has never been this bad." Social media is often used to magnify every sensational, horrible thing as if it is happening right next door, which is made worse by many not knowing their next-door neighbors.

An example of this is the drama surrounding the *Titan* submersible from OceanGate and their expedition to *Titanic*. This was an experimental craft in nonmilitary submersibles, an industry few had heard of, involving people even fewer had heard of, in what turned into being the first loss of a nonmilitary submarine in decades despite the steady increase in the number of submersibles in use. The people running the operations were intentionally avoiding rules and regulations in terms of design, testing, and operations.

The *Titan* submersible captivated the news cycle for several weeks, displacing the shipwreck of the *Adriana*, a fishing boat carrying 750 people where over 600 died, making it the worst shipwreck in years. While the Titan was a one-off experimental submarine, the issues with the *Adriana* were the ongoing migrant crisis where the same overloading of boats and ships is likely, theoretically making it a bigger story. That's not the way it worked out.

Contrast the *Titan* coverage to that of the submersible *Limiting Factor* from Triton Submarines. It is rated for 11,00 meters (36,000 feet) of salt water depth. The Five Deeps Expedition began in early 2018 to dive to the deepest points of all five of the world's oceans, mapping the vicinity and collecting scientific samples. The expedition finished in August of 2019, making unprecedented hadal-depth dives on a repeated basis. Everything worked. This was an unprecedented engineering feat and heralded a new era in exploring our oceans. Even with the climate change hook, it didn't sell because our society takes it for granted that something will work.

The hard reality is there were ten non-military submersibles besides the *Titan* that could dive to the 3,800 meters (12,500 feet) depth of the *Titanic* without incident. The *Limiting Factor* is still in use and performing critical hadal-depth science. The main technical difference between the *Titan* and hundreds of non-military submersibles around the world that can dive hundreds of meters or more, well beyond SCUBA recovery, is that the *Titan* is the only one that avoided engineering design codes and third party oversight.

In terms of coverage, though, it was simply "the other boats worked." No matter how remarkable the engineering, no matter how fascinating the science, the media appears to take these things for granted and doesn't want to feature finding solutions (the *Limiting Factor*) or addressing problems (the *Adriana*) when a spectacle is available. Even when I tried to steer the media coverage as one of the subject matter experts being interviewed, there was little interest in "things that go right".

Tomorrow's Hope is about finding solutions. My love of science fiction and writing goes back to my childhood. My father came up reading Doc Smith, Asimov, Bradbury, and Heinlein. He left his *Analogs* and *Asimov* magazines where I could read them and made it clear I could borrow anything as long as it was not in his current "read stack." We watched *Star Trek* together. He took me to my first science fiction conventions.

Les writes about *Star Trek* inspiring others to study math, sciences, and other subjects to improve the world. "They saw the problems of their world, a fictional and inspiring future in which those problems had been solved and then decided to work on ways to make that future their future." Like Les, I am one of those people. There is more than just how to survive with a problem. I believe that solutions can be developed.

I have enjoyed working on this anthology. It shows the spirit of using science to inspire stories is alive and well. I'm looking forward to seeing more from all of the authors. As Arlan tells us, "I want to find new delights in the unknown futures and unimaginable worlds that only science fiction can provide. I look forward to reading your stuff." Here is what our authors from around the world have gifted to us:

A Can of Worms by Sarina Dorie has a space-punk musician facing an alien invasion of seemingly unstoppable massive worm-like beings that had already devastated Earth.

Mallory Cooper's *Europa's Javelin* puts the captain of a wildcatting asteroid mining ship at odds with corporate machinations and the hazards of being the first to drill Jupiter's moon Europa.

We go to Venus with Benjamin Tyler Smith's *Heavy Air*, where three women astronaut/scientists find their exploration mission jeopardized by Venusian hellish atmosphere of acid rains and lightning strikes. We then get a partially terraformed Venus with *The Hyper Vaulter*, by Michael Anthony Dioguardi, where the hostile atmosphere is still the antagonist, only now it's about settlers on the planet surface.

Messenger of Emptiness by Gustavo Bondoni has a young system explorer confronting a massive cryogenic ship entering the system with its power failing, putting the sleepers on a countdown to dying just as they reached their destination after hundreds of years asleep.

Shields by Charli Cox gives us a retro-feel with a young trainee pilot uncovering a secret enemy that threatens their entire society.

A maintenance robot takes on a blue-collar role with four disembodied AIs, modeled on four of the smartest people on Earth, sent on a first contact mission in *The Oracle at Tau Ceti* by Jetse de Vries.

My esteemed co-editor William Joseph Roberts shows us a different kind of hope in Orbital Odds, showing wisdom comes in different forms and lessons.

Finally, I've added *Bobtail Anni*, a story about a Gordian knot of corporate and government interests on Earth strangling developing commerce and expansion on the moon, and how it caused a disaster that threatens Lunar autonomy with just one person who is at the wrong place at the wrong time to do the right thing.

Humanity has a way of finding solutions. Often solutions for one problem leads to new problems down the road, or the initial solution did not take us as far toward the goal as we later want. People can choose to look at the world, sip a complicated soy-coffee-sweetener concoction, and proclaim it all to be "simply the worst" before turning their back and resume doom-scrolling on their phones. This anthology is dedicated to those who envision how we will look at the problem, roll up our sleeves, and do what we can to make tomorrow a better place.

Orbital Odds

By William Joseph Roberts

"Yeah, you're almost there. Just over to your left a bit more, Ray." Henry directed the other maintenance technician as he drifted along the outside of the observation deck of training station Nobel. He peered away into the far distance. Heavy lift space elevator station Walker orbited high above the Brazilian rainforest. A sudden plume of flame and smoke erupted far below, surrounded by the visible exhaust streaks of four aircraft. "Hu. Looks like someone got too close to the elevator again. When the hell will those idiot protesters just give up?" Henry said more to himself than to Ray. "It's not like they are going to stop it from happening."

"Who knows. Damned bleeding hearts. It's not like there's any life out there for us to destroy. Jupiter and its moons are just resources to use. Hey, I can't see the spot. There's too much glare from out here. Which way do I need to go?"

"Oh, sorry," Henry replied. "Down about six inches from where your left hand is. You're right on it. Do you feel the divot? It looks pretty damned deep from in here."

"Yeah, I feel it, but just barely. It would be nice if the pane wasn't mirrored on this side. then you could just point at it for me."

Henry scoffed. "Are you kidding? That would be too easy then. Do you really think that the eggheads who dreamed up this station thought about routine maintenance?"

"Probably not," Ray replied.

"Maintenance to training bay gamma. Maintenance to training bay gamma," a voice announced over the station's intercoms.

"Dammit," Henry growled.

"Ha, sucks to be you," Ray laughed. He positioned a suction cup type apparatus over the divot in the massive viewport.

"Who was in gamma today?"

"Um…," Ray thought. "I think the newest class. The ones that arrived just last week. They should be working on their basic zero-G movement techniques.

"Well, that's just great. They probably puked all over the place then." Henry tapped on the viewport. "Right there Ray, that looks perfectly centered from this side.

Ray pressed the device against the glass and squeezed the trigger.

"I swear to God, the worst part of this job is cleaning up after these young pups. Hell, I bet half of them were sucking on their mamma's tits just before they boarded the shuttle to fly up here.

"You're probably right. They are so green, the zero-G ain't got nothing to do with it."

"Yup," Henry laughed. "You good Ray?"

"Yeah Henry. I got this. You go on and have fun cleaning up puke."

"God, I hope that's all it is." Henry pushed away from the massive viewport and floated backward toward the rear wall of the observation compartment. "Ya know, if the Independent Alliance had any real sense about them, they would seal the training areas completely. That way nothing could get into the cracks and crevices of the station and screw with the systems."

"We could only be so lucky," Ray huffed. "Hey, does this look alright from in there?"

Henry turned as he reached the rear wall. "Yeah, that looks good. If they ain't careful this viewport is going to blow out the next time a bolt or rock decides to come crashing into it. They need to just replace the damn thing."

"Are you kidding? This thing will be all laminate patch before they replace it," Ray groused. "They are sinking every penny they got into the expansion program. I heard that they are supposed to start terraforming Mars and then pushing to the outer planets to establish a beachhead for operations.

"At this point, why even bother? They'll just ruin those places like they did the earth. Henry shook his head in disgust. "I tell you what. You dream way too much, you old coot."

"I may be an old coot, but at least I'm not the one going to clean up puke."

"Bite me, Ray," Henry said, then opened the hatchway and floated through.

"You're too tough and grisly ya old grump ass. And besides, you might like it." Ray chuckled over the radio.

"Yup," Henry proudly replied, then closed the hatch. He pushed off and floated down the corridor, greeting another crewman in passing.

"Hey Henry," a voice shouted from a side corridor as Henry floated along the main thoroughfare of the training station. He quickly caught a handhold along the wall and stopped his forward momentum, swinging from the point then landing flat against the wall with a soft, padded thud. Crewman Randel Drake, a small hobbit of a man, floated freely into the main corridor from the side junction.

"We got a pool going on the next crew of cadets. You want in?"

Henry furrowed his brows in thought. "Well, that depends. How long do I have?"

"We'll close out bidding in the next hour or so."

Henry's brow knitted with thought. "Who's at the top of the leaderboard right now?"

"At the moment, the odds are against Cadet Hanson with McKool in a close second. Both of them seem to be shaky and have a fair amount of anxiety issues according to their records.

Henry squinted, assessing the young soldier. "You do realize that looking at another crewman's records is illegal, don't you?" Before Drake could answer, Henry continued. "What odds are you offering?"

"Two to one for Hanson, five to one for McKool."

Henry thought for a moment. "Well, who's the least likely to quit?"

"Wainwright," Drake instantly replied. "He's the typical egotistical alpha jock that thinks he is the answer to any of the world's problems."

Wainwright," Henry whispered under his breath as he gazed off into blind thought. "I don't recall the cadet's face.

"Oh, you'd know him right away if you'd met him. Dark black hair, six foot six, square-jawed and freaking massive. He looks like he was a comic book superhero that fell out of the pages or something."

"What kind of odds are you giving on him?

Drake looked up at Henry with a skeptical glance. "I'll give ya fifty to one," he replied.

"Pshh, that's it? Fifty to one for a long shot like this? You're the one that said he looked like a superhero."

Drake squinted, suspicious of Henry. "What are you planning to do?"

"What makes you think that I'm going to do anything? It isn't like I have some magical ace up my sleeve or anything." Henry pulled up the sleeves on his coveralls as a friendly gesture. "You'll have to give me a better spread than that for me to put my hard-earned cash down. And you know I ain't going to go half-assed into it. I might even bet a month's pay if it's worth my time."

"Fine," Drake sighed. "Sixty to one."

"Nope, not good enough," Henry scoffed as he turned to leave. "You know that I like the stupid long-shot bets."

"And the last time that I gave you crazy odds, you put me into some serious debt after you rigged the outcome."

"What? How do you figure that? Is it my fault that the kid was too cocky for his own good? I just helped him to see the error of his ways is all that was."

"By making him have a full mental breakdown and nearly floating himself? That just isn't right, Henry. And besides, you made a killing off of that one."

"Now how is any of that my fault? Here," Henry paused. He reached into his pocket for a personal datapad and pulled up his bank account balance. "You see right here? Do you see what that says?"

"Yeah. Oh wow…"

"Yeah, exactly. Wow," Henry sarcastically grunted. "It's not like I don't have the money to play with. I'll put down one thousand credits on Hanson, and one thousand on McKool. Then I want you to put me down for five thousand on Wainwright." Henry jabbed an aged, boney finger at Drake, "but I want eighty to one odds that your superhero boyfriend quits on his own accord."

"You have to be insane to think I'd give you those kind of odds."

"Oh, so my money isn't good enough for you? Alrighty then. Hey man, that's your loss." Henry tucked away his datapad and pushed away down the corridor.

"Hold on. Wait! Um…Fine…" Drake's eyes darted back and forth with internal thought. "Eighty to one, but he has to quit the program cold, no medical hold or anything in the next twenty-four hours."

Henry grabbed another handhold to stop his momentum. He hung there, in weightless thought for a long moment. "Alright, I'll take it." He kicked off and floated back over toward Drake, his hand extended to shake, impacting with the hobbit of a man as their hands locked in agreement. "Deal," Henry said with a happy intonation.

Drake reluctantly shook. "I have one question, Henry. If you're a millionaire, then why the hell are you still up here working?"

"Are you kidding? What the hell else am I supposed to do? I do it because I like the work and it keeps me busy. Besides the fact that my asthma is so much better up here than down there. You know the part per million count of pollution in the air on most of the planet is worse than working your whole life in a coal mine? Anyways, I've got to git." He pushed away from the small crewman.

"Oh, I heard the call over the intercoms. Who's in bay G?"

"The newest group of Cadets fresh off of the shuttle."

"Hopefully it isn't as bad as the last class. One blegh that begets another blegh that begets another blegh," he laughed.

"Oh, so you think that was funny? Laugh it up, Chuckles." Henry scowled toward Drake. "It sure as hell isn't funny to the guy that's gotta clean it all up.

"You just remember to have fun and enjoy your job. I'll come by to see ya tomorrow and collect on that bet.

"Uh huh. I ain't scared none. My luck ain't never let me down." Henry grabbed a handhold and propelled himself forward. He soared effortlessly down the main corridor of the station. His fingers grazed the walls gradually to make slight corrections to his course. He soared, nose first through the weightless nothing. "And here comes my exit," he muttered to himself, twisting to reposition himself so that his chest faced the wall on the side of the turn. "Three...two...one..." He grasped the handle that protruded from the corner of the intersection and used it as the pivot point to redirect his momentum ninety degrees down the side corridor. He pushed outward on the far wall and corrected his direction. Wisps of thin, white hair on the top of his head skimmed the wall. He twisted his potbellied, eighty-year-old frame in mid-flight and tapped the wall to rotate himself in the corridor. He tucked his knees and tumbled backward as he soared forward, adjusting his tumble with taps along the wall to aim himself feet first at the oncoming hatchway that was designated as training room G by the large military-style G stenciled on the door. Henry braced himself for touchdown on the hatchway, knees bent and ready to cushion the impact just as the hatchway opened, revealing a tall, broad-shouldered sergeant.

"Make way," Henry yelled. His hands shot out, grasping for any handhold along the corridor walls to either side and scratched along for purchase.

The red-headed sergeant quickly pushed off from the hatchway frame and out of Henry's path, tucking himself along the curved surface of the corridor wall. "What the crap, Henry. One of these days you and your superhero landings are going to get someone hurt!"

"Ha! Not if I can help it. I'm pretty damn sure that this is going to hurt, but watch this," Henry laughed. He stretched, spread eagle in the corridor, unable to grasp any surface. He continued toward the opening and caught the frame of the hatchway. His limbs flexed and overextended awkwardly as his body's pear-shaped bulk continued forward with the momentum of his flight. He groaned from the strain as his limbs eased, then relaxed. The energy of his movement nullified, Henry gently floated backward away from the hatchway. He moved and stretched out the kinks. Rubbing at his left shoulder, he spun around to look at the Sergeant.

"You just aren't right in the head, you know that don't you?" The sergeant shook his head.

"Sergeant Hooker," Henry gruffly demanded. "Does it look like I give a good God damn about what you think?"

"I know that you don't, and that's the scary part." He laughed.

"Well good then," Henry nodded with a smile. "At least we're both on the same page about it. So what did these wanna be space Marines do that y'all had to call for me? Don't you know that I've got important stuff to be doing? I'm not about to start babysitting or changing diapers for y'all. That's what fellers like you signed up for." Henry jabbed a boney finger into Sergeant Hookers' shoulder. "Not me."

"I know, Henry, I know," Hooker defended, then sighed. "It's really bad this time, Henry. And I don't just mean a little upchuck. I mean epic level bad. Honestly, I'm not sure what to do in this particular situation, and I would really rather not go in there any farther than I have too."

Henry glanced away from the sergeant, back toward the open hatchway. "Why the hell is it so quiet in there? Did they kill each other and it's some sort of scene from a bloody slasher film or something?"

Sergeant Hooker set his jaw and firmly replied. "I ordered them to shut up and stay calm. I honestly didn't know what else to do," he reluctantly admitted. "I just don't know how much longer that will last before they give up and utter chaos erupts," he admittedly whispered. A disgusted look painted his face a sickly shade of pale green.

"Oookay." Henry gently pushed off from the wall, away from Sergeant Hooker and back toward the open hatchway. Catching himself on the frame, he cautiously peeked into the compartment. Padded gray panels lined most of the compartment's surfaces. Barrier sections floated aimlessly in the middle of the room. To one side of the compartment, just out of reach from any surface was the newest class of cadets. They floated as a huddled mass, in amicable zero-G disgust among yellowish puddles and globules of partially digested alliance rations. "Oh hell," Henry gasped as he looked back to Hooker.

"Yeah. My thoughts exactly," Hooker replied as he floated to Henry's side. "Do you have any suggestions?"

Henry turned back to the nightmarish scene in the training bay. "Are all of y'all still alive?" Quietly mumbled, yes sirs found his ears in reply. "Is anyone of you in immediate danger," Henry shouted at the group of trainees.

"What the hell do you think old man? Are you going to stand around asking stupid questions all day or are you going to help us out of this," a deep baritone voice demanded from the mass of unmoving bodies. "How about you quit screwing around with stupid questions and do something about this before I report you for dereliction of duty and insubordination."

Henry looked back to Sergeant Hooker, chuckling. "Who the hell does this little ass wipe think he is?"

Sergeant Hooker restrained his own laughter. "If I'm not mistaken, that would be Cadet Ian Graham Wainwright. He has annoyingly reminded us daily that his father is a senator and a major investor and supporter of our efforts here, after the lunar riots."

"Oh, so what you're saying is that he thinks his shit don't stink. Is that what you're trying to politely tell me?"

Hooker suppressed a laugh, "Yeah pretty much, Henry. That about sums him up."

"Well then cut the bullshit and just tell me things like that already. It saves time and keeps me from wanting to shove a boot up your ass."

"Hey gramps, aren't you forgetting something," the male voice shouted from among the clump of students.

"Hold your horses, pretty boy," Henry shouted over his shoulder, then turned back to Hooker. "If you can keep them calm for about twenty minutes, then I can get the vacuum hoses down here. We can peel them away one by one and suck up any of that mess as we do." Henry leaned down in Hooker's direction. "Who the hell let the nervous piddler on the station? Didn't the higher-ups learn their lesson the last freaking time?"

"Hey Methuselah," the young baritone voice shouted.

Henry glanced back up at the mass of cadets. "What in the hell do you want?"

"How about you get your ancient ass in gear and do something instead of standing there, using up oxygen."

"Are you done yet? There ain't nothing going to happen if you keep up the whining like you're doing," Henry shouted back. "Pampered little bastard," he mumbled so only he and Hooker could hear.

"I have the power to make your life a living hell if you don't do what you're told, old man. See, this is why they should have never made it illegal to beat the hired help," Wainwright chided. Nervous scoffs and light chuckles escaped from others among the putrid mass.

"Oh now, really," Henry chuckled with surprise. His face twisted in heavy contemplation.

"I know that look, Henry. What are you getting ready to do," Hooker asked.

"Something," he said, smiling at Hooker. "You just be patient and wait for it."

"This can't be good," Hooker snickered.

Henry pulled a personal communicator from his pocket, flipped it open and held it at arm's length as he thumbed through a menu. "There you are," he mumbled, then pressed a button and held the communicator to his ear. "Hey, Drake. What kind of bonus would you offer me for say...if that Wainwright kid shits himself in the process of quitting?"

Henry nodded as he listened to the crewman on the other end of the call.

"I am personally offended by that sort of attack, Drake. I didn't say that I was going to do anything. It's just a random curiosity question." He nodded and picked at some flaking paint on the hatchway frame.

"No, you won't regret this. It's a sure thing, trust me. I'll even add ten thousand credits to my bet. You know you can just taste the money, Drake." He listened intently, one finger in his other ear as he floated in the open hatchway. "Alright. A double rider if he shits himself in the process of quitting. I'll take it. I'll talk to you later." Henry hung up the phone and tucked it away.

"Hey smart ass," Henry shouted in the direction of the class. "Don't you think a little gratitude or at least a please would be in order? You have had ample opportunity since I've been here, trying to help y'all." Henry moved into the compartment and drifted along the inside wall to a series of maintenance panels near the hatchway.

"What are you about to do, Henry?" A concerned look washed over Sergeant Hooker's face.

"Don't you worry none about that. But I would be either in or out, take your pick right now. You don't want to be floating there when I close the hatchway."

"What the hell does that have to do with you keeping your job, old man," Wainwright retorted.

Henry scowled back toward the spoiled voice, then opened the first maintenance panel and removed three relays from their slots. He tucked the relays inside the panel, closed it securely and moved to the second panel. There, he pulled a series of circuit breakers and a number of relays from their slots.

"What are you about to do, Henry?"

"Just watch and learn," Henry replied. He wrapped his feet into the anchor straps attached to the wall. "You might want to hold onto something," he suggested with a nod of his chin to the straps on the wall. Unsure, Hooker did as he was told and watched the ancient mechanic work his magic. "One good thing about helping to put this station together all of those years ago is that I've managed to learn how to manipulate every system and every function of this space station." With practiced ease, Henry pulled a length of wire from his pocket, twisted the bare copper ends and inserted one end into a relay slot.

"Hey asshole," Henry shouted back. "How long can you hold your breath?" He touched the other end of the bare wire to the main buss bar of the panel. Dull amber emergency lights flashed as a warning klaxon screamed. The hatchway door slammed shut and a robotic voice bellowed through the room's speakers. "Decompression warning. Unauthorized override of airlock safety protocols. Evacuate compartment immediately."

The class of cadets screamed as one with cries of horrific panic. Pressure latches clanged and released. A high pitched whistle overshadowed the rumbling roar of the klaxon alarm. The outer airlock doors opened a crack, then stopped suddenly. The compartment erupted in a blast of mist and rushing air from the sudden explosive decompression. Henry's ears painfully popped from the pressure change. The barriers that hovered in the middle of the compartment were instantly sucked toward the outer airlock. They impacted the heavy metal doors with a metallic twunk that shook the air. Screaming cadets bobbed and undulated toward the airlock en masse and collapsed upon contact. They sprawled across the barriers and airlock door, each of the cadets screaming or crying for help. Some could be heard over the roar of the atmosphere escaping the compartment, begging Wainwright to apologize.

"What are you doing? Are you insane," Hooker shouted at Henry.

"Naw, sir. I'm teaching these punks a little life lesson. Just hang on and watch." Henry smiled wide.

"Warning," the computerized voice announced. "Full decompression imminent. All personnel, please evacuate the compartment to a secure location."

"You're going to kill us all, Henry!"

"Do you really think that I'm suicidal," Henry shouted over the sound of the wind then let out a full bellowing gut laugh. He disconnected the wire from the main bus bar in the maintenance panel, replaced the relays and reinserted the push button style breakers. "Huh. Well, that ain't good."

"What isn't good," Sergeant Hooker shouted over the roar of the wind.

"That should have shut off the alarms and closed the door."

"What? Should have? You are trying to kill us, aren't you?"

"Don't get your panties in a wad, Sergeant. I know how to fix it. Just give me a minute or two." Henry braced his feet against the wall and leaped away with all of his might toward the opening door and the class of terrified cadets. He tucked his knees, rotating backward until his feet aimed toward the door. "Move out of my way or it's going to really hurt," he warned the cadets as he fell toward them. He landed on the surface of the door with a solid thud. His knees bending on impact, distributing the force of the landing.

"What are you doing old man? Help us! Or did you just want an up-close and personal view as we all die?" Wainwright shouted. He clawed at the surface of the door as he pulled himself toward Henry.

"Just set still and you'll be fine!" Henry opened an access panel on the airlock door that flew from his hand and sucked against the opening crack of the doorway. "Hell, I'll have to fix that later." He dug into the access hatch and extended a long metal handle that telescoped outward. "Grab and pull," he ordered Wainwright.

"I swear to God…"

"Swear later, pump the handle now!" Henry reached into the hatch and shifted another small lever.

Wainwright braced his feet against the surface of the airlock and furiously pumped the lever. The airlock door inched closed with each swing of the handle. The Klaxon alarm ceased as the latching mechanism of the door clunked into place and sent a metallic shudder throughout the frame of the compartment. Thankful sobs and gasps of relief escaped from the class of cadets.

"Open that door and let these kids out of here," Henry directed the sergeant. "I need to put the rest of these relays back into place." He pushed off, less forcefully this time, in the direction of the maintenance panels.

Shaken, Sergeant Hooker pushed himself back along the wall to the hatchway and opened the door. He turned, taking in the site of the milling cadets. "Get out and get into the showers, you pukes," he bellowed. "If you cannot adapt to and handle an emergency situation then you do not belong in my beloved corps. If that is the case, then clean yourselves up and be at my office door in twenty to file your 214. Do you get me?"

"Yes sir," erupted in uniformed response from the class of cadets. One by one the cadets pushed off from the far wall and soared toward the exit. Grumbles and half-hearted comments of asshole aimed at Henry could be heard muttered under their breaths as they passed by, entering the corridor.

"You'll wish that you hadn't done that," Wainwright threatened as he approached. He pointed a stiff, angrily shaky finger in Henry's direction.

He wiped his eyes on the backs of his sleeves. "My father will hear about this incident, I assure you," he growled.

"You're welcome," Henry replied in a sarcastic sing-song tone. He half-heartedly saluted Wainwright with his middle finger as the cadet passed through the open hatchway.

"Crewman Johnson," a voice announced over the station's intercoms. "Report to Commander Godwin's office immediately."

Henry looked up at the speaker mounted on the wall. "Really? That didn't take them long." Henry sighed. "Y'all will have to wait a bit. I've still got cleanup to do down here," he shouted in the direction of the speaker.

"Hey, as far as I know, you were trying to repair a malfunction," Sergeant Hooker admitted.

"No, no need in that" Henry replied. "It's alright. Besides, I'm sure that they were watching everything on the internal security feeds once the alarms went off." Henry opened the first maintenance panel and replaced the relays to their original slots.

"Well good luck then," Hooker said with a nod. "I hope they don't rake you over the coals too badly. I need to get ready for the cadets."

"Eh," Henry shrugged. "I'm not too worried about it. What are they going to do? Fire me?" He closed the panel and pushed off toward the hatchway.

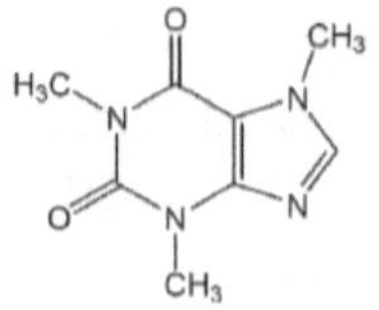

Henry drifted through the main hatchway of the station's Command Information Center, or CIC. Large, wrap-around display screens curved with the inner surface of the spherical compartment and dominated the wall on one side. Four crewmen monitored the information displayed on the screens, lounging against the odd-looking zero-G couches that faced the display wall. Henry never understood the need for the couches. They were sold to the Independent Alliance as a morale enhancer. They guaranteed that the crew who strapped themselves onto the couches during normal duty hours would feel more relaxed and less strained than if they'd have been using the tried and true bars or straps to hold themselves in place.

"Oh, hey Henry," a cute little blond said after noticing Henry enter the compartment. "The old man is not at all happy with you this time. You endangered the lives of fifteen cadets, plus their instructor."

"Morning Carol," Henry replied, stopping himself against the side of her duty station. "I'm not too worried. The commander can pull that stick out of his ass and get over himself."

She giggled.

He nodded acknowledgment with the other three crewmen, then continued. "They were never in any kind of danger. I don't understand how he hasn't figured out that I know this station like it was the back of my own hand. It's frustrating sometimes, ya know. In my forty years of maintaining this station, no commander has bothered to learn even a fraction of the systems aboard." He shook his head. "It's just pitiful if you ask me. You'd think they'd take a bit more interest in the things that are keeping them warm and breathing at a minimum."

"I don't know, Henry. Just the way they are trained I suppose," she innocently suggested. "He's been impatiently waiting on you." She glanced back over her shoulder toward the commander's door.

"He can just deal. I had important maintenance tasks that had to be done or they could have caused a threat to all hands aboard." He smiled and gave her a knowing wink. "Now come here and give me my hug before I enter the lair of the devil, himself."

"Do you really think that you deserve a hug after scaring all of those poor cadets like you did?" She unlatched the harness straps that held her to the couch.

"Oh absolutely. I was the hero in that situation. Weren't you watching on the videos?"

"We may have been." She giggled again as she turned and wrapped her short arms not even halfway around Henry's grandfatherly round torso. "You'd better get in there. He really is upset at you this time." She hooked her foot on a couch strap and pulled herself back down to her station.

"I'm not too worried." He pushed off from her station toward the commander's door. "You just wait. I'll have him thanking me for setting that asshole Wainwright straight."

"Oh, I almost forgot. Wainwright is already in with the commander," Carol warned.

"Well now, that'll make things a bit more interesting." Henry laughed. He tapped the control panel next to the commander's door and it slid open with a hiss.

"What in the wide wild world did you think you were doing, crewman," Commander Godwin bellowed. "What if your hair-brained actions had injured, let alone killed even just one of those cadets? This particular class has a high visibility all because of Wainwright and his father's senate seat." Wainwright floated at nearly motionless attention before the commander's desk. His feet hooked into small depressions in the decking just in front of the desk to accommodate cadets reporting for disciplinary action.

"Are you kidding me," Henry said plainly. "Look. It was a good learning experience for all of them because," he emphasized, "they were never in any real danger whatsoever. If they get that knee jerk panic reaction out of their systems now, then when there is a real emergency, they will be able to react and actually be helpful in that situation."

"Twelve! Twelve of the class resigned their commissions and are waiting for the next earthbound shuttle," the commander shouted.

"Oh, really," Henry murmured. "Who all quit?"

"Does it really matter," Commander Godwin shouted. A large vein pulsed along the left side of the commander's head. "That's twelve cadets whose two years of training are now a total wash. That's two years of lost time and resources. We'll have to replace them with new troops and that costs time and money that we really don't have. Now that the I.A. is sinking everything they have into the expansion program, our resources have been cut to the bare minimum."

"If those kids couldn't handle this, then they were a liability anyhow," Henry argued. "Back in my day we were just shoved into suits and told to make it happen. It didn't matter if we had any kind of training or not. They'd give us a crash course of what we were supposed to accomplish on the ride to the location and then they'd send us on our merry way. We learned how to improvise and how to adapt."

"You could have killed them with this stunt of yours, crewman! You are irresponsible, conceded, reckless! I should have you court-marshaled."

"I might be scared of that threat if I were still enlisted. But I'm not, now am I? I'm a civilian contract and you'll have to do better than speculate anything to get me fired, buddy. I have the most senior tenure of any I.A. civilian employee." Henry forced a wide, kiss my ass smile toward Commander Godwin. "I'll have you know that no one in the Independent Alliance knows this station like I do," Henry interrupted. "I helped to bolt this coffee can station together. I'm the one that initially programmed most of the systems on board and I am the one who has maintained this station for the last forty freaking years. You think I don't know this station? I was turning wrenches up here before you could even be a wet stain on your mamma's bedsheets," Henry growled. "Irresponsible? Ha! Conceded, well, maybe. But that's beside the point. Now excuse me if I question any opinions against my ability to repair and manipulate this station and its systems. Because I will in a heartbeat. Every last one of you pups thinks you know anything about this station? I call horse shit. And as for this pampered prince and his daddy," Henry growled in Wainwrights direction, "the I.A. would be better off without him or any of the other pampered pretty boys that they want to use for publicity stunts."

Commander Godwin sucked in a calming breath. "One of the other cadets recorded a video that has already managed to slip its way onto social media before we could catch it," Commander Godwin admitted.

"Oh," Henry said, curiously. "And what did this supposed video contain?"

"It was a video of Cadet Wainwright, having a slight mental breakdown in his quarters just after your little stunt," the commander said with a nod at the cadet. "We think that the video was removed before it could cause any permanent damage to either the cadet's or the senator's reputations. Though in all honest truth, we won't know for sure unless it resurfaces somewhere on the net.

"And exactly why am I supposed to care if Wainwright was crying to his teddy?"

"Because," commander Godwin reluctantly began, "the I.A. is already stretched thin across the globe, in orbit, and on the moon. Our recruitment numbers are way below where they should be and if this expansion program fails, the fate of mankind could hang in the balance." Godwin looked up at Wainwright with a pitiful countenance. "Officers like Wainwright here, if trained and guided properly, could make all the difference in the end. We need more, properly trained individuals that want to make a difference. Surprisingly enough, Henry, you were the topic of discussion just before you arrived, but not for the reason you'd think." Godwin smiled.

"Oh hell," Henry huffed. "That look has bad news written all over it. Did pretty boy break something else that I need to go fix?"

"No, nothing like that. But I believe that I'll let Cadet Wainwright explain the idea to you." He motioned for Wainwright to enter the conversation.

"Permission to speak freely sir," Wainwright asked.

"Permission granted, Cadet," Godwin replied.

Wainwright nodded toward his commander then turned to address Henry. "I nearly made the worst mistake of my life, just a short time ago. I had joined my crewmates outside of Sergeant Hooker's office when I realized what a horrible mistake it was that I was making. That I would just be giving up on yet one more thing that had been pushed upon me. Something not of my choosing, but something that my father had decided would be good for me and his career. I have honestly enjoyed my time in service. I had actually thought about retirement from the I.A. at some point down the road, for no other reason than to accomplish something for myself. So I thank you, sir. Thank you for opening my eyes about my attitude. I thank you for showing me that the obvious is not always the answer. If you would allow it, Mister Johnson, I would like to learn whatever you are willing to teach about ship systems and how to bypass or manipulate them. I think that knowledge such as this could provide a tactical advantage in certain situations, such as ship boarding operations."

Henry slowly looked from Cadet Wainwright to Commander Godwin and swallowed the dry, unsure thought. "Well, I'll be damned."

"I told you it wasn't what you'd think it was about," Godwin chided.

Henry reached into his pocket and produced his ancient, flip out communicator. He held the device at arm's length in an attempt to read the tiny, digital lettering, tapped a key, then held it up to his ear.

Godwin's stare of consternation toward Henry was unnerving. "What the hell are you doing now?"

"Just hold your horses, Commander." Henry waggled an ancient, boney finger at Godwin.

"Hey Drake, this is Henry." He paused, a look of confusion twisted his features. "I know you can see who's calling you, dumb ass. It's just polite to announce yourself is all. Didn't anyone ever teach you good manners? Anyways, that's not what I called you for. Is it too late to change any of those previous bookings?" He nodded as he listened to the voice on the other end. "Dammit. Alright then, you have my account info. Go ahead and square up on Wainwright and we can look at the others later. Hu? What do you mean you hadn't heard anything? I'm telling you now. I'm standing here looking at him as we speak and he's not going anywhere soon. He wants me to teach him a thing or two," Henry said in a sarcastic, grousing tone.

Godwin shrugged at Wainwright and motioned for Henry to hurry.

"Alright, well I gotta go. People to do and things to see. Yeah yeah. Alright, bye." He closed up the communicator and tucked it back into his pocket.

"What exactly was that all about?" Godwin scowled, the large vein that ran across his forehead pulsed with anger and frustration.

"Oh, that was nothing. Just squaring up real quick with my bookie on a bet I'd placed earlier."

"What the…"

"Just sit and hush Commander. It's done and over with and nothing you can do about it anyways. So what do you want me to do with Cadet Wainwright, Commander?"

Godwin closed his eyes and sucked in a long, deep breath. "He does not have a class to continue his training with at the moment, thanks to you." Godwin glowered at Henry. "The next class isn't scheduled to be on station for another two months. Since he has expressed interest in learning from you, I suppose that he should be assigned to special duty for the time being. Would that be acceptable Cadet?"

"Sir yes, sir! That would be completely acceptable, sir."

"Good, then that's settled. Until further notice, you are to report to Crewman Johnson here for your daily tasks and assignments."

"Whoa now, hold on just a second here. Don't I get a say in any of this?" Henry crossed his arms and shot a questioning look toward the commander.

"Not one word," Godwin replied. A wide smile crossed his face. "You are right about one thing, Henry. I can't fire you. Unless there is a loss of life or something equally bad, no one can touch you. But as the commander of this station, I can make amendments to your assignment as required in order to accomplish our mission." His smile seemingly grew wider.

"So legally, you can make my life a living hell if you want."

"Yes, that's pretty much it exactly." Godwin laughed. "I will make an amendment to your contract stating that you are, as of this moment, a part-time instructor and due the pay increase of such a position. So it isn't like you will be doing it for nothing. Just make sure that Cadet Wainwright learns something. I expect a full report of his progress at the end of every week and a list of goals set in place for him to achieve that I want by the end of today."

"I hate you," Henry said plainly.

"I know you do, Henry. Now if you would please," Godwin motioned for Henry and Wainwright to leave. "I have work to do." Godwin chuckled under his breath.

The End

Heavy Air

By: Benjamin Tyler Smith

I leaned back in the pilot's seat and glared at the orange sky beyond the windscreen. "If I hear that notification bell one more time, I'm throwing her tablet out the airlock."

Next to me, meteorologist Miuna Yamaguchi pressed a petite hand to her lips to stifle a giggle. "Helen, please! That's not very commander-like."

A series of loud dings echoed up from the passenger compartment, bounced around the cockpit, and rattled my brain. "Lord, here we go," I muttered.

"Shall I get the airlock ready?"

"We'll see." I reached past the EVA helmet resting next to me and turned on a small monitor. A freckle-faced redhead stared back at me through the screen. *Her and her damn livestreams...*

The redhead held the camera out as far as her arm would go, revealing a blue jumpsuit with a NASA logo emblazoned on it. "Hey, viewers! Dr. Jenna Connolly here! Today is the twenty-sixth day of *Aphrodite*'s month-long mission high in the skies of planet Venus. We're down to the wire here, and today will be super busy. Isn't that right, Commander Helen?"

I clenched my jaw. My nametape says "Barnes", but Jenna sold the brass that it is better for the ratings if I am "less military." *It's for the mission, Helen. It's for the mission.* I spun my pilot's chair to face the open doorway. Jenna stood there, the camera now aimed at me. "Every day's been busy, but yes. Today we'll be—"

"Conducting a retrieval mission!" Jenna spun the camera back to herself. "Atmospheric probe *Soyokaze* has been floating in and out of the acid clouds ever since JAXA sent her here in June of 2026, almost two years ago!" She turned the lens toward us again. "Miuna, as JAXA's representative on this mission, what are your thoughts?"

Miuna blanched, and I tried not to laugh. The tiny Japanese woman was downright shy where cameras were involved. It didn't matter that we were under near constant NASA surveillance everywhere except the bathroom and bunks. Make her conscious of it, and she became Miuna the Mortified. She made a show of studying her console as she said,

"Retrieving the *Soyokaze* is a critical goal of JAXA and NASA. It'll be the first time a probe has been brought back to Earth from Venus."

"We'll be supervising the retrieval effort, not conducting it," I added. "An unmanned version of the dirigible *Aphrodite* called Eurus will descend from space, grab the probe, blast off into orbit, and rendezvous with *Hermes*, our return ship. All through a NASA-programmed AI that we'll be monitoring."

"All we can do is sit and watch?" Jenna made a show of pouting for the camera. "That doesn't sound very exciting."

I bared my teeth. "You can push the start button, though I'd think being here would be exciting enough. Many wish they could be right where you're standing, Doctor." *Including the one bumped off the roster for you.*

Jenna laughed, but it sounded as forced as my smile felt. "Absolutely correct as always, Commander. Who wouldn't want to be on what could very well be the agency's last crewed spaceflight?"

Before I could reply, she stepped back into the passenger compartment and sat at her console. "Now, let's speak with our other crewmate. Give me a sec to get the camera feeds switched."

Last crewed spaceflight. I turned back to the airship's controls. I hoped our CAPCOM was on a bathroom break, or he'd hear that statement in about three minutes, when the transmission reached Earth. Dr. Scott Barnes had been *Aphrodite*'s physician before being sidelined to let Jenna on the mission. She had Scott's same medical qualifications, and she ran a highly successful space tech blog and streaming channel. An online petition signed by tens of thousands of her subscribers had caught the attention of NASA's private backers. I could only imagine the emails that flooded Administrator Nelson's inbox. "Give *Aphrodite* an all-female crew! Oh, and bring this loudmouth ginger along while you're at it!"

Well, maybe the emails weren't worded *quite* like that, but I liked to think they were.

And of course, it didn't hurt that men far and wide thought Jenna had a pretty face and a hot body that nicely filled out the skintight environmental suits we all wore for EVA missions. That alone had bolstered our ratings, from launch through two months of deep space to the weeks spent floating over the hellish Venusian surface in a blimp as oversized as her chest. If we were judging our mission based solely on that, it had been a huge success. That publicity alone made the decision to boot Scott a sensible one, but it didn't sit right with me.

Did I mention Scott's my husband? Yeah, I'm biased, but still. This had been his turn, his chance, and that had all been dashed for likes and shares.

"One more second, chat," Jenna said, bringing my attention back to the present. "The connection's acting a little funny, but I've almost got the cameras up on screen. CosmicPsycho, thank you for the generous Super Chat! I won't be reading any messages until after we sign off with the rest of the crew, so bear with me."

I stifled a snort. Where did people come up with these internet handles? CosmicPsycho was one of Jenna's most frequent "Super Chatters" who paid good money to have his messages read to the thousands of viewers tuning in to the livestream. He was her top donor, followed by FluffyDuffy and MoonWaffler84. It was hard to take any of them seriously.

"As you can see," Jenna said, "NASA astronaut Ria Ponce is outside conducting minor repairs on *Aphrodite*. Ria, how is everything?"

The monitor next to me switched from Jenna's camera to a view of a tarnished liquid oxygen tank mounted to the exterior of *Aphrodite*. A caption at the bottom of the screen read "Helmet Cam: R. Ponce."

One of Ria's gloved hands grasped a handrail fixed to the dirigible's hull. She reached out for another but paused to look down. Her camera captured a grand view of the dark haze below us, its depths illuminated by the occasional flash of sheet lightning. "The last few trips through the acid clouds have damaged some of the exposed cables out here," she said, her voice coming in through the cockpit's speakers. "I've patched what I could with protective tape, but I'll need to get more."

I stood. "Let me take over, Ria." Our protocol was to have one astronaut on standby when another was performing an EVA. All I needed to do was secure my oxygen tank, snap on my helmet, and I was ready to go.

"That would be nice. It's a bit chilly."

"Chilly?" I checked the atmospheric instruments. "It's a balmy 15 degrees Celsius out there!"

"Add 220 kilometer an hour winds into the equation, then tell me how balmy it is."

"We're going with the current! It's not gonna drop the temperature that much."

"I'm from Pasadena! Anything below 24 C is frigid. My nipples are hard enough to cut glass out here!"

Miuna gasped, and Jenna chuckled. In a few minutes, Ria's husband Jack would be dealing with two young daughters demanding to know what mommy was talking about. I laughed at the image. "All right, all right. I'll meet you in the airlock."

"Once you're finished, should we get into position to record the probe retrieval?" Miuna asked.

"Sure. And we can even let Jenna push the button—"

A blinding flash filled the windows, and an explosion rocked the whole ship. Aphrodite shuddered and bucked as warning lights flashed red in the cockpit. I grabbed the stick and steadied the airship. "Miuna, status!"

"Complete loss of pressure in the Oxygen-1 and Hydrogen-1 tanks. Reduced pressure in Oxygen-2."

That was near where Ria had been. "Ria, you there?"

Silence.

A wave of dread washed over me. "Ria?"

"Helen!" Jenna shouted. She waved at me from the passenger compartment, then aimed her camera out the bubbled window.

The monitor showed Ria hanging close to the airlock door, her arm hooked in one of the handrails. Something had shattered her faceplate, and blood leaked onto her white environmental suit.

She wasn't moving.

Images of little Debora and Blanca pointing at the TV flashed through my mind. I could already hear their screams. "Take the stick, Miuna." I grabbed my helmet. "Jenna, with me!"

Jenna beat me to the airlock by a few strides and already had my oxygen tank in her hands. She snapped it into place while I pulled on the breath-mask. There was an audible hiss, then cool air brushed my nose and lips. I donned my helmet and snapped it in place as Jenna ran her hands along my arms and legs, inspecting for any tears or weaknesses in the thin environmental suit. As annoying as Jenna could be, she knew her spacesuits through and through.

She gave me the thumbs-up, and I nodded my thanks. I stepped into the airlock, the door sliding shut behind me. A blower fan cranked to high speed and sucked the air from the chamber as I picked up the end of a long, coiled tether. I hooked it to my waist and gave it a few tugs. It would keep me secured to the dirigible once I stepped outside.

I ground my teeth as the airlock cycled from air to carbon dioxide rich atmosphere. It only took thirty seconds, but it felt like thirty hours.

The wind buffeted me as soon as the outer door slid open. It wasn't my first time outside, but I was just as happy for the tether now as I was then. As much as I loved skydiving and rock climbing, I didn't relish the idea of falling into an acid bath hot enough to melt lead.

I leaned out the airlock to reach for Ria, but she slipped from the rung she was on and plummeted a few meters until her tether went taut. A jolt of fear shot through me as she bounced once, twice, three times. She spun slowly, dangling beneath the airship. I sighed in relief. The tether had held, thank God.

Now came the hard part. I planted my boots against either side of the airlock door, grabbed her tether in my gloved hands, and started pulling. After only a few tugs my muscles burned with the effort. "Lord, give me strength," I said through clenched teeth. Next to Miuna, Ria was the lightest among us, a fact I was grateful for. It also helped that I hadn't been as affected by deep space travel as the others had been. The first couple days on Venus's near one-gee gravity had been rough for me, but it had taken a full week for the others to recover.

Please, don't be dead. Tears stung my eyes, but I blinked them away. We'd been part of the same astronauts' class, and we lived across the street from one another in the Clear Lake area of Houston, a few streets over from her parents' home in Pasadena. Debora and Blanca were like nieces to Scott and me. I'd be damned if I let their mother die. Not on my watch!

After a few agonizing moments, Ria's oxygen tank crested the lip of the airlock, followed by her backside. I pulled her higher and snatched the drag-strap built into her suit. With the last of my strength, I hauled her over the edge, and we tumbled to the airlock floor in a tangle of limbs. Panting heavily, I slapped the button to close the outer door, then hit the adjacent button to activate the shower. Water sprayed from nozzles mounted to the ceiling and walls, rinsing our suits clean of sulfuric acid.

My limbs shook from fatigue and adrenaline as I knelt in the cramped space to examine Ria. Her face was bloody and blistered, but her breath-mask was still secure. Whatever else, she hadn't breathed in the planet's corrosive atmosphere. *Thank you, God.* I carefully removed her helmet and tilted her head back to rinse her face. "She's alive, Jack," I said between gasps for air. I wasn't sure if NASA would cut the public feed, but at the moment I didn't care. "Debora, Blanca, your mama's gonna be alright."

I hoped.

After the shower finished, both liquids and gases were drained from the room and replaced with breathable air. The inner door opened, and Jenna helped me drag Ria out. Jenna leaned in to study her closely. "Shrapnel cut. Possible concussion. Was she conscious?"

"No. She's been out this whole time. Is she…." I hesitated. "Are you broadcasting?"

"Only to NASA on the ship's camera feeds." Jenna gestured toward Ria. "You think I want to show my viewers *this*?"

The sudden venom in her tone surprised me. "Sorry. I just—"

"Assumed that I'm a ghoul looking for clicks and views." She glared up at me. "Before all else, I'm a doctor. And I have a patient to see to, Commander. Please excuse me."

Anger burned within me. I opened my mouth to respond, then snapped it shut with a click. She was right.

"Helen, is Ria all right?" Miuna asked.

"She's hurt but breathing. Jenna's working on her."

Miuna murmured something in Japanese. I didn't understand much of it, but I did catch the last part: "Onegai, Kami-sama." Please, God.

Amen to that. "How are things up in the cockpit?"

"The storm's gone, but we have another problem: the altimeter shows us at fifty thousand meters and dropping."

My stomach clenched. Fifty? We were supposed to be at fifty-one. Any further and we'd sink into the sulfuric haze. "Can you get us to climb?"

"No."

"There must be balloon damage. Anything on the cameras?"

"Port side shows nothing out of the ordinary, but two of the starboard cameras are offline."

Ria had been on that side. I chewed my lip. We needed to know what was going on, and I was still suited up. "Keep us steady."

Seconds later, I was outside again. I reached for the same rung that Ria had dangled from only a short while ago. I whispered a quick prayer as I climbed from rung to rung, leaning out to avoid exposed tanks and coils of insulated wires and tubes. *Aphrodite's* fore section had all sorts of equipment sticking out of its otherwise smooth hull. The original plan had been to encase the whole thing in aluminum, but they scrapped that in favor of acid-resistant titanium. Titanium was heavier and more expensive, though, so full encasement was out of the question. Everything had been sheltered from micrometeoroids and other space debris during the trip by a protective sled, but that was dropped to the planet's surface on arrival, to free the housing where the balloon was sealed.

Miuna and I hadn't liked the idea of exposed equipment and had argued against it, citing lightning strikes as a possible concern, as well as the ever-present acid. If it was detrimental to aluminum plating, why were we risking tanks of pressurized gasses and wiring? I understood the weight-reduction argument, but I worried we could reenact Apollo 13 if an oxygen tank blew or a bit of wiring shorted and started a fire. "Venus's atmosphere is mostly carbon dioxide," I'd been told. "Little risk for an explosion or a sustained fire."

Tell that to my ship.

"*Aphrodite*, Houston." Scott's voice crackled slightly in my helmet's speakers. "Helen, is everything okay? We saw the explosion and Jenna's video of Ria. Is she—Hang on, Miuna's transmission is coming in now. Stand by, and please stay safe."

"Houston, *Aphrodite*. Scott, I'm all right." It felt good to hear his voice. I thought about telling him Ria's status, but he would be caught up by the time this transmission reached him. "I'm inspecting the outer hull for damage. I'm on the starboard side and approaching *Aeneas*."

Aphrodite was actually two ships in one, and the distinction was obvious: the fore section, with its festoon of tanks and wiring, was where most of our food and supplies were stored, as well as where we could observe our surroundings and take meteorological readings. The aft section, what we called *Aeneas*, was a two-stage rocket that would send us back into orbit once our mission was complete. Unlike the craggy monstrosity that was *Aphrodite*, Aeneas's sleek, white surface looked more like a traditional rocket.

Two tanks lay closest to this bisection of the ship: Oxygen-1 and Hydrogen-1. Both had ruptured like rotten pomegranates, their flat bottoms turned into jagged, blackened metal. Lightning must have struck a vulnerable point in the tanks and the exposed wiring Ria hadn't yet patched up. A bolt from the blue, or orange in the case of Venus.

Shrapnel damage was everywhere, from jagged pieces of steel embedded in the hull to a sliced tube that explained the drop in pressure from the Oxygen-2 tank to holes in the fabric of the thirty-meter-long balloon that kept us afloat. The balloon sagged strangely at different points, which meant some of the gas-filled ballonets that helped maintain the shape and balance of the larger balloon were damaged. I paused my inspection long enough to repair the sliced tube with protective tape. After wrapping it several times, the tube looked like it had an aneurysm about to burst. Better safe than sorry.

I pocketed the tape and turned toward *Aeneas* and froze. A large piece of shrapnel had smashed its cockpit windscreen, exposing the rocket's interior to the corrosive atmosphere. My heart sank. "Houston, *Aphrodite*. You there, Scott? After you see this, you may be glad you got bumped from the mission." I knew I was glad.

No sense in both of us dying, after all.

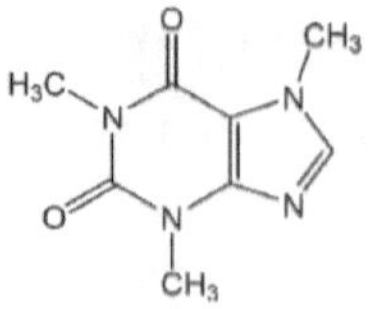

"And that's the long and short of it," I said, ending my report. I flipped a few control switches in *Aeneas's* cockpit. The computer booted up, but immediately crashed. Behind me, one of the instrument panels sparked and died. "No computer, no launch sequence, no navigation, and no windscreen. Please advise."

Scott acknowledged receipt of the transmission a few minutes later, as I finished cleaning my suit of residual acid. "*Aphrodite*, Houston. We're reviewing everything now. Stand by. And no, I'm not glad I was bumped, for the record. Ria's in good hands with Dr. Connolly, but I wish I was there, too. I'll do what I can for you here. Stay safe, Helen. We'll get you through this."

A lump formed in my throat as I stepped into the airlock separating our broken escape rocket and our equally broken dirigible. I wished Scott was with us, too. Not because he was my husband, and not because I doubted Jenna's medical skills. Scott had been our team's anchor. Always level headed, always able to settle any disputes that arose during the stress of training, always able to reason his way out of any of the emergencies that NASA threw at us in the simulators. He had continued to serve in that capacity as CAPCOM, but the three-minute transmission lag was really starting to get to me.

Once the airlock had cycled through its chemical shower and pressurization, the door to *Aphrodite* slid open and I stepped through. "Just keep the pressure on the eggheads, Scott." I removed my helmet and pulled down my breath-mask. "They need to get us a solution, and fast."

I was sure the engineers back in Houston and the Cape would come up with something, but I couldn't sit idly by, not with three crewmen who had families to return to; Jenna with her parents and siblings, Ria and Miuna with their husbands and children. I worried the most about the kids. No child should have to grow up without a mother. I'd lost mine at an early age to cancer, and it was the reason why Scott and I hadn't had any children yet. Astronauts lived in a dangerous world, where the slightest mistake in action or flaw in design could lead to death.

Had I been wrong? Scott had always wanted children but had respected my thought process. Would my death be easier for him if he had kids to remind him of me? His parents could have helped raise them and would have loved the opportunity. Or would it be easier for him to move on, without anything to tie him down except memories? Could he even move on? Would I be able to if our positions were reversed? Would I want him to?

God, what about my dad? I was an only child! He'd never have grandchildren now.

Tears welled up in my eyes, and I scrubbed them away along with the dark thoughts echoing through my soul. Too late to worry about any of it now. I had a crew with actual children to return to, and I needed to protect them.

And if—no, when we made it back, Scott and I could revisit this issue.

We gathered in *Aphrodite's* cockpit a short while later. Miuna sat in the pilot's chair, and Jenna stood behind her, her blue sleeves flecked with blood. "Is Ria all right?" I asked.

"She's still unconscious," Jenna said, and for once she didn't sound bubbly or snarky. "She stirred a little but wouldn't wake. She has massive contusions on her forehead and neck, in addition to the lacerated face. I found the culprit inside her helmet." She held up a clear plastic bag with a bloody piece of shrapnel inside. "Another couple centimeters and she'd be missing an eye, or worse."

I shivered at the thought. "Thank you, Jenna."

She seemed taken aback at the sudden praise. "Uh, you're welcome?"

"I mean it." I squeezed her shoulder. "You did good work back there, first in helping me suit up, then with Ria." To Miuna I asked, "Would you like me to take over?"

"No, you should take a break. You've been up and about this whole time." Miuna frowned. "That's more than I can say about *Aphrodite*. We're still sinking."

"Can we repair the damage to the balloon?" Jenna asked.

I shook my head. "The dirigible was never designed for that. The fabric the balloon's made of was meant to be impervious to anything we'd find on Venus." They just hadn't accounted for damage by something we'd brought to Venus.

"Can we repair *Aeneas?*" Miuna asked.

"With time, maybe." I chewed the inside of my lip. "The damage to the cockpit is pretty severe, and I'm not sure how we'll repair the windscreen unless we remove *Aphrodite's* and try to Frankenstein it onto *Aeneas*. And that's before the issue of fried electronics. You saw the damage."

"It didn't look good from the camera feed, that's for sure." Jenna crossed her arms. "Think the eggheads at NASA can figure something out?"

"They're trying." I wasn't optimistic, but I wouldn't voice that. "They need the same thing we do: time."

"What about dropping weight?" Miuna asked. "There's a lot we can toss overboard."

Jenna's tablet dinged loudly. I pointed at her hip pocket. "Want to poll your viewers?"

"I'm surprised you didn't suggest throwing it out."

Miuna and I glanced at each other. "Oh, believe me, the temptation is there."

Jenna laughed. "Help me get into my environmental suit, and we'll get to work."

I rolled my eyes. "CosmicPsycho and MoonWaffler84 will definitely enjoy that."

"Oh, stop!"

We spent the next half-hour gathering everything that could fit in the airlock: chairs, electronics, bedding, and yes: even the kitchen sink. Anything not crucial to our survival was getting a one-way ticket to the ground. We piled everything up in the airlock with us, careful not to scratch the paint on the walls. I'd already seen what Venus's atmosphere could do to bare metal inside *Aeneas's* cockpit, and I didn't want to see that in the airlock.

Jenna pressed her back against the inner door and fed items to me. It was my duty to toss them to their final destination. "Sorry for snapping at you before," she said, her voice coming through my helmet's earpiece.

I grunted as I threw a sack full of cookware out the door. "Don't be. I was in the way of a doctor treating her patient. And you were right." I turned back to look into her wide eyes. "I really did think you were a ghoul looking for clicks and views."

She flashed a grin. "Well, finally, some honesty! And here I thought I was going to go the whole mission dealing with your passive-aggressiveness."

"I'll have you know I'm active-aggressive!"

"Yeah, no." She tossed a roll of bedding my way, followed by another, and another. "I'm not seeing it. Maybe your husband—"

She and I froze. Jenna reached up to cover her mouth, and her gloved hand smacked against the faceplate of her helmet. That made her jump, and I laughed. She glared at me at first, but anger quickly gave way to mirth. "These stupid suits get in the way of everything!"

"Hey, be glad they're as slender as they are." I held up an arm and flexed my bicep, the muscle clearly showing through the material. "If we were in deep space, we'd be stuck in climate-controlled suits many times thicker, and a lot more constrictive."

"I thought they gave us these because they wanted us to look hot in them." She tucked an arm under her breasts to emphasize her point.

I tossed the bedding out the door, then dragged a chair over and shoved it out. "Well, I didn't sit in on the design meetings, but it would surprise me if that was part of it. They are more concerned with functionality." I held up my arm again and tugged at the rubbery material. "0.1 millimeters thick. Now I know how my husband feels with a condom on."

"Well, that's one way of looking at it!" She pushed another chair within my grasp. "Sorry for bringing him up like that. You probably wish he was here."

"Scott's our CAPCOM. He's never far away." I sighed. "Part of me wishes he was here, but it was the right call for you to replace him, if only for the sake of the mission."

"You really think so?"

"Yes, much as I hate to admit it." I tossed the second chair out and reached for a third. "Your viewers are a blessing that NASA needed. A manned mission to Venus is exciting, but your presence has made that excitement a daily part of so many lives."

"Woah. Commander Helen Barnes, the no-nonsense Amazon of NASA, complimenting my vlogger skills?" She gently tapped the camera mounted to the top of her helmet. "I'm glad this thing's recording."

"Don't get used to it."

"I'm appreciative, too." Miuna's voice was strained. "My parents tune in to your livestreams every day, even with the time difference in Hokkaido. They're so thankful they can see us this way."

"Will wonders never cease? Shy Miuna happy to have the camera on her?"

Miuna giggled. "They love seeing me in action, and my son—" There was a long pause, followed by a scraping sound, possibly from Miuna wiping her eyes and bumping her headset in the process. "Riku enjoys it. It's the talk of his fifth grade class."

"Debora and Blanca, too," I said. "They love watching their mama, Aunt Miuna, and Aunt Helen at work. Oh, and I guess they like you, too, Jenna."

"Gee, thanks."

The three of us spent the next several minutes talking about everything from vlogs and livestreams to favorite Houston haunts to our favorite bits of NASA history. Miuna filled us in on some of JAXA's accomplishments over the last few years, and Jenna even had a couple funny ER stories to share. While we talked, the tension in my shoulders and neck eased.

Jenna pushed the last item, the aforementioned kitchen sink, toward me. "Hey, if we don't make it, think they'll build a statue for us somewhere?"

"If they do, I hope it's not of us doing this." I shoved the heavy sink out the door and over the side, then shut the airlock and started the shower cycle. "I can just see us in bronze, pitching bags of crap out the airlock with a plaque reading 'Venus Deflowered by Interstellar Dumpage, February 2028.'"

Jenna's cackling laughter filled my helmet. "Interstellar Dumpage. Sounds like a great name for a band!"

"As does Venus Deflowered," Miuna said.

I gasped in faux outrage. "Miuna! You're the last person I expected to hear that kind of talk from!"

"Where do you think Riku came from? A peach? I know that's a Japanese myth but come on."

All three of us laughed. The crude jokes and even the gallows humor were a welcome change of pace. They took our minds off our impending mortality, if only for a short time. Jenna and I were still giggling when we stepped back inside, our environmental suits dripping from the fresh shower. She removed her helmet and ran a hand through her auburn hair. "Amazing what a little spring cleaning can do for one's mood."

"It's still winter!" I objected.

"Does Venus even have seasons?"

"You make a good point."

"Helen, come up front," Miuna called. "Another storm is approaching."

Our smiles faded. "Have we gained any lift?" I asked.

"Not enough. We need to lose more weight."

"What else can we toss?" Jenna spread her damp arms. "Should we rip up the floor? Smash the consoles? Break up the furniture?"

"*Aphrodite*, Houston." Scott's voice sounded tense in my headset. "Helen, we're still looking into the problem with *Aeneas*, but it doesn't look good. We hadn't planned for catastrophic windscreen and cockpit damage. Stand by."

I shared a long look with Jenna. Damn it, Scott, couldn't you have done a little better than that? I hadn't expected much, but the news still hit like a gut-punch. Our escape rocket had been reduced to a multi-billion dollar anchor that was dragging us down. I pressed my hand to my forehead and squeezed my eyes shut. How were we going to get out of this? What else could we drop?

The sick feeling in my stomach slowly dissipated and was replaced with a sense of grim resolve. I knew what we had to do.

"We'll drop *Aeneas*," I said once we gathered in the cockpit.

"We need it to get home!" Miuna objected just as Jenna said, "Are you insane?"

I held up a hand. "I'm well aware that *Aeneas* is our only means of escape. However, it's not going anywhere. And we're sinking into a storm that could very well kill us." I looked from one to the other. "Do either of you have a better idea? I'm open to them."

Jenna shrugged. "Got any more kitchen sinks we can toss?"

I smirked, but it faded quickly. "Look, I don't like it, either, but I think our chances will be better if we can get higher in the atmosphere. If we sink any lower, we might not be able to make it back out, even if we can get *Aeneas* repaired."

And at that point, it'd be a toss-up as to what would kill us first: the lightning storm, the sulfuric acid haze, or the pressure of the increasingly heavy Venusian air.

Miuna stayed silent for a long moment, her lips pressed into a thin line. Finally, she said, "It's a good plan, Helen. You have my support."

Jenna shook her head, then sighed. "Ah, what the hell. It's not like I paid for the stupid rocket."

"Only if you didn't pay any taxes in the last three years." I grinned, but it felt forced. "I'll man the stick. Get strapped in. Dropping *Aeneas* is going to be a wild ride."

Jenna headed aft to restrain Ria. While she was gone, I brought up the emergency jettison program for *Aeneas*. I never thought I'd have to use this, especially without any of us onboard. Yet here we were, dealing with a problem we'd never prepared for, even with all our careful planning and training regimens. Regardless of the outcome of this mission, our actions would be studied for years in order to better prepare the next generation of astronauts.

I hoped we'd be around to help with that training. It'd be worth surviving just so we could prank the new crew in the simulators.

After Jenna returned and seated herself, I brought up the only camera still active in the stern of the ship and turned it toward the damaged escape rocket. *Aeneas*. Depending on the interpretation, it either meant "man of praise" or "horrible man." Which version fit the rocket now? It was also the name of the paralyzed man Peter healed in the book of Acts. Maybe if the good saint were here, he could lay his hands on *Aeneas* and "healed" our stricken ship.

I was hesitating, I realized. My finger hovered over the release button, and my lungs burned from the breath I was holding. I forced myself to breathe normally. Saint Peter wasn't here, and the only way he'd involve himself is if we met him at Heaven's pearly gates. It was my job to keep that meeting as far off as possible.

No more hesitation, Helen. I pushed the release button. "*Aeneas*, jettison."

A shudder ran through *Aphrodite*, and we shot up like a rocket. Forty-nine thousand meters became fifty, then fifty-one. I fought the controls to keep her steady during our crazed climb. A proximity alert shrieked through the cockpit once, as we came within a few hundred meters of the *Soyokaze* probe and the doughnut-shaped balloon that kept it aloft.

I reached over and muted the siren. We weren't in any risk of striking the *Soyokaze*. What a stupid alert—

"Wait, that's it!" I cried as the dirigible's ascent slowed to a halt.

"What's it?" Jenna demanded, her voice tight. "Oh, I think I'm going to be sick."

"The *Soyokaze*. It's supposed to be picked up by *Eurus*!"

Miuna clapped her hands together. "And *Eurus* has an escape rocket, too!"

"You're right, it does!" Jenna grinned. "We'll board it when it gets here, then."

"Not quite." I shaped my hands into fists and bumped them together. "Both it and *Aphrodite's* balloons are too big. We wouldn't be able to get close enough."

"How do we escape on it?"

Miuna leaned back in her seat and looked at the ceiling. "Ah, I think I understand. We'll use the *Soyokaze*, right?"

Jenna cocked her head. "Use it how?"

"We'll… how do you Americans say…hitch a ride?"

"Hitch a—" Jenna's eyes widened. "That's crazy!"

"Crazy enough that it might work," I said. "And we don't have a choice, not with *Aeneas* gone. We'll climb aboard the *Soyokaze*, wait for *Eurus* to scoop it up, and board *Eurus* before launch. Once in orbit, she'll take us to *Hermes*, and we can get back to Earth as planned."

"That's crazy," Jenna repeated, her pale features growing paler.

"I'm for it," Miuna said. "Get me close enough, and I'll hook us to the probe."

"Can it even support our weight?"

"*Soyokaze* weighs four hundred kilograms. Its balloon is rated for twice that. We'll be fine."

"I'll let the brass know," I said. "Houston, Aphrodite, we've—"

"*Aphrodite*, Houston," Scott said, his delayed transmission interrupting me. "Helen, we've got a... Well, a bit of an unorthodox plan. We see you're still in position near the JAXA weather probe *Soyokaze*. Is that correct? Over."

The three of us shared a look. I chuckled. "Houston, *Aphrodite*. Scott, when did NASA start employing mind readers?"

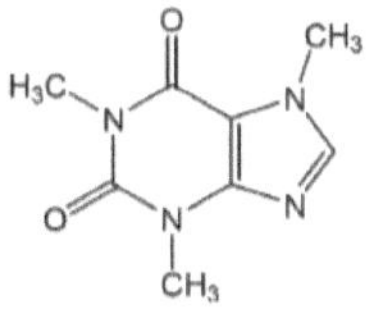

Jenna hooked a long tether to one of the airlock's anchor points. She tried to wipe her forehead but smacked the faceplate of her helmet. She cursed and cast a dubious eye at the pile of tethers we'd gathered together. "Are we sure about this?" she asked.

"As sure as the engineers back in Houston." I shrugged. "It'll be fine, I think."

"She thinks," Jenna murmured. "How reassuring."

NASA's plan had been the same as mine: activate *Eurus's* retrieval program and be on the *Soyokaze* before it arrived. To do that, we would first need to connect *Aphrodite* to the probe with a cable and use that as a makeshift zip-line. Once we were on the probe, we'd just wait for our ride home. "Simple, right?" Scott had asked with a dry chuckle.

Yeah, I thought. *Real simple.*

We were all suited up, our oxygen tanks on. Once we got started, we wouldn't have time to fiddle with equipment. Jenna inspected us one last time. First me, then Miuna, then Ria. The unconscious astronaut lay on her side in the hallway, the bulky oxygen tank preventing her from resting on her back. Jenna checked to make sure the replacement helmet was secured before she joined Miuna and me. She stared at the airlock door, her hands fidgeting. "We're as ready as we'll ever be."

I looked at Miuna. "Are you ready? You've got the most dangerous job."

"As Jenna said, I'm as ready as ever." Miuna grinned. "I can finally put those gymnastics classes to good use."

Scott gave an update as I returned to the cockpit. "*Eurus* will be in position for descent for another twenty-two minutes. Miss that window, and it'll be seventeen hours before you can try again."

Our balloon was still leaking precious lift gases, so how much would be left in that many hours? It was now or never, and we all knew it.

"Our thoughts and prayers are with you, *Aphrodite*." There was a pause. "Get these ladies home, Helen. We're all waiting for you."

That damned lump formed in my throat again. "Amen to that," I murmured.

I spent the next several minutes coaxing *Aphrodite* into position over the *Soyokaze*. It wasn't easy. The airship's balance was completely off-kilter with the damaged balloon and the loss of *Aeneas*. I could practically hear the propellers whining in protest as I banked and turned the stricken craft until it hovered about ten meters above the probe's doughnut-shaped balloon. Way too close for comfort, but we couldn't be any further away. "In position," I said, and switched the craft to autopilot.

I turned to the console where we had routed *Eurus's* descent command and pushed the enter button. "*Eurus* is go. Ten minutes to retrieval."

No turning back now.

Back in the airlock, Jenna and I carefully lowered Miuna with one of the safety tethers. Once she was as low as she could go, she started swinging her body, first toward the *Soyokaze*, then away. Her pendulum arc gained momentum and distance, and after a few more swings she was able to grab hold of the probe and haul herself onto its cylindrical surface. She hooked the tether to a stout piece of railing that ran along the circumference of the probe. "The zip-line is in place! I'm ready for you, Jenna."

Jenna edged away from the airlock door as I clipped a long tether to her utility belt. "This is a meter shorter than the zip-line. It'll act as your brake when you reach bottom."

"A brake." Jenna swallowed hard. "Good."

I picked up a half-meter cable, hooked one end to the taut cable tying *Aphrodite* to the *Soyokaze*, and connected the other end to Jenna. "And this will keep you secured to the zip-line."

"Are you sure this is going to work?" Jenna asked, her voice cracking.

"It'll be fine. Think of this as the solar system's greatest ropes course."

"I hated that course," she muttered. She looked down toward the *Soyokaze*, then back at me, her eyes wide. "Uh, maybe you should go first. In case something happens and you need me to help with Ria."

"No, we stick to the plan. Miuna was first, then you, then me with Ria in tow. I need both of you to haul us up." I studied her. "Are you all right?"

"I, um—" Jenna cast her eyes about nervously. "I'm afraid of heights."

I gaped at her. "We've been here damn near a month, and now you're worried about how high up we are?"

"I didn't think I'd have to go outside!" She looked down again and let out a squeak.

Oh, for the love of— "Jenna, calm down. Close your eyes and take a deep breath. All right? A deep breath."

It took her a few seconds to comply, but she did. "Good, now hold it. Hold it. Release. Take another deep breath. There. Think calm, happy little vlogger thoughts. Now, put your hands to your chest."

As soon as her hands cleared the airlock's door frame, I planted a boot on her butt and shoved.

Jenna screamed the whole way down. I winced as the high-pitched shriek filled my helmet. It wasn't the safest—or nicest—thing for me to do, but we didn't have time to talk her out of a panic attack.

"Jenna, I've got you!" Miuna said. "Take my hand!"

Miuna pulled Jenna onto the probe's rounded surface. The redhead clung to the JAXA astronaut and wouldn't let go until she was secured to the *Soyokaze*. Then she flipped me off and sent a string of cuss words over the comms.

"Woah, girl, language!" I cautioned with a laugh. "What'll your chat buddies think? Hey, are you able to do instant replays of your ride down? That should earn you some big Super Chats."

"Just get down here, you crazy Amazon!"

"Be careful, Helen," Miuna added.

I dragged Ria into the airlock with me and leaned her against the wall. I moved to the outer door and hauled up the brake-line, coiling it in my arms one length at a time. Once it was back aboard, I attached the free end to my belt and grabbed two more short tethers. The first I hooked to myself and the zip-line as I'd done with Jenna, and the other I used to connect Ria and me. I yanked on each several times to make sure they were secure.

Satisfied, I pulled Ria into an awkward embrace and backed toward the airlock door. "Debora, Blanca, Aunt Helen's gonna bring your mama home." I inhaled deeply to steady my racing heart, mouthed a silent prayer, then took the final step backward.

As we slid down the zip-line, we left the shade cast by *Aphrodite's* partially deflated balloon and came into the bright sunlight of the Venusian daytime. I squinted at the sudden glare and studied *Aphrodite*. She appeared so small without *Aeneas* attached to her. *Had we really lived there for nearly a month?*

We came to a jarring stop as the brake-line went taut, leaving us suspended about a meter away from the probe itself. Miuna held out a hand. "Let the brake-line go, and we'll haul you up."

I detached the brake-line, and we slid the last meter to bump against the *Soyokaze*. Hands grabbed my shoulders. I let Ria dangle just long enough to help Miuna and Jenna pull me aboard the probe's slick surface. Together we hauled the unconscious astronaut up and hooked her to the probe.

Miuna unhooked the zip-line cable and cast it off. We were free from *Aphrodite*, and very much on our own. Jenna's helmet cam rotated this way and that, taking in all the sights and transmitting them back to Earth. She pointed. "Here it comes!"

Eurus plummeted into the orange atmosphere like a missile. A drag-chute deployed from the aft section to slow her down, and then her balloon inflated into a shiny mushroom cap. The balloon arrested the ship's fall in a sudden jolt that I remembered all too well during our entry maneuver. It hadn't been pleasant.

Jenna whooped. "It made it! Did we look that cool when we first arrived?"

Miuna laughed, and I smiled. Despite being scared out of her mind, Jenna's space geek exuberance was on full display.

Aphrodite's navigation program drew her away from us, out of the path of the approaching *Eurus*. The *Soyokaze* suddenly bucked as several motors drew in the cables attached to the support balloon. For the retrieval to succeed, the probe's profile had to be as short as possible. Miuna and Jenna squatted down, and I pressed myself against Ria.

Our helmets touched, and one of Ria's eyes opened. She tried to sit up, but I pushed her back down. "What'd I miss?" she croaked.

I blinked away tears as I grinned. "Oh, not much. Lightning strike, explosions, the ship sinking, some zip-line fun. You're just in time to ride a probe into the sunset, though."

She chuckled weakly. "Sounds like a blast."

"Oh, it's gonna be."

Eurus didn't have a windowed cockpit like *Aeneas*. Instead, there was a cup-shaped divot that the *Soyokaze* locked into. After the two craft docked, the probe's doughnut balloon released. It bounced off *Eurus's* elongated balloon and careened off into the orange sky.

With our rubbery roof no longer over our heads, Miuna set to work. She scrambled up onto *Eurus's* shiny surface and made for the hatch on top, just in front of the place where the airship's balloon met the hull. Even though she was an unmanned craft, the rocket was based off *Aeneas's* design and had a compartment that could be used for crewed configurations. It was unfurnished, which meant it didn't have the acceleration couches of our original escape rocket. The launch was going to suck, but I'd take extreme gee-forces over a slow, acidic crush any day of the week.

Once the hatch was open, Jenna helped me get Ria to her feet. We each took one of her hands and kept her between us. "This rocket's going to launch any minute now. Shake a leg, ginger!"

"Just hurry it up! I want off this crappy rock as much as you do!"

"Glad to hear it!"

We dropped down into the empty module just as the launch sequence began. Miuna shut the hatch and hit the deck next to us. A series of shudders and bangs reverberated through *Eurus* as the clamps holding it to its balloon released. The rocket fell, and for a moment fear gripped my heart. *What if the rockets failed to ignite? What if the computer didn't react in time? What if—*

With a deafening roar, *Eurus* flew skyward. Tremendous force slammed me against the module's rear wall. I wrapped my arms around Ria as *Eurus's* maneuvering thrusters kicked in. While the four of us rolled and slid, our celestial chariot steered itself into a steeper incline. I focused on my high-gee breathing exercises and was grateful for the pure oxygen in my tank: inhale, hold, sharp exhale, repeat.

As *Eurus* finished the turn, the first stage rocket cut out and severed itself. Silence filled the cabin, but I knew it wouldn't last. "Hang on!" I shouted. "This is where the fun begins!"

"Hang on?" Jenna objected. "Hang on to—"

The rest of her statement—and her subsequent screams—were lost as the second-stage engine kicked in.

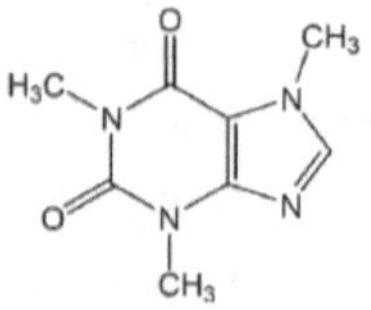

"Hey, viewers! Dr. Jenna Connolly here, back aboard *Hermes*, in case the zero-gee wasn't enough of an indicator." She floated about the cabin, pointing her camera this way and that. "We've just finished the Trans-Earth Injection burn, and in two months we'll be back on sweet terra firma. If you'll look with me outside, you'll see *Eurus* docked alongside us. Let me tell you, there is no better set of sounds than the thud and hiss of both airlocks connecting when we got back up here. Oh, and there's the *Soyokaze* still attached to the tip of *Eurus*! You didn't think we'd leave it behind, did you?"

I hung in front of a computer console, my hips strapped against the wall with Velcro. I shook my head. Less than twelve hours had passed since our miraculous escape, and the celebrity vlogger was back to business. And business was booming. Her average live audience of several thousand had turned into several million in the time since the explosion, and more were tuning in by the hour. When all was said and done, we'd learn that the raw feed of our last few hours on Venus was viewed and re-viewed more than a billion times.

Try topping that with a cute cat video.

For NASA and its private sector sponsors, this was an amazing turn. Houston was still celebrating, and there had even been talk of going ahead with the proposed follow-up missions; missions where numerous airships would link together into a floating base. From there, we'd conduct surveys of the ground via drones and rovers. The planet had a lot to offer, in scientific findings and material resources.

"I'm happy to report that Ria Ponce is going to be just fine," Jenna continued. "Her head's wrapped up like a mummy, but her spirits are high. I'm still monitoring her for a concussion, so it's about time for me to head back and make sure she isn't dozing."

That made me smile. Debora and Blanca's mama was coming home, as was Riku's mother. I looked forward to their respective reunions in a couple months, along with my own. I'd spoken briefly to Scott on a private line, but I hadn't told him about my possible change of heart on having children. I think that was best left for when I made it back to Earth. Why use words when actions would explain it so much better?

"And what's that expression about, Commander Helen?" Jenna aimed the camera at me. "Is someone thinking good thoughts?"

"Just happy to be headed home," I snapped, and hoped my cheeks weren't as red as they felt.

"Uh-huh." She turned the camera toward herself and winked. "I'm sure CAPCOM Scott Barnes feels the same way, wouldn't you all agree?"

She shoved the camera into Miuna's face. "Before we go, is there anything you'd like to say? Everyone's calling you the female Tarzan after your rope swinging stunt. There's even talk of making you an honorary member of Japan's gymnastics team at the Summer Olympics in L.A., provided we get back in time."

Miuna squirmed, and I tried not to laugh. After all we'd been through, the camera still mortified her. "That might be nice," she murmured.

Jenna turned back to me. "And how about you, Commander Helen? Any final words for the people back home?"

Other than we came, we saw, and we kicked Venus's ass? I wanted to say that, but settled for something a little more professional:

"Thank you for your prayers and support. Though it nearly ended in disaster, I would still count this mission a success." I grinned. "And as exciting as it was to be the first humans to visit Venus, the crew of *Aphrodite* can't wait to be the first to return!"

END

The Hyper Vaulter

by Michael Anthony Dioguardi

The acid burned Gena's lips. Although she double-checked before vaulting, she could feel it on the inside of her mask. Tonguing her cheek, Gena swallowed the acrid taste, knowing she'd have to accept this discomfort throughout the whole jump. The young Venusian vaulted through a bright, amber CS-tier cloud.

"3,800 feet up," she said, watching the altitude meter projected on her visor. Droplets of yellow acid beaded across the glass. She shrugged her shoulder, adjusted herself on the pole. Crunching her abs, she swept up her legs and bent the pole. *Hand to the pocket*, she thought. *Top hand strong.*

Her feet pierced the cloud first, her body a straight line oriented at Venus's stratosphere. The droplets sped off her visor, her vision now cleared. The sun grew in size, glistening down on the acidic dew that remained on Gena's suit. Whenever Gena breached the sulfuric clouds, she imagined cold cascading over her body.

Lifting her top hand off the pole, she touched a button on her forearm interface. Four bags unfurled from the lateral compartment of her suit. Thin metallic strings reached their maximum length, giving way to wrinkly balloons, Venusian aquifers. She gripped the pole with both hands and glanced back. "Great, no duds. Four water receptacles, ready to go."

Reaching the maximum ascent of her jump, she shielded the sun with her arm and looked out at the horizon. On a clear day, she could see Maxwell Montes, the rust-dyed massif. She beheld the unfettered sky until she started to descend into the clouds.

"Damn bags!" she reached over and tapped her forearm interface. The bags collapsed, their orifices closing shut before their metal guidelines retracted into her suit. The commotion tilted her trajectory. Gena fought to grip the pole without pulling it in. But her bottom hand gave, and she fell beneath the pole. "Not good! Not good!" she shouted.

She straightened out her arms with her top hand above her head. The altitude gauge inside her visor blinked red. Gena couldn't see ahead; she stared aghast at the swirling deluge of brown and yellow. If it weren't for her many years of vaulting, Gena would have landed on the cinders of

Venus's surface, breaking each bone in her body before the suit-punctures filled with acid.

Gena kicked her boots together; fiery exhaust flowed out from their heels. A line of fire swiveled beneath her, slowing her descent. The warning system increased its cadence, beeping and flashing red. She felt around for the switch—a small latch on her left heel—and when she found it, kicked down. Fire roared from her feet, kicking up the scorched iron dust beneath her. Gena's boots crunched against the surface. The altitude gauge decreased, and the temperature gauge replaced its resonance, returning to its standard state.

With her left hand still gripping the pole, Gena's fingers crept up the confines of the metal and located the edges of a small latch. She unhinged it and pressed down on the pole. The sound of the pole contracting echoed between the low-lying clouds overhead. *Szoom szoom szoom*, the metal ends collided against one another, driving coupling into coupling. Gena dug her boots into the ground, bracing for the final impact. She placed her right hand over her left and closed her eyes. *Szoom szoom, thwank…*

A shock rippled throughout her body. She felt it in her toes; she felt it in her teeth. But years of water runs gave her unique brawn to stand her ground. Modern hyper vaulting poles were light, weighing around fifty pounds. Gena's was a scrappy build. The pole's shaft was sourced from materials she'd scavenged: unwanted and abandoned poles from the lower decks of Дом.

Gena hauled the pole onto her shoulder. It collapsed into itself like a baton, a cylinder of around two feet in diameter and four in length. The temperature gauge in her visor continued to rise.

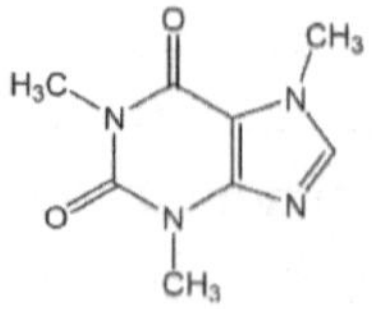

Дом stood stalwart among the clouds, its shadow looming on the Venusian plane. The majority of vaulters stayed within the confines of Дом; Gena's walk would be a short one. She reached behind her and patted the aquifers that filled during her jump. She sighed, knowing that it would only sell for around 16-20 *Behepas*.

Dozens of shanty pods lay at the base of Дом. The roofs and walls on each one varied depending on the builder and material. Gena, along with any other *krysa* (bottom dweller in old Ven'ûs) could recognize when the habs had been built, with their siding showing acidic decay. Nearly two hundred years ago, when the first explorers from Earth set foot on Venus, they laid down the foundations for Дом, not knowing what it would become. Under constant renovation and repair, Дом had recently risen to the height of 4,288 feet.

Gena kicked a rock in front of her. She smiled and kicked it with her other foot. It bounced over a modest molehill and hurried down toward the nearest hab. She shrugged her shoulder, adjusting the collapsed pole against her body. Her muscles burned, but it was something she'd become accustomed to. Gena had tolerated much longer walks before.

Three *venurete* pipes jutted out from the exterior wall of the hab. Venurete was the Venusian counterpart to Earthen concrete, crafted in a similar fashion with a mixture of cinder, blackstone, acid, and peroxide. As venurete aged, thin, scribbly lines like microscopic lightning bolts decorated its flesh. Black flakes crumbled off its corroded surface layer, joining the landscape below. Gena paused at the end of the pipe and lifted the latch to the remote box on the inside wall. As she pressed the button, she glanced down the end of the pipe at an unmoved door.

Reaching around the box, Gena ripped the frame from the pipe's wall. Exposed wire jutted out; each one painted a different color before fraying out into thin bushy strands. Knotting together the red and yellow wires, the door budged, rising an inch from its starting position. With another twist and turn of the copper ends, the door slid open. Gena replaced the wall panel and climbed up into the hole, placing her foot atop the lip and pulling herself inside the pipe.

The outside light faded as she crawled further down. She slinked forward until her entire body filled the space. Not able to see behind her, Gena used her feet to blindly locate the malfunctioning door and forced it close. Pushing forward, she arrived at the second door.

She pressed her hands against the pipe where she knew the operating box was hidden. She lifted the hatch and pressed the button; she could hear a mechanical hissing noise from above. Gaps opened up in the pipe.

Sodium bicarbonate spewed out in a concentrated spray from the perforated venurete, showering her. On the upper decks of Дом, Gena imagined they used water, or perhaps a fancy concoction of specialized alkaline solution to counteract the layers of sulfuric acid.

Poking out her head from the pipe, Gena pushed her torso through and jumped down from the lip. She stood in a hexagonal room, with several shower heads protruding from the ceiling, and one mirror on the wall. The floor was an altered type of interior venurete, and outside of the room was the remainder of the docking facility.

Gena undressed, her reflection a faint blur on the glass. She removed her helmet, letting her hair fall onto her shoulders. She continued by decompressing her shoulder attachments from her pectoral attachments, folding the suit parts on top of one another. From head to toe, she was coated in sweat. Exposure to the cool air sent chills throughout Gena's body; as hot as it was in the lower decks, it was brisk in comparison to the scorching terrain of Venus. She flipped the suit upside down to remove the aquifers from the lateral receptacles. Gena felt a slight burn where her neck and chin met—sulfuric residue, a familiar sensation for all who lived on Venus, regardless of lower or upper decks. Gena stepped forward, catching her reflection in the glass.

Her skin was dark—a deep umber from years of melanin build-up. Genetic melanin overproduction became commonplace on Venus after two hundred years. The rapid onset of the mutation came as a surprise to Earthen and Venusian scientists alike. The lower your dwelling was in Дом, the higher your likelihood was of having the distinct Venusian skin tone. Naturally, this created a visible division among the population. Although over ninety percent of Venus's population was indigenous—with Earthen migration steadily decreasing over the last twenty years—there was a bifurcation in DNA among the population. Gena could always tell where someone came from, or at least label them with an approximate height of their dwelling.

In addition to her skin tone, Gena was covered in *shrams*: white specks, scars from sulfuric burns. Gena kept count when she was little. She'd count until she ran out of numbers. By the time she was a teenager, her entire body was covered in them.

Gena rubbed her chin; the burning sensation followed her fingernail. She stuck out her hand, touching the lever on another control pad. After a rumble of mechanical parts, sodium bicarbonate solution drizzled down from the showerheads. Gena stepped into the mist and watched as it beaded up on her skin before sliding down to the floor drain. She looked back up at the glass, watching her reflection blur. Brown skin marbled with white like paint on a pallet.

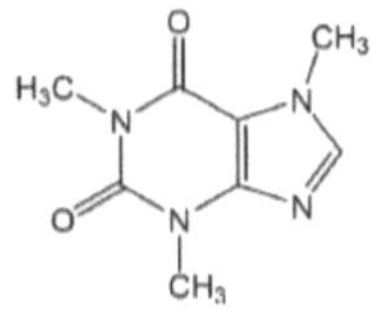

Gena walked out of the excursion room and stepped into the general habitat. Forming a part of Дом's foundation, the room itself was the largest of the local cluster. It smelled old and musty. People joked that the true mark of a lower-deck Venusian is to look up their nostrils; they'd not have a single hair due to elevated levels of ambient acidity. Mechanical timbre provided a consistent background noise in the entirety of the space.

Patting down her hair with a towel, Gena noticed the commotion within the gen-hab. Two children, Janus and Abril, ran up to Gena, embracing her legs and shouting in a mixture of English, Russian, and Ven'ûs.

"*Gena'dare! Dare, heru tap tap*! Hyper vault!" the girl shouted, looking up at Gena with a huge grin.

"She always brings *heru*!" the boy said in a snarky tone,

Gena sighed, looking behind her at the door to the excursion room. "I have only enough for 16-20 Behepas." She watched the expression on their faces diminish.

"A few drops now?" Gena continued. "Or mas-toy later?"

The girl's face lit up at the sound of mas-toy, a sugary mixture that could only be obtained above deck 50.

"Can I have some too?" the boy asked, his arms clutched around Gena's thighs.

Gena lifted both arms. "Only if you can hang on!"

She tickled the boy until he giggled himself off her leg. The girl let go, before moving in and nestling against Gena's knee.

Serra and Geoff walked out from the consumption wing, each one staring at their forearm interfaces. They lifted their heads to acknowledge Gena and proceeded across the hab toward their destination, the central lift.

"Hey, Serra!" Gena said, louder than she wanted to.

Serra turned around halfway, glancing down at her interface and then back up again. Geoff stopped, shifting his weight onto one leg as he exhaled.

"Had a nice solo run before," Gena said. Her heart started to thump.

Serra nodded; her eyes wide underneath arched eyebrows. Geoff turned his attention from Gena back to his interface. Serra wore mid-tier silk drapes, only slightly yellowed in certain blotches. Her skin was an olive beige, with a few notable shrams on her face and neck area.

"Cool…I, uh…," Serra replied, "I didn't know we were allowed to do solo runs with the Gaska mandate."

Gena's stomach churned. She'd forgotten about the new restrictions.

"No Gaska mandate is going to stop me," Gena said, trying to sound confident and dismissive at the same time.

Geoff let out a huff. He turned toward the lift while tapping his forearm interface.

Serra squinted at Gena. "You're crazy girl. Don't gas out. We still got today's jump. Gaska-sanctioned and all. Supposed to storm out too." She turned to follow Geoff.

The children ran off toward the sounds of the conversation. Gena followed while rubbing her hair with a towel. A dozen vaulters sat on stools, surrounding a venurete table. Gena could tell the table had once been an outdoor fixture; it was littered with scars. At the table's center sat Mother Buñuel, her white hair flowing over her back, almost hitting the ground.

"Excuse me, *perdón*," Gena said as she squeezed by a group of vaulters, some sitting, others standing.

She paused behind Mother Buñuel, admiring the old woman's body. Her bones protruded from underneath her drapes: bony shoulders and wrinkly neck behind a long maim of acid-stained hair. Mother Buñuel's skin was covered almost entirely with *shrams,* her natural tone now just a scarce remnant among a sea of scarred white. Wrinkles hung down from her cheeks and neck—her earlobes drooped with age.

"Mother Buñuel," Gena whispered, bent next to the old woman's side. Mother Buñuel turned, revealing a toothless mouth. "*Mijita*," she leaned over to kiss Gena on the cheek.

"There were cumulonimbus clouds right outside Maxwell Montes base. I was able to break through at 3,500 feet."

Mother Buñuel rubbed Gena's shoulder. "Did you find a *doraposa*?"

"No. I didn't see one."

"You just have to keep searching."

At the mention of the doraposa, Janus and April scurried out from under the table and ran to Mother Buñuel's sides.

"La doraposa!" April said. "Tell us the story!"

The conversations hushed to murmurs. The old vaulter cleared her throat. With a warm smile, she began.

"The golden Venusian flower; it exists, I have seen it with my own eyes. When I was a little girl, before Дом was more than 2,000 feet, we'd jump far and wide searching for water. A storm was scheduled to hit our jump zone. We were a hearty bunch. We jumped anyway. You see, after Venusian storms, something happens way up in the clouds..."

Gena watched as the room filled with smiles. This was everyone's favorite part of the story.

"Some say it's magic, while others say it's a scientific anomaly. Believe what you want, but after these storms, seeds appear in the sky—some of them so *pequeñin* you can't see them… but they're there! And sometimes, if the seed gets enough sunlight…"

"It grows!" Janus quipped.

A few giggles escaped the crowd.

"Yes, up from the seed sprouts a golden stem. If that golden stem survives, a bulb forms. White petals, delicate as silk, bloom and reach out to the sun. And then, when the sun recedes and the doraposa is left in darkness, it sheds its petals as tears. Those tears…they are the sweetest droplets of water you'll ever taste. The doraposa needs a lifetime to grow tired, gifting their fresh water for centuries..."

Suspense filled the room.

"…She thinks not of their life
She thinks not of their love
Venus knows no life
Venus bears no love
Her heart, an ashen rock
Cut from her sister long ago
One filled with fire and hate
The other with water and love
And when the amber wind blows
The doraposa takes root
Only then does Venus remember
Only then does Venus love…

And that is why we jump. For water, for life…for the doraposa."

As Mother Buñuel concluded her story, Gena stepped into the shadow of the hallway corridor. The conversations resumed. Janus pleaded for Mother Buñuel to tell it again. Gena held her aquifers close to her body, her destination: the Sham'liue marketplace.

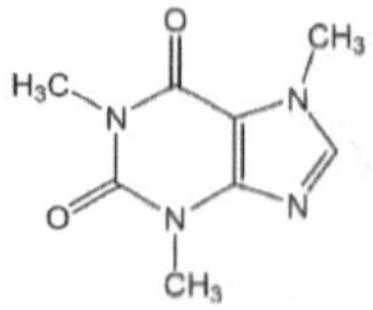

People packed into the central lift more with each passing level. The different decks had their own distinct aromas. The rotten eggs smell of the lower decks eventually dissipated as the elevator chugged along. As the entry corridor slid open, permitting entry to level fourteen dwellers, Gena's nose itched at something she would never be accustomed to. She was attuned to the lower levels and the change in scent was the most pungent—*Stale, sterilized, too clean,* she thought.

A man stepped into the elevator, standing in front of her. The lift was large enough for around thirty people to stand. Gena held onto the string handles of a cloth sack. Inside the sack, Gena stowed away her aquifers, filled with a modest but nonetheless profitable amount of potable water.

The elevator transitioned from its vertical ascent to a horizontal rewind. Дом's internal structure—particularly around the mid-to-lower sections—lacked traditional intuitive design. Governmental officials rarely traveled lower than deck thirty, so it was natural that the lower decks had questionable infrastructure.

The lift came to a stop and the doors opened. A group of children led by their teacher entered and surrounded Gena. She scooched her bag over, so they were between her legs. Children clad in grey uniforms piled in around her, speaking in English with a few Ven'ûs words thrown in.

"Pardon," she said, raising her arm to prevent a scurrying boy from stepping on her bag.

The boy looked at her and scrunched his face. Gena knew he'd rarely—if ever—heard a lower deck accent. She stood in place, quietly monitoring her surroundings. Soon they'd arrive at level forty-nine, to Sham'liue.

Gena hefted the bag into her arms, its weight assuring her that the aquifers were all present. The elevator open and all exited, stepping out into the Sham'liue marketplace. Neon green signs and globular lights decked the ceiling and walls. The corridor itself was only about fifteen feet wide. The storefronts and side-rooms varied in size depending on when they were built and who the developers paid off to skirt regulation.

Being a lower deck jumper, Gena had exposure to a decent hodgepodge of languages and cultures, yet nothing compared to being in the thick of Sham'liue. Over a century ago, Chinese settlers constructed the marketplace in their vision of the ancient city of Hong Kong. Gena had heard Mother Buñuel talk about some of the old Earthen cities before. When Gena was younger, she'd close her eyes and imagine herself roaming the streets of Hong Kong. Skies blue and grey. The air cold and wet. No egg smells.

"Shuǐ yào! Sweet water!" a man shouted as he approached Gena.

"No thank you," Gena replied, dodging out of his path as she passed.

Storefront counters displayed food and beverages, while others sold parts, scrap, water components, and hydrogen splitters from Mars. If you couldn't scavenge it yourself from the planes of Imdr Regio, you could always find someone in Sham'liue who sold it.

Groups of shoppers gathered around each of the storefronts. Children played with their *volchkis,* a spinning top toy containing anti-gravity proton receptors. They floated in the air like oversized flies. Sweet water junkies aligned the curb in front of the storefronts, bubbles exiting their eyeballs every few seconds—a common side effect of overdosing on *shuǐ yào*.

Four Gaska guardians marched down the corridor, each one armed with a Mag-rifle, their stocks sleek with off-Venus metals. Gena maneuvered to the right side of the corridor, trying to blend into the crowd as they passed. If a Gaska guardian saw what she carried, they might ask questions about how and where she'd retrieved the water.

She glimpsed bright white hands. Most men and women that entered the Gaska unit came from the upper decks. Rumors floated around that some of them, if not all, were bred specifically to become guards.

Gena caught the glare of the foremost guard. His lip lifted into a condescending snarl and his eyes narrowed onto her bag. She switched arms, hoisting the bag in her left hand. Gena remembered that she was the darkest person in the corridor, and that her sheer number of shrams was a telling sign of where she'd come from. She thought for a moment that the guard might have noticed her, striking a pulse of fear in her heart.

"Almost there, almost there," she muttered to herself. She glanced at the storefront signs as she passed. Some glowed in neon and argon light, while others were crudely etched onto brightstone with cinder.

Gena was looking for Kuku Corn, an otherwise innocuous storefront that specialized in Venusian Corn, of the Kuku variant—stalks the size of an enlarged human finger. Gena had used them before to trade water in for mas-toy. They paid in standard Behepas as well, but Gena—like lower-tier dwellers—had less need for tangible currency.

With his back facing the central causeway, Gena recognized Wo'las standing in the back of the unlit Kuku Corn storefront. Wo'las was fatter than the average Venusian, but Gena supposed he was normal-sized for a middle-tier dweller. Gena checked the busy street and stepped toward Kuku Corn.

"Let's just get this over with," she whispered to herself. She was on edge from the lift ride and the dirty look the Gaska guardian had given her moments prior. And although he tried not show it, Wo'las preferred not to associate with people from the lower sections; he didn't want to draw the ire of the Gaska guardians.

Venturing out into the Venusian planes was considered grunt work by many, with the only exception being held for military or scientific personnel. Long gone were the days of glory from exploration. Venus had been thoroughly navigated a century prior, with the first of many circumnavigations occurring more than one hundred and fifty years ago.

"Gena vaulter! *Privet,*" Wo'las said as he emerged from the shadowed storefront.

Suddenly, Gena felt something clinch her on both elbows. Four hands wrapped around her biceps, forcing her knees to buckle. She dropped down, her feet no longer supporting her body. She felt another hand press on the back of her neck. She couldn't turn her head. From the corner of her eye, she noticed the teal-blue Gaska coupling. She smelled the stench of shuǐ yào emanating from one of her accoster's mouths.

"*Violent Krysa this one!*" she heard a man's voice from behind her. She smelled the sweet water breath again.

"*On a heru run, were we?*" the man said with a cackle, his upper-tier accent almost as pungent as his breath.

She thrashed about, screaming and jerking her head. She lunged forward, cranking her head sideways and brandishing her teeth.

"Frenz! Elektroshoker!" shouted someone else. Gena a pinch on her back. From her face to her toes, every muscle in her body contracted. She felt warm. Her eyes shut.

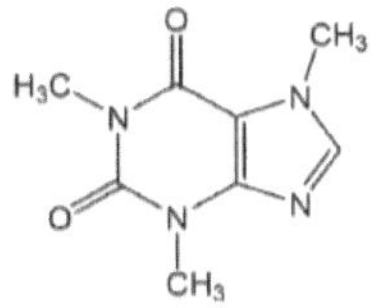

Gena awakened with her face pressed against a cool surface. She remembered touching something cold once when she was little. It was too long ago for her to recall. But she knew it felt like this—like air biting into flesh.

Gena peeled her tongue off the roof of her mouth, swallowing a grainy sliver of spit. The air was dry. She blinked. Everything looked blurry and wavy, her head felt like it was spinning. Her body vibrated but she did not know why. The tingling she'd felt on her cheek had spread to every hair follicle on her skin.

She reached up to rub her eyes, bracing herself before making contact with the back of her hand. As a lower-tier dweller, Gena had learned to tolerate the slight acidic burn in her eyes whenever she touched them. But this time, there was no burning. No sensation at all. She rubbed her eyes, massaging them like she'd never done before. Images invaded her thoughts. Walking around. People everywhere. The central lift.

As her vision returned to normal, Gena looked around and realized she was in a jail cell. Gena's body revolted as she tried to sit up. It was as if every muscle in her body had been stretched beyond their limits—a million tears on each tendon and ligament.

Gena noticed a porthole, and the latch along its edge. She reached over and lifted it up, filtering in a blinding light. Gena fell backward, guarding her eyes. After a few moments of recovering from the initial blast of light, she grabbed the porthole frame and pulled herself up.

At first, she had to shield her eyes with her hand, as she would when vaulting at the apex of a jump. Once adjusted, Gena removed her hand and saw a beautiful view of the planet below. She'd only seen sights similar to this while vaulting on clear days. She could see Sol and she swore she could see Earth if she squinted hard enough.

Gena turned around at the sound of approaching footsteps. She watched as three men dressed in Gaska uniforms filled the doorway; the foremost guard stepped into the cell and glared at her.

"*Krysa!*" the guard said, his voice deep and gravelly. Gena could tell he'd suffered a sulfuric burn in his throat at some point. *A pity*, she thought, *as if his accent wasn't bad enough.*

"Cuff her," he said.

The two guards stepped out and approached Gena. Hooking underneath each arm, they hoisted her onto her feet and dragged her forward. She tried to protest, but her voice only cracked. *This air…so dry*, she thought. She knew she couldn't fight back; her muscles were too sore, and her thoughts still scattered.

After walking through a series of cold, barren corridors, the guards paused before a door that slid open to what Gena thought could only be an elevator. She didn't see them press any buttons nor did she hear them mutter a single word; the lift appeared to move independently from their input. Gena was not aware of where they were taking her.

The subtly of the elevator was alien to a bottom-dweller. But before she knew it, the elevator arrived at its destination. The door opened and Gena felt a blast of cool air.

She kept her head up and stepped forward, inadvertently assisting the guards with their duty. Her vision had nearly recovered or at least she thought that it did. She could make out the details of the walls and ceiling. Everything had a yellow tint to it. She couldn't tell if the interior material was a type of venurete she'd never seen before or if it was something entirely different.

The guards took a few more steps before stopping in front of a door. The door slid upward; light poured into the hallway. The two guards loosened their grips on her arms, assuming a more humane hold.

Moisture returned to the tip of her tongue as if the air around her had been injected with water. She began to glisten; except this time, it was not a fault of the oppressive Venusian heat but from the humidity concealed in the quarter. Gena licked her lips and noticed that this was something she never tasted before. There was no familiar sulfuric taste that spiced all food on Venus, and Gena realized this was her first sample of untainted water.

Opposite her was a massive window that occupied the whole wall. Gena gasped at the sight before her—at the grays and golds, swirling in whirlwinds and clouds right outside the window's glass. The view was more beautiful than the one from the jail cell. Gena fell to her knees; partially in awe, partially in exhaustion.

There was a desk in the center of the room, with a singular chair facing the raging storm outside. The guards raised Gena back to her feet, pushing her forward. After she took a few steps, they turned around and walked out the door. It closed softly, with only a faint whistle.

Gena was in a daze. She crossed her arms over her stomach, feeling like she hadn't eaten in days. She thought about the last time she'd eaten and couldn't remember anything before the jail cell.

Before she could lose herself in her thoughts, the chair in front of her swung around. Seated in the chair was a woman not like anyone else Gena had ever seen, not even in her dreams. Her skin was an alabaster white, the color of a shram, but without any of the scarring. Her hair was as light as her skin—her eyes a reddish-orange, intensified by a shimmering gold collar necklace. She wore a dark blue dress that seemed to pulse in color as if it was alive.

Entranced by her appearance, Gena hardly noticed that the woman looked back upon her with equal admiration. Gena suddenly felt self-conscious, unsure about what she looked like since awakening in the jail cell. She imagined her hair, braids unraveling and unkempt. She hoped that they still covered her most hideous shrams.

"Salu, Gena…," the woman said, her accent soft and fragile, as if it the words would fall apart if not carefully lifted from her lips.

Gena winced. She felt a wave of terror reverberate down her spine. An upper-level dweller would never speak with someone so far beneath them, let alone set eyes on such a lower-deck scoundrel.

"Excuse my hesitancy to speak," the woman continued. "I have watched you for many years. You are Gena, of level…one. You follow the great vaulter they call Mother Buñuel."

"Salu…," Gena swallowed, "I'm sorry…I'm not used to being noticed." She squinted at the woman. "Who are you?"

The woman cocked her head and smiled; her teeth as bright as Sol. "I always wanted to be a vaulter just like you. When I was young, I would beg my parents, but they never let me go out onto the surface." She paused, breathed out. "I am Hedra. The Executor of Level 191."

Gena remembered studying the breakdown of Δoм's government in school. She recalled the three separations: the Lembos, the merchant body, the Gaskas, the military body, and the Executor, the most powerful of the elected.

"It's the newest extension—" Hedra said.

"Why am I here?" Gena interrupted.

She cleared her throat. "Please excuse your seizure, I needed to find you. I needed you…in particular."

Gena blinked and shook her head. She knew Δoм was ever-expanding but never imagined the building reaching this level. Before she could think of a response, Hedra lowered her head and continued, "We are in crisis, although it does not appear to be. Our water comes from the Aqua-nexus reservoir; it is the main water-supply line for this level and twenty below it." Hedra exhaled. "Our hydrogen splitters are running dry. I'm afraid Venus has given us what she can, and now we must rely on other methods to obtain our water."

Gena struggled to contain her reaction, trying not to smirk at this strange woman. *Why do I care if your reservoirs are drying up? What have you done for me? For my people?* she thought. *We're lucky if our reservoirs hold enough water for a week.*

Hedra lifted her head, signaling at the center of the table. A projection device beamed a light above the table. After the initial fuzziness had cleared, Gena watched as the light took shape and blossomed in a flower, its petals golden and shaped like butterflies. Gena remembered this projection, thinking back to the ancient image logs she'd seen in school that came from Earth. In the center of the flower grew a black, porous bulb, beaded with droplets that raced down onto the petals. Remembering Mother Buñuel's story, Gena thought, *It is true! All the stories!*

"There is native flora on this planet," Hedra said. "You are looking at the *gerbera primula sulphuris*, known in Ven'ûs as *the doraposa*. It has a proclivity to appear during times of great storms, although it can be found in naturally occurring weather. One doraposa is capable of creating a nearly endless supply of water. That is how the legend goes…"

Hedra looked down. She began again, her voice frailer than before. "We need your help. You are the most capable of vaulters. More capable than your matron Buñuel. A storm approaches; you must retrieve the doraposa. Even if that means giving your life to Venus…"

At that moment, the floor shuddered, and the projection began flickering. Amber-colored liquid splattered over the window. The skies darkened, clouds shielding out the sunlight. A storm raged outside. Gena looked beyond Hedra at the wildness that brewed outside Дом.

Hedra followed Gena's gaze and turned to look out the window. "It has come…"

The restrictions Gaska had issued just a few days prior started to make sense. Did they plan this all along? she thought.

Hedra stood up from her chair and walked closer to the window. She repeated lines from the poem Gena knew too well:

"…She thinks not of their life
She thinks not of their love
Venus knows no life
Venus bears no love

Her heart, an ashen rock
Cut from her sister long ago
One filled with fire and hate
The other with water and love
And when the amber wind blows
The doraposa takes root
Only then does Venus remember
Only then does Venus love…"

Gena walked around the desk and paused next to Hedra, taking a moment to admire her beauty and strangeness. She wanted to touch her skin but feared any residual acid would burn her frail body. She looked back out at the maddening clouds. A brown whirlwind rushed from one to another, creating a churning river of acid. Lightning crashed in the distance, illuminating the darkness within. Gena stared, entranced by the devastating beauty. She'd seen storms before but nothing like this.

Hedra turned to face Gena and said flatly, "You have violated the Gaska mandate…"

Taken aback by the change in Hedra's tone, Gena said, "It was only for…w…how…how did you know…?"

"I watch you," Hedra replied. "I know what times you jump. Have no fear. The Executor has no interest in pursuing disciplinary actions."

Gena let out a breath of relief. Her heart weighed down in her chest. Gena remembered vaulting earlier in the day. She'd retrieved water and was going to sell it in Sham'liue. *Did I make it there?* she thought.

Hedra continued, "Rather, I wanted to show you…" She pointed down through the window.

Gena leaned close to the window to see below. One by one, vaulters pierced the storm clouds, headed for Дом. Two more jumpers pulled through the top of the clouds, their poles firing from different heights as they increased their altitude. Gena swore she recognized them. *Serra?* she thought, *Possibly, next to Geoff.* She watched as they pushed their hips up, extending their bodies upward. But at the apex of the jump, no aquifers jettisoned from their lateral compartments. This was no collection mission; they were fighting to survive.

Gena's heart skipped, realizing the likely fate of the jumpers in a storm like this. She noticed a third jumper bursting through the cloud as the two in front began their descent. A small vaulter with idiosyncratic form, leaping higher than anyone she'd seen before—they flew over the underlying storm cloud as if they were naturally airborne. A red trail of dust followed, the mark of the lead vaulter.

"Mother Buñuel…," Gena whispered.

Hedra reached for Gena's hand, her touch a freezing sensation that could entrance any Venusian. The Executor didn't say a word, but Gena knew she wanted her to go.

Gena started toward the opposite end of the room. The door opened without any direct operation. She ran down the hall, not knowing where she was heading.

Down, she thought, as she picked up speed. *Down!*

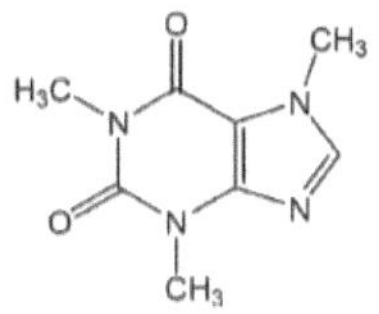

Gena's leg itched. It was too late though. Any attempt at itching would be a weak rub on her suit's fabric. She took a step forward, wind pelting her suit as she walked. Sulfuric acid sprayed against her visor, dirtied by the silt whipped up by the storm. The scent of acid reacquainted with her senses.

Six jumps, she calculated, *maybe seven or eight?* Gena knew the average distance of each jump could vary, especially with the storm conditions. Checking her oxygen and temperature gauges, she knelt down and unfurled the pole.

Holding the pole underneath her arm, Gena grasped on top with her other hand and started jogging. She picked up speed, her feet digging into the dirt more with each passing step. Once at a sprint, her knees raised to her waist as her arms lifted straight away from her chest. In one motion she extended the pole above her head and slammed it down into the dirt. The coils protracted, pushing the height of the pole above ten feet. Gena held on, her arms held out straight, her abs crunched. She swung her body upward as the pole continued its expansion. The pole's propulsion rockets fired beneath her, pushing the pole skyward. Gena's feet came into view, her body now vertical. She brought in her arm to her hip. The pole continued to expand.

The storm buffeted her suit with strong and sudden gusts. Acid splashed against her suit, eating away slowly at the specialized fabric. As she approached the maximum ascent of her first jump, she could make out the exhaust trails of the other jumpers lingering in the troposphere. The smoke was thick and unmoving; Gena knew they were near.

During her first descent, acid accumulations obscured her vision. Thick CS-tier clouds clumped together beneath her feet. Rockets fired as she neared the ground, the pole collapsing more with each passing second. Her feet landed on scorched rock.

In front of her huddled a group of five jumpers, each of their poles wrapped under their arms or strung atop their shoulders. Switching to a communal voice channel, she noticed their voices, scratchy and exacerbated by the storm.

"It's Gena," one of the jumpers said. Gena recognized the man's voice.

"Geoff!" she shouted. "Where are the others?"

Geoff panted. "Only seven of us went out. We were desperate. The storm…it was too strong.…"

Reaching the group, Gena took a moment to regain her composure and looked around at the rest of the group. Familiar faces but no Buñuel, no Serra. Gena began to imagine them stranded in the storm.

Geoff coughed and said, "Serra went back in—"

"And Mother Buñuel?"

Geoff panted without response. He turned and readied his pole. "We need to go back and regroup."

"We need to help them, now!"

"I'm sorry, Gena…," he said before jogging back in the direction of Дом. The rest of the jumpers followed Geoff. Gena watched them vault into the clouds, knowing that they'd given up on Serra and Mother Buñuel. She turned back around and faced the approaching storm. She'd jumped in the edges of the maelstrom before, and now she needed to jump into the thick of it.

The storm whipped up a deluge of cinder. The particles collided against Gena, each collision just enough to bruise her beneath her suit. For the first time in a long time, Gena's arms trembled as she clasped the pole. She thought of Serra and of Mother Buñuel, and the diminishing likelihood of finding them in these conditions. She came down from her second jump, landing with the assistance of her gauges; the view of the ground was all but washed away by the storm. She looked around hoping to spot Serra's chemtrails, but it was impossible with the wind.

Gena took a bearing of her vital signs and started her third jump. Gena doubted she could make another; there was simply not enough fuel, oxygen, or suit resistance. She dived through another set of thick clouds, traversing to the other side.

Sunlight gleamed between the nimbus clouds above; she had entered the eye of the storm. Gena knew that in these precious moments she could gain some semblance of visibility. She rocked her head from side to side, looking out for any chemtrails that hadn't been swallowed by the storm. As she grazed the underbelly of a cloud overhead, she glimpsed a meandering coil of smoke. She shifted, throwing off her trajectory going into her descent. For a moment she fell, her pole collapsing as she gained speed rocketing through cloud after cloud. Then she saw it: the midsection of an oncoming pole.

Reacting quickly, she initiated her pole's thrusters, driving her toward the passing pole. At first, she wasn't sure if it was Serra or Mother Buñuel, but it didn't take long to confirm it—no red smoky residue. It was Serra.

Both poles collapsed only a few feet apart, their vaulters returning to the ground while the storm raged around them. Their heat signatures increased, emitting the emergency beacon from both of their suits. Gena tried opening a communication channel; all she could hear was static and fuzz. Despite the rising pain, Gena ran to Serra.

Serra stumbled. She had improvised repairs all over her suit—taped up shoulder spaulders, a patched waist tear. She was in bad shape. Serra placed her hands on her knees and doubled over.

"Serra!" Gena broke through. "Serra!"

Gena ran up and embraced Serra. She was relieved to see her still alive. But their moment came to an abrupt end, as Gena needed to press on.

"Can you make it back?" she asked, already preparing herself for a fourth jump.

"I think so…," Serra replied, her voice hoarse with acid burns. "Gena…I…" she struggled. "Don't go. You'll die out there, and I can't let you do that."

"We don't have time for this!" Gena shouted. "Mother Buñuel is out there. We need to find her!"

Serra stepped forward and threw her arms around Gena's neck and pressed their visors together.

"Please be safe. I want to see you again—"

Serra's communication channel cut out. Gena turned and set out on her next jump.

As Gena climbed through the air on her fourth jump, anxiety flooded her veins. Her vision fogged and her hair matted with sweat. *How far am I from base?* she thought. Most jumps—unless accompanied by a transport—were within a comfortable distance of home. The storm must have taken Mother Buñuel far off-course.

She felt in her gut that she was at the steppe of the Aphrodite Terra Mountain Range. At any moment, her jump could be jeopardized by an unexpected crag or jetty. As she reached the top of her jump, Gena choked on her own breath. A rugged mountain face stood before her, taller than her pole. In a few seconds, she'd smash against the wall.

She engaged her foot thrusters while clinging to her pole, contracting it as she flew upward. She closed her eyes and braced herself as the pole inched closer to the wall. The tips of her boots scraped against the ground. She felt pressure in her thighs, a strong counter-leverage in her returning pole. She landed on a plateaued section of the mountain.

Gena tucked the pole as it retreated into its final coupling. She took a bearing of her surroundings. Red dust trickled down from the clouds above her; Mother Buñuel had been here. Gena looked down at the footprints. With every ounce of remaining energy, Gena pressed on, following the path veiled in red dust. The storm had passed this area, leaving a breeze interrupted by gusts of substrate and small rocks.

This was the furthest Gena had ever ventured before. To any Earthen observer, the landscape would have looked hellish, filled with smoldering craters, storms raging across the horizon raining down with their acidic torrents. But to Gena, it was the purest beauty.

The shadow crept up from behind her. Gena turned to face Mother Buñuel, collapsed against a rock and beckoning for Gena.

"Mamí!" Gena shouted. She switched to interpersonal coms and shouted again. The static had dissipated; she could hear Mother Buñuel breathing.

Mother Buñuel attempted to speak but could only utter a few whispers. Gena ran over, kneeling at her side. Through her visor, Gena made out the details of Mother Buñuel's face. Their faces resembled each other's, dark with white scars decorating every curve and corner of their figure. Gena forced a smile.

"We have to bring you back," she said, grasping Mother Buñuel's hands. The heat radiated through her gloves, nearly burning Gena's skin.

"*Mijita…*," Mother Buñuel whispered.

Her heat index was rising quickly; they both would need to move soon before their suit systems broke down.

"There's no *regresa*…for me…" Mother Buñuel said. She pointed beyond Gena. She smiled and said, "The doraposa… I saw it…"

Gena's heart jumped at the mention of the mysterious flower. She shook her head and said, "No, Mamí, no doraposa, we have to get you back."

Gena reached around the old woman's torso and tried to lift her up, fighting through the burning on her hands and arms.

"No!" Mother Buñuel shouted, pushing Gena away.

Tears rolled down Gena's cheeks while a trail of yellow acid rolled down Mother Buñuel's.

"*Mosaka!*" Mother Buñuel said: the Old Ven'ûs word for *death*. She pressed her visor against Gena's, waiting for her response.

"Mosaka…," Gena said, her lips trembling.

Mother Buñuel grabbed Gena's hand and gave it a long squeeze. Then, the old woman let go, reached for her release valve, and removed her helmet. Mother Buñuel was set aflame. Gena backed away, watching with somber understanding as the woman's skin deteriorated into ashes. Gena picked up her aquifers.

"Mosaka," Gena repeated.

Gena turned around; in front of her, she saw the legendary pole of Mother Buñuel. She stepped forward and lifted it from the ground. The weight surprised her. She was accustomed to heavier poles; this was the lightest she'd ever held. Gena felt magic in her hands, as if she was holding something powerful.

She looked westward over a sun-splashed sky. Clouds drifted by, chasing the storm's wake. All she needed was one jump, one chance to see if the doraposa was real, if what Mother Buñuel said was actually true. If Gena found a single doraposa, water could be provided for centuries. She took off running.

The control mechanism was similar to her pole. Following her plant, Gena rose frightfully fast, the pole extending faster than hers ever could. In its wake, the exhaust outlets exuded a red-dyed gas.

Gena completed all the expected body movements in her jump, the surface beneath her becoming more obscure with each second. She breached the clouds overhead, looking for the doraposa flower. Gena ignored the flashes of red and beeping noises in her helmet, alerting her of her suit's limitations.

Rays of light pushed through the upper stratosphere, illuminating the tops of the clouds. Gena closed her eyes, her head feeling light from the onset of oxygen deprivation. The air felt different. It smelled sweet. The typical acidic taste that she'd grown so accustomed to was replaced by a new sensation.

Another gust whisked in front of her, revealing in its aftermath a small dark object, spindly and meek, floating softly above the path of the gust. Gena recognized it instantly.

The images mixed with the tall tales recounted to her hundreds of times before. Gena's arms trembled. Time slowed as she passed by the flower. Its leaves shined in the light that came through the clouds; its body shivered in the wind. Gena felt a coldness within her, a soothing sensation. She felt as if the flower had a familiar presence.

Gena unleashed her aquifers. Following a course correction from her rear foot thruster, she drove herself forward, now descending on her jump. The doraposa was only a few feet away from her. Gena reached out; confident she could grab the flower. As her gloves grazed its petals, everything went black. Gena's arms relaxed and all was quiet.

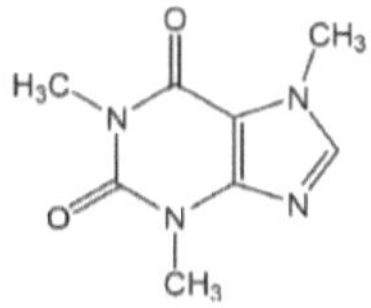

The dankness of the air hit her first. Acid tinged her tongue. Every new shram, every burn, cut, and bruise ached all at once. Gena opened her eyes. Pale light dangled from a bulb above her head. She was lying down, her view surrounded by faces covered in shadows.

"She's awake!"

"Serra…" Gena said, her voice raspy from acid burns.

"You made it back…we thought we lost you too."

Serra nodded, tears streaming down her face. She gripped Gena's hands. Gena's thoughts raced back to her. She tried not to choke up, but the tears fought their way through. Mother Buñuel was gone, becoming one with Venus.

The light adjusted in the room. More people gathered around Gena. She helped herself up and looked around the room. Vaulters, children, lower-tier dwellers—they all gathered by Gena's bedside. Their faces ranged from deep sorrow to subdued excitement at seeing her awake and fully lucid.

The people in front of her parted in the middle, granting passage to several large figures looming behind the crowd. Three Gaska guardians walked forward with their faces covered in masks, protection from the sub-standard air of the lower decks. Then they stepped to the side; from behind stepped out a blindingly pale woman.

Hedra approached the bed. Gena looked at her red eyes. "We found you by a miracle of Venus. You'd been unconscious for nearly an hour."

Gena instinctively reached behind her back. "My bags… where are they?" she asked.

Hedra closed her eyes and nodded, "We were unable to recover your aquifers from the surface. You were clutching onto their remains when we found you." She then held out two bags, their sides perspiring. Gena recognized them as her own, from earlier that morning. "However, I believe these belong to you…"

Gena grabbed the bags and placed them atop her legs. "Thanks," she said.

Hedra bowed her head and added, "We are sorry to hear of your matron's fate."

A veil of solemnity washed over the faces of the people.

"You should get some rest."

Hedra turned to leave; the rest of the company followed her.

As Serra bent down closer to Gena, two children poked their heads up from the bed's end.

"Janus! Abril!" Gena said.

The two children climbed atop the bed, flanking Gena, and hugging her. Although her skin burned and her muscles ached, she held them tightly, feeling their genuine love.

"Heru! Heru! Share the heru!" Janus shouted.

Gena rolled her eyes, loosened the cap from the aquifer in between her legs.

"You know I was going to trade this for something better," Gena said.

Abril pushed out her lower lip in protest.

"All right. There's enough for you two and probably everyone else. Get yourself something to drink with. It's not like I'm going anywhere."

Janus and Abril leaped from the bed and scurried into the commissary. Serra smiled at Gena and followed the children. Gena sat alone in her room, staring at the ripples in the water. She shook her head, dipped her finger into the liquid. It felt cool, sending a chilling sensation up her arm.

She felt something in the water. Something delicate and small. She pulled out a pale stem, then a leaf, blackened by Venusian cinder. Another leaf, this one brighter, then another, that one gold. Cold water dripped from its petals and landed on her legs, streaming down into the fabric of the bed. Gena held a baby doraposa in her hands.

END

Shields

By: Charli Cox

"Lieutenant, you're next. Fasten your helmet and enter the simulator," his training officer ordered. James dreamed of this day for nineteen years. His dad served in the Army, but James saw his future differently. He wanted to fly, not the friendly skies… but in space.

The Space Force was still working out their kinks, but he heard if he wanted to pilot an interstellar aircraft, he needed to learn to fly first. The Air Force needed pilots, and his ASVAB scores were in the top 1%. Before he approached the recruiting office, his phone blew up with calls begging him to enlist.

He chuckled as he recalled the feeling of being wanted, of being courted, to do something he had dreamed of doing for as long as he could remember. A rap on his helmet brought him back to the present.

"Earth to Lieutenant, are you with us Colby?" asked the Training Officer.

"Sorry, Ma'am. Yes, I'm here, and I'm ready," he answered confidently.

Captain Ava "Raven" Crane shrugged and pointed him towards the cockpit. "Buckle up! It's going to be a bumpy ride."

James grinned from ear to ear. He heard stories from others who had flown these simulators. Most of them had crashed after less than five minutes. He knew he could do better. His hands shook with anticipation as he strapped in to the pilot seat. This was it! He was living his dream, and it was here, and it was now. He ran through the pre-flight checks just like they taught him during orientation. Keying his mic, he reported, "Lieutenant Colby ready!"

"Copy, Lieutenant! Follow the navigation on your HUD and listen for your orders. Happy hunting!"

"Aye, Ma'am!" He beamed in the cockpit and his face started to hurt from the strain on its muscles. He must resemble the Joker at this point. Focusing on the present, he gripped the stick and followed the prompts in front of him. His HUD displayed a runway in the middle of the desert. Giving the stick a little push, he edged forward towards the tarmac and adjusted his flaps in preparation for takeoff.

He was in a Tomcat, his dad's favorite jet, and over the years he had learned everything about it from the sleek fuselage to the twin jet engines. He could see everything with his eyes closed, including the cockpit controls.

Opening his eyes, he looked out at the tarmac and got ready for takeoff.

"Lieutenant, you are a go for mission, say again, your mission is a go," his instructor's voice came through the speakers in his helmet.

"Copy, Ma'am. Lieutenant following flight plan Delta," he responded.

"Delta, huh? Interesting choice. We'll see you when you get back. Raven out."

He clicked his microphone twice to acknowledge his training officer and prepared to take off.

Increasing in speed, he pulled the stick back and his F-14 started lifting into the sky. He leveled his wings and followed the flight path to the north over Las Vegas. As he flew over the strip and headed southeast towards the Hoover Dam, his speakers crackled to life.

"Raven to Lieutenant, we have a bogie on your three o-clock. Unknown craft is heading your direction at Mach speeds. Be advised, it is going too fast for a positive ID."

"Lieutenant to Raven, copy all. Sending out IFF." He hit his transmit button to send out a prerecorded message to the unknown craft. IFF was short for Identification, Friend or Foe. He waited for a reply when his speakers roared at him.

"Raven to Lieutenant, evasive maneuvers, I repeat, evasive maneuvers! The bogie is armed and headed right for you."

He slammed his throttle into the firewall and banked to the left, climbing high into the clouds to make himself a more difficult target.

"The bandit is gaining on you."

Searching the instruments, James found the bandit right on his tail. He punched the throttle harder and climbed steeper into the atmosphere. The bogie followed, but he pulled away. Climbing higher, he inverted the jet and swooped down behind the enemy craft.

"Permission to engage?" James asked.

"Granted. You are weapons free."

Activating his weapons systems, James saw the target reticle right on top of the bogie. He gave it a five-count and launched a missile. "FOX one!" The missile streaked away and walloped the bogie, but the radio said otherwise.

"Negative splash, he is still in front of you."

Confused, James asked, "Say again?"

"Target not destroyed."

James shook his head in frustration. Activating the missiles, he fired again. "Switching to FOX two."

"Negative splash."

As he got closer to the bandit, James saw that it wasn't an aircraft he had ever seen before. Switching to guns, he reached for the trigger, only for the bogie to lift straight up into the sky and disappear. It didn't climb and fly higher. It levitated and vanished from sight.

"Lieutenant to Raven, do you have a location on the bandit?"

"Negative, Lieutenant, it just disappeared."

"Charlie Mike, or RTB?" he asked, wondering if he should continue the mission or return to base.

"RTB, Lieutenant. That was enough excitement for one day."

"Roger, returning to base."

He pulled the stick around and flew back over Las Vegas just as the sun started to set over the Strip. There was something about the bright orange hues in the sky that he found unsettling. *Just what was that craft, and why didn't the missiles destroy it,* he wondered.

The Tomcat landed perfectly on the airstrip at Area 51, and he decelerated to a taxi speed. Over the radio, he heard, "Mission fail. Prepare for debrief."

James slumped as the HUD went dark, and the canopy lifted over his head. Raven waited for him just outside. "Ma'am, what happened out there?" he asked.

"Debrief in thirty. Grab a shower and some chow."

"Ma'am?"

"That's an order, Lieutenant."

He nodded and climbed out of the simulator.

Anticipation clawed up James' esophagus and across his tongue with such force, he thought he would vomit all over Raven and the rest of the command staff waiting in the briefing room.

"Have a seat, Son," General Abe Hawthorne said and pointed to a lone chair at the far end of a very long conference table. James nodded and walked along the table for what felt like an eternity. Finally, he reached the end and stood at attention waiting for instructions.

"At ease, Lieutenant. Take your seat."

"Yes, Sir," James replied, and sat slowly.

"Tell us what you encountered out there."

Starting with the radio transmission indicating a bogie, James proceeded to recall the events of the flight in the simulator. "Then the craft levitated straight *up* and disappeared! I've never seen anything like it."

The general nodded and looked at Raven. She stood and walked to the front of the table. A white screen dropped down from the ceiling as the lights dimmed. James heard the click of a projector and an image of the craft he had witnessed appeared in front of him.

"Is this what you saw?" Raven asked.

"Yes, Ma'am, that's it. Wait, is this an actual photograph? It's not CGI?" Colby gulped audibly. "Is that thing real?"

Everyone in the room chuckled as James melted into his chair, trying to hide his embarrassment.

"It's OK, Lieutenant," Raven continued. "Our pilots first encountered this craft a few months back orbiting the Bandiagara Escarpment in Mali. The locals are primitive but had no fear when they noticed it in their airspace. We received a call from Bamako through AFRICOM to check it out.

"Every time we send a plane up, we are not able to get any closer than you did in the simulator. The crafts all ascend, like you saw, and disappear."

"Do they have cloaking capabilities, then?"

Raven sighed. "That's just it. We don't know how they do it. We also don't understand how they ascend. Our scientists are working on a way to analyze the craft each time it ascends to see if there are any fluctuations in the immediate airspace, but our technology isn't there, yet. Any drones we send out are destabilized and fall out of the sky before they get close!"

Taking a deep breath, she continued, "Long story short, we are at a loss regarding these crafts. We don't know if they are manned or remotely operated, where they come from, and most importantly, their purpose in being here."

General Hawthorne took over, "That's why you're here, Lieutenant Colby. You're showing promise in your flying abilities, and you have history with an extraterrestrial. Maybe they will talk to you."

James raised his eyebrows and gave the general a quizzical look.

The general chuckled and said, "Don't worry, everyone in this room has clearance. We know about your father's mission back in Eastern Washington and the lifeform that he contacted. We are hoping his ability to communicate with the dog-like alien is genetic and that you can, too."

"Me?" James stammered. "Sir, I have so many questions. First, you said 'these', that implies there are more than one of these crafts. Yes, I have been near an alien, but my dad is the one who communicates with him. It's been nineteen years, and he is still the only one who can! For some reason, Njerum won't work with any other humans."

The general put his hands up in a placating gesture, "I know it's a lot to take in. Given your genetic makeup and the relationship your dad has with Njerum, we believe that you will be able to contact whoever, or whatever is in the crafts.

"Make no mistake, we're not asking. These are your orders, and you won't be doing it alone."

Raven interjected, "We'll fly you up in the family model and you'll ride backseat. Once your pilot opens a channel, you'll attempt communication with the entity."

The general added, "Get some rest; you go up in the morning. Dismissed."

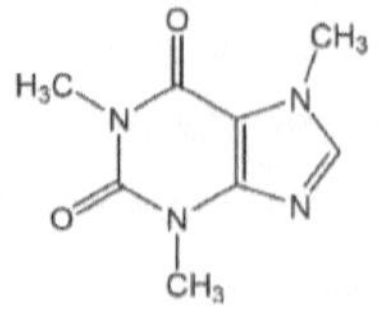

"Do you think he's ready?" General Hawthorne asked Raven.

"Is anyone ready for a mission like this, Sir?" she asked with a raised eyebrow.

The general sighed and stood. Pacing along the table, he responded, "First contact with Njerum was a shitshow. Those boys were lucky that he was as friendly as they thought. I don't want to make the same mistake this time around."

"As it is, we are no closer to getting Njerum back home to Emme Ya. We didn't even know there were three stars in the Sirius system until Njerum crashed here. The more the eggheads at Area 51 dick with his ship, the worse it seems to get. If we can't get his craft space worthy, or reverse engineer it enough to replicate, he is stuck here for the duration.

"Without a viable interstellar craft, we are just as stuck. That is why it is of the utmost importance that we find out who, or what, we are dealing with. Lieutenant Colby may just be our best chance."

"With respect, Sir, why don't we have his father do it? He is the one who can communicate with Njerum. Why are we so focused on the kid?"

General Hawthorne stopped pacing and gave Raven a piercing glare. "Are you questioning my reasoning, young lady?"

Raven blushed and shook her head. "No, Sir. Just trying to get a better understanding is all."

"Don't worry about your understanding. Get the kid ready and follow your orders. Is that clear enough?"

"Yes, Sir," Raven said as she stood and saluted. "I'll go prep for my part of the mission."

"That's my girl," the general beamed.

Raven walked around the table and gave him a kiss on the cheek. "Don't worry. I won't let you down."

Once the room was clear, General Hawthorne reviewed the image of the alien vessel on the screen. It was a thing of beauty. Shaped like a dolphin, its fore looked bulbous in comparison with the sleekness of the rest of its frame. Its aft tapered into two engines that were adjustable depending on the direction of flight. On each side of the fuselage was a wing that angled down and away from the sides of the craft like fins.

They knew these vessels were able to fly in atmosphere, but were they able to travel in vacuum? What about underwater? These damn things looked so much like aquatic mammals; he wondered if they had been swimming in the deeps before leaping up to the sky.

Shaking his head, he looked over the written report that Lieutenant Colby had turned in after the simulation. *The kid did everything by the letter. He followed protocol, communicated with Raven, and listened to orders even when he disagreed.*

General Hawthorne knew he had made the right call. *This kid's going places!*

James woke drenched in sweat. *That was a crazy dream!* he thought to himself. Swinging his legs out of his bunk, he stood and stretched before dropping to the prone in a front-leaning rest position.

Push-ups, as much as he hated them, helped to clear his head. He reflected on his dream and tried to make sense of what his subconscious was telling him.

In it, Njerum had warned him about the Nommos, an aquatic race from Emme Ya that resembled mermaids. "They are coming! You must prepare," he urged. Njerum's muzzle hadn't moved, yet the words drifted urgently into his mind. *This must be what it is like for Dad when he talks to him,* James thought.

"Fasten your shields around you and whatever you do, do not let them in. Once they are inside your mind, they will control you. Heed my warning. Fasten your shields."

The words made little sense to James. His aircraft didn't have shields. Their tech wasn't that developed, as far as he knew. If it did have shields, how would he wrap them around him?

At the count of one hundred, with more sweat dripping down his body and onto the concrete floor, James was just as confused as before.

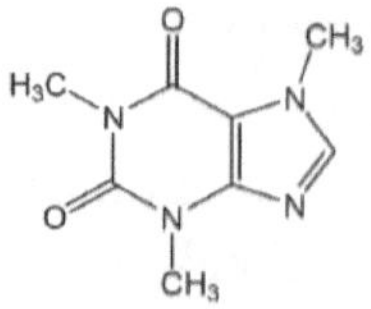

"Are you ready, Lieutenant?" asked Raven as James stepped onto the flight deck.

"Ready as I'll ever be, Ma'am," he replied hesitantly.

Raven nodded and pointed to the cockpit. "Hop in. We've got work to do."

James obliged and climbed up the ladder. Slipping into the back seat of the F-15EX Eagle II, he mused on how cramped it was. *How do WSOs do this all the time?* he wondered silently.

Raven went through the pre-flight checklist from memory and asked, "Comm check?"

"Got you five by five, Ma'am," he replied.

"Don't call me 'Ma'am' in my bird, Lieutenant. Out here it's 'Raven.'"

"Yes, Ma'am, I mean, yes, Raven."

"That's better," she said with a giggle. "You all set back there?"

"Let's do this," he replied.

"Control, this is Raven. We are ready to proceed."

"Roger, Raven, this is control. Execute."

With that, Raven pushed forward on the stick and exited the hangar. They approached the runway and accelerated. As they reached takeoff speed, Raven pulled back on the stick, and they climbed into the sky.

"Control, Raven. I'm reading a bogie at my five o-clock. Lieutenant, do you see anything?"

James looked out the cockpit window and replied, "Negative," but kept looking. As he stared at the clouds, he thought he saw a bird approaching them.

"Raven? Is that a-?"

"Control, bandit confirmed! Approaching rapidly and moving to intercept. Do we engage?"

Over the radio, James heard, "Affirmative, Raven. Let them get close, but do not fire unless you are fired upon. Copy?"

Raven let out a sigh and replied, "Copy all Control. Raven out."

To James, she asked, "Do you have visual contact?"

"Yes, I mean, I think so…I thought it was a bird at first, but now it looks more like a flying dolphin."

Raven chuckled, "Yep, that's our guy. You remember your orders?"

"Yes, Raven. Get us close and I will do my best."

"I have a feeling they will get close on their own."

Sure enough, the craft flew right toward them. James' eyes opened wide in shock, but the craft slowed and pulled alongside. Looking at the craft's cockpit section, James couldn't see inside, but he felt his anxiety peak when he heard a voice.

This is new. What have we here?

"Uh, Raven? Did you hear that?" asked James.

"No, all I hear is 'Bitching Betty'. Do they have to be so close to us up here? Their proximity is giving me the willies."

James swallowed, and thought, *Hello. Who is this?*

In response, he heard, *Oh, you can understand me. Very interesting. Tell your leader this is our planet now, and you all should leave.*

James shook his head and thought back, *WHAT!*

The voice chuckled and replied, *You understood me. The skies and the seas belong to us. Soon the stars will as well. Leave while you still can.*

Gulping, James spoke to Raven, "I think we need to get out of here. They definitely are not friendly."

"Wait, you spoke to them already?"

"Yes, now we should go."

Your pilot should have listened when she had the chance. Too late! The enemy craft ascended quickly and vanished.

No, please… pleaded James, but the only thing he received in response was a missile lock alarm.

Raven tried to get out of the way, but they were too close. As the missile impacted their jet, James heard, "Control, this is Raven. Mayday, mayday mayday mayday, we've been fired upon and…"

As their plane plummeted to the ground, James pulled his eject handle. "Eject, eject, eject!" The canopy flew away from their bird and his seat punched up. The last thing he heard as he shot into the sky was another missile striking their plane. Heat blossomed below him and he fought for breath despite the oxygen mask strapped to his face.

His parachute deployed a white mantle protecting him from the gravity that pulled him towards the ground. As he descended, he caught a glimpse of the fireball that used to be Raven's plane.

James awoke to the *whumpa, whumpa, whumpa* of a helicopter's rotor blades and the stench of decaying plant matter. Slowly, he opened his eyes and peered into the darkness. *How long was I out? Where is Ra-?* He remembered seeing the fireball and a tear dropped onto the ground. Wiping his grimy face, he winced as his hand caressed his nose. *Great, it must be broken.*

The noise of the helo got louder, and he looked towards the source of the sound. Above him, he saw lights heading his direction. James stood and almost fell right back down. The world around him swam in his vision and he felt nauseous. *Must have hit my head when I landed,* he surmised.

"Lieutenant!" he heard behind him. James turned around slowly and saw a man he had not encountered before. He was not much taller than him, but more well-built, with a tanned face, sandy brown hair, and brown eyes filled with concern. "Are you alright? Do you need a medic?"

James regarded him and noticed Captain's bars on his flight suit. "No, Captain," he replied respectfully. "Not right away. Did anyone find Raven?" he asked pleadingly.

The captain walked closer to James and held his hand out. James took it and they walked together towards the waiting HH-60W Jolly Green II. "I'll let the general answer that question. Right now, let's get you back to base."

James didn't like the sound of that but nodded in understanding. The captain helped him into the helicopter and sat down next to him. "By the way, I'm Joseph Catalan. Nice to meet you."

"You, too, *Captain*," grumbled James. Manners be damned; he had just conversed with an alien and gotten blasted out of the sky. As he contemplated unloading on the man beside him, he thought better of it. For one, this guy outranked him. For two, he had just pulled him out of the desert and gotten him safely onto the Sikorsky.

"Sorry," he muttered. "I'm not usually this cranky."

"No worries," Joseph remarked. "I remember the first time I lost a brother, or sister, in your case."

James nodded, and they rode the rest of the way to the base in companionable silence.

After James was checked by the flight surgeon, he went to the general's office for debriefing. General Hawthorne met James at the door and gave him a hug, of all things.

"Sorry, Lieutenant, it's just been a long day," he remarked as he made his way around his desk and sat down.

James took the opposite seat and sat slowly. "Yes, Sir, that it has."

"So, tell me what happened out there."

James recounted the conversation with the presumed pilot in the other craft and ended his story with the fireball. "Is Raven OK? Did the rescue team find her?"

"Don't worry about Raven. She is a tough gal," the general replied, but James noticed his voice quivered just a touch and his eyes blinked away unshed tears.

Just as James was about to offer his thoughts, he was interrupted by a knock at the door. "Enter," said the general.

Joseph walked into the office and popped a crisp salute.

"At ease, Guardian," said the general. "What can I do for you?"

Joseph shifted his position to a parade rest and said, "Sir, I was thinking. Not to step on any toes, but with Raven MIA, our Lieutenant here needs a pilot. I would like to volunteer."

The general looked up at Joseph, then at James, deep in thought. After a few moments he replied, "We might just scrub everything. If a simple conversation resulted in the injury, and possible death, of our men, I wonder if the risk is worth it."

Joseph opened his mouth to reply, but James beat him to it.

"With respect, Sir, they did warn us, in a way, before opening fire."

"Are you defending their hostile actions?"

"No, Sir, I was just about to go into more detail when Joseph entered."

The general turned to Joseph and said, "I will take your offer under advisement. Dismissed."

"Yes, Sir, thank you," said Joseph as he saluted the general, executed a parade ground about face and made for the door. Before leaving, he turned to James, gave him an encouraging grin, and closed the door behind him.

James turned back to the general and continued, "Sir, if what the occupant of the other vessel said is true, we need to gather more intelligence. They said that we needed to vacate the planet. I don't know about you, but I'm curious how they think they can get rid of us so easily."

The general nodded in thought. "I have a meeting in an hour. Go get some rest and I'll let you know what is decided. I'll be in touch in the morning."

"Yes, Sir," James responded and headed to his quarters.

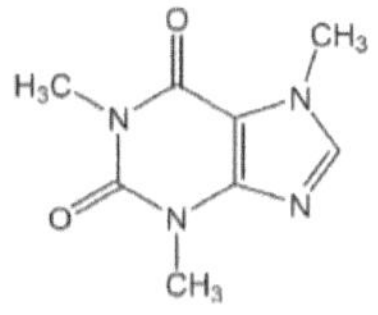

As exhausted as he was, James couldn't sleep. He tried meditating, counting sheep, even the glass of milk on his nightstand was empty. Finally, he reached for the sleeping aids the flight surgeon prescribed.

He popped two pills into his mouth and swallowed them dry. Lying back down, his head barely touched the pillow, and he was back in the cockpit.

This time, Njerum was his pilot. "James, are you well?"

"Um, yes, I think so. I didn't know you could fly a plane."

"I cannot. I also cannot talk to you, but here I am. You are manifesting me in your dream."

"Oh, that makes sense."

Njerum continued, "How was your mission?"

"How do you know about that?"

"I hear things. I am still in a cage in the basement, remember?" Njerum uttered haughtily.

"Right, sorry, I forgot."

"Anyway, tell me what happened."

James recounted his experience with the other craft and the warning he was given.

"Hmm, that is interesting," remarked Njerum. "Did you remember what I said about your shields?"

"Yes, but I don't understand."

Njerum sighed, if dog-analog aliens could sigh, and said, "Your shields are your mental barriers. You must open them, a little, to interface with telepathic beings; however, you do not want to open them fully, or else you risk being taken over."

"Taken over? What are you talking about?"

Njerum continued, "When you open your mind to outside influences, you risk being overrun. To communicate telepathically, you must open your mind to let in their thoughts. If you open too much, they can take over and leave you out of control."

"That sounds scary," James remarked.

"Indeed, but if you maintain your shields, they will not be able to overpower you."

"How do I do that?" asked James.

"When you are communicating with them, think of the entrance to your mind like a door. You want to open it just enough to let in a nice breeze on a pretty spring day. If you open the door fully, the wind can gust, throw the door open, and knock you onto the floor.

"When you open the door to your mind, be aware of just how much you are letting in. If they push against your door too hard, and attempt to force their way in, slam the door, and turn the deadbolt."

"What if I don't realize that my 'door' is opening too far?" asked James.

"Then you must find them and throw them out a window."

"What?"

Next thing James knew, someone was knocking on the cockpit glass. He turned to Njerum who shrugged and vanished. The plane started to plummet, and James reached for the controls to steady its flight and avoid crashing. As soon as his butt hit the pilot seat, he heard, "Terrain, terrain. Pull. *Up!* Pull. *Up!*"

He pulled on the stick and the plane climbed, but not high enough. As he drew closer to the side of a mountain and was just about to collide, he heard an obnoxious buzzing sound. He turned towards the sound and felt wetness on his face.

"Huh?" he thought and sat up. His personal comm was blaring, and someone was knocking frantically on the door to his room. "Coming!" he shouted.

James threw the blanket onto the floor and sat up on the side of his bed. He made his way to the door and, remembering what Njerum had said, opened it just a crack.

Joseph was standing there. He opened the door a little wider.

James took a step back and asked, "What's up?"

"The general has been looking for you. We have another date with a dolphin."

James cast a confused look in Joseph's direction.

"Wow, man, you really must be out of it," Joseph remarked. "We're going up again, later this afternoon." Taking stock of James' appearance, he added, "No offense, but you look like shit."

James chuckled, "I bet. Let me hit the showers and grab coffee."

Raven awoke in a hospital. There were tubes everywhere protruding from her body, and the bed she was in was uncomfortable. The more she looked around, the more she realized this place was unlike any other hospital room she had been in before.

As if on cue, someone entered. In retrospect, there was no door, just an archway at the far end of the room, set in walls that looked like crystals.

Before the women who entered could speak, Raven asked, "Where am I?"

"You are safe, and you are alive." The woman looked down at her with golden eyes. "Your current location is irrelevant."

Swallowing a gasp, Raven asked, "Who are you?"

"Again, that is irrelevant. For now, you must rest."

Raven started to struggle, but the Nurse, Doctor, whoever she was pressed a button over Raven's head, and she could no longer move. She tried to scream, but her jaw would not open, nor would her throat allow any sound to escape. In frustration, she let out a tear and the woman with the golden eyes said, "You must rest. Everything else will be revealed to you soon."

With that, the woman spun on her tail, *TAIL?* and slithered away. Raven tried to follow her path, but she could not keep her eyes open, and fell into a darkness that enveloped her.

Before climbing up the ladder into the cockpit, James asked the general, "Sir, does Joseph have clearance? How much does he know?"

"I'm glad you asked. All he knows is that you and Raven were shot down by an enemy that we need to talk to. He doesn't know about the capabilities of their craft, nor does he know that we believe them to be extraterrestrial in nature. In short, all he knows is that he needs to fly you out where they can find you, so you and the craft can have a chat. And I'd like to keep it that way. Come back safe, you understand?"

"Yes, Sir. I shall do my best."

With that, the general clasped James on the shoulder and left the flight deck.

James was about to climb the ladder when Joseph asked, "Everything OK?"

With a sigh, James responded, "I wish everyone would stop asking me that."

"Sorry, Kid, it's just that we understand you've been through a lot. I don't mean to pry."

James guffawed, "Just who are you calling 'Kid'? You can't be much older than me."

Joseph's tanned complexion paled, and he responded, "Sorry, you're right. I'm twenty-five."

James chuckled, "That's what I thought. I'm twenty-three, not exactly young enough to be your 'Kid.'"

Joseph relented, "Fair enough, what should I call you anyway?"

Shrugging, James said, "Raven always called me 'Lieutenant.' The pilots in training nicknamed me 'Gouda.'"

"Gouda, huh? Sounds like a story for another day. Up here, my callsign is 'Acheron.'"

"Roger that, Sir." James got settled into the back seat of the "family model," as Raven called it, and put on his helmet. With shaking hands, he fastened his harness and checked his comms.

"Ready back there?" asked Joseph.

"Yup, let's do this!"

Joseph took the plane out of the hangar and onto the tarmac. With practiced ease, the jet climbed into the atmosphere and banked away from the base.

"Keep an eye on radar and let me know when you see something," Joseph instructed.

James acknowledged by zippering his mic.

They flew further away from the base than he had in his flight with Raven, and James wondered where they were going.

"Hey, Acheron, aren't we a little far from the base?"

"We are, but I was told to get you as close to the enemy as possible. They must be out here somewhere, right?"

Right, thought James, but his feeling of unease increased. They were flying even further when the radio crackled to life.

"Pathfinder One, what is your status? You dropped off our radar."

Joseph replied, "Control, Acheron. We are A-OK. Just trying to get our Lieutenant up close and personal."

"Copy that, Pathfinder, keep at it for another few minutes, then RTB. We don't want you too far in case you need support out there, copy?"

It was Joseph's turn to zipper his mic, and he looked behind him towards James.

"See anything, yet? I'd hate for our first flight together to be a disappointment."

James studied the radar but didn't notice anything out there. After a few breaths, the hairs on the back of his neck stood up, and his heart rate increased.

"Hey, Acheron?"

"What do you have?"

"Nothing on radar, but I feel like we are being watched."

"Explain."

"I don't know, it just feels like we aren't alone up here."

Just as James closed his mouth, one of the "dolphins" appeared at their eight o-clock. Joseph giggled, and said, "There they are."

James looked at his radar, but still nothing appeared on the screen.

"How are they invisible to radar?" James asked Joseph.

"Must be one of the mysteries of the Universe."

That's helpful, thought James. Then he remembered his mission.

He sent to the approaching craft, *Why did you shoot us down yesterday? What do you want?*

In reply, he received, *You were warned. The other pilot did not listen. Now you are with a pilot who will. Return to where you came from and leave this planet!*

Or what? James shot back.

A moment passed, and then their plane swung around behind the enemy craft.

"What are you doing?" James asked Joseph.

"Following orders."

"What orders?"

"The ones that don't come from humans."

James suppressed a scream as their jet kicked in the afterburners in pursuit of the alien vessel. They dove down and followed it out towards the Coast and over the Pacific Ocean.

"Where are we going?" asked James.

Joseph looked back at him and simply said, "Home."

In a moment of panic, James reached for his emergency ejection handle, but it wasn't there.

"Sorry, Bud, there's no escape this time." Their jet accelerated and dove into the sea.

Raven awoke to the sounds of movement all around her. The nurse from before was back, and with her a half-dozen other tailed creatures bringing in someone familiar.

"Lieutenant!" she cried. "What have you done to him?" Raven demanded.

The nurse looked down at her and reached for the button to put her back to sleep. "Please, no, not again," Raven pleaded groggily.

"Very well, but no further outbursts," the nurse ordered. Raven simply nodded in reply.

The creatures laid James on another bed-shaped object and fastened his limbs like they did to her. A large male, wearing a flight suit, lifted a helmet-shaped device over James' head and said, "OK, Lieutenant. This won't hurt too much," he added with a sinister grin.

Raven was about to protest when the female nurse glared in her direction. She closed her mouth and choked back the words on her tongue.

The male approached Raven and looked her over. "So, you're the Pilot?" he asked. Raven glanced at the nurse for permission, and she inclined her head slightly before turning her attention to James.

"Yes, I am a pilot. What is it to you?"

The male replied, "I am Joseph, and I don't believe I've had the pleasure."

"You look familiar…" then it hit her. Joseph was amongst a group of new recruits they brought in a couple of months ago. He had flight experience and a willingness to fight for God and Country. So, why was he down here?

"I remember you now," she continued. "Were you captured, too?"

Joseph laughed. "Not exactly. You see, I have lived among the merfolk for fifty years. I didn't lie about being an aviator; I truly did fly for the Army back in Nam."

Raven regarded him and her eyes grew wide. "But, how? There is no way you could have been alive that long ago. How old are you?"

"What age do I appear?" he asked.

"Twenty something, maybe…" she hesitated. "If you flew during the Vietnam War, you would have to be pushing seventy by now."

"Yes, if I was a typical human." He looked over to the archway of the room and smiled at another female creature listening from the doorway. "The Mami Wata saved me all those years ago and brought me here."

Confused, Raven asked, "What is a 'Mami Wata?'"

Joseph continued, "Mami and her daughters found me after my plane was shot down. They brought me here, healed my body and my mind, and filled me with purpose. Now, I live to serve them, not the whims of simple humans."

"But you *are* human, or you were, at least."

"Yes, I was born human. Thanks to Mami, I am now so much more, and you can be, too." He leaned towards her, and Raven recoiled in fear. They heard someone clearing their throat from across the room. Joseph looked up, and then back at Raven, "I'll be back later," he promised, and turned to leave.

Joseph walked to the archway where a mermaid waited for him. He appreciated her curvaceous figure and honey-gold eyes. Her dark hair flowed around an oval face with skin the color of coffee mixed with a healthy amount of cream.

The gills on her neck, just behind her round ears, undulated as she spoke. "I take it your mission was a success?"

She moved down the hallway, her green scaled tail writhing underneath her, as she glided across the smooth floor.

"Yes, Mami. The female pilot is here, and I was able to bring the youngling to you as well."

"Well done," she praised. "For now, let him rest. We will study him and his abilities later."

James was floating. Not in the water, nor in the air. He seemed to be suspended. Everything was dark. The more he strained his vision, the darker everything became. Out of nowhere, he felt a presence behind him. From afar, he heard Njerum, "Remember, use your shields." Then, the comforting voice was gone.

Next, he heard, "Hello little human. Tell us how you came to be here."

James wasn't sure how to answer. He tried in vain to recall his "Evasion and Conduct After Capture (ECAC) Course" training. He hesitated, not wanting to endanger his people, or himself, unnecessarily.

The voice asked again, "Tell us how you came to be here."

He decided to start with the obvious, "The plane I was in crashed into the water."

He heard laughter, "Nice try. Tell us again, the truth this time."

James started to open his mouth and felt an indescribable pain lance through his body. He shuddered and panted, fighting to bring his heart rate down.

"Are you ready to be honest now?" the voice taunted.

James took a deep breath and told the voice about his flight, the new pilot, and then the crash. "But it wasn't exactly a crash, was it?"

"No, your plane was flown here intentionally," the voice acknowledged.

"Why?" James asked weakly.

"You have a gift, and we would like to study you," the voice replied.

James shuddered despite himself. "What gift?"

"Do not play coy with us. We know much more than you realize."

"I don't know what you are talking about."

Another lancing pain, and it felt like forever before James could properly breathe again.

"Perhaps, you need some motivation."

In an instant, James was blinded by pure white light, and laying in a bed. Once his eyes adjusted to the brightness, he tried to wipe them, but his hands were restrained. He turned his head and saw Raven in the bed across from him.

It wasn't exactly a bed, more a padded bench with shackles bolted to the sides and end. He looked down and found his ankles bound.

Raven shouted, "Are you alright?"

He tried to shush her, but no sound came out. Clearing his throat, he tried again, but still nothing. He mouthed to her, "I can't talk. Where are we?"

"I don't know," she shouted again, and he cringed away from the oppressive noise.

Noticing his distress, she tried whispering, "Are you alright?"

He nodded at her in appreciation for the change in volume. Before he could answer, Joseph and a female mermaid entered the room.

The mermaid laid her hands on his throat, and he felt a wash of comforting warmth spread throughout his neck and chest. He swallowed and tried to speak. Only a croak escaped his lips.

Joseph held out a cup of water with a straw, and James chugged it.

The mermaid asked, "Is that better?" and he recognized the voice from earlier.

"Yes," he answered shortly, then added, "Thanks."

"You are most welcome. Now, where were we?"

James tried to sit up on the bench, but the restraints were too tight. Joseph adjusted them and the bed, so James could recline more comfortably. Answering the earlier question, James said, "You were asking me about a gift."

"Oh, yes. You were less than forthcoming." The mermaid loomed over his face, the stench of dead fish emanating from her open maw.

James gagged and turned away. Joseph grabbed his chin and yanked him back towards the mermaid.

"Perhaps, introductions are in order," she began. "I am Sagla, leader of these Mami Wata. We are from another world and came here many years ago. Now, our own world has failed us, and we are looking to – how do you humans phrase it? Oh yes, relocate." The last she said with a smile.

James shook his head. "Why here?"

"Because we have been here for a very long time. We gave you humans many gifts and it is time for your people to return our generosity. One little planet certainly is not too much to ask, is it?"

James protested, "But this is our *home*. We don't have anywhere else to go!"

Sagla nodded and replied, "Not our problem. What is it you say, 'survival of the fittest'? If you refuse to leave peacefully, then we will conquer you, or erase you from history. Your choice!" She waved her arm at him dismissively.

James tried to reach out to strangle this creature, but the restraints bit into his wrists and Joseph punched him in the side of his head.

"No, stop!" Raven cried. One look from Sagla ceased any further protests.

James' eyes fluttered with the force of Joseph's attack, and he slumped onto the padding, losing consciousness.

Sagla glared at Joseph, "I do not need you to defend me. Do not do that again!"

"Yes, Mami," Joseph replied sheepishly.

With that, they both left the room to their captives.

James' vision swam and he leaned over the side of his "bed" to vomit. Raven saw the nurse from earlier bringing him a towel and a bucket.

"What is your deal?" Raven asked her.

She looked from Raven to the doorway, then approached her. "I wasn't always one of them," she said. "My name is Lorelei and I used to be human, too."

James looked at her and asked, "Can you help us?"

"Even if I could, escape is hopeless. We are thousands of meters beneath the Ocean surface. Once we leave this crystalline prison, the pressure of the water will crush us. Not to mention, you humans don't have gills."

"You do," Raven observed.

Lorelei laughed, "Right, a lot of good they will do me if I'm devoured by orcas on my way to the surface."

James interjected, "There must be another way."

"If you think of one, let me know. I'm tired of being a slave to their merkids."

"What do you mean?" asked Raven.

"Like Joseph, I am much older in age than I appear. When I was young, my father and I were captured and brought here. He became a member of the Mami's harem. Once I matured enough, I earned my keep by being used by the younger male merkin…"

Raven replied, "Sorry I asked."

"It's OK. Father died last year. He was old even when we came here. Their 'treatments' didn't do much for him, except allow him to sire more hybrids. Now that he is gone, there is nothing keeping me here."

James stammered, "So the mermaids are mating with humans?"

"Yes, there used to be only a handful of them. Now, they have an army of hundreds. Coupled with the orcas who do their bidding, they are formidable."

"I can see why you are afraid to leave," remarked Raven.

"Well, I never had hope before. If we work together, maybe we can find a way. For now, I must go, before anyone gets suspicious."

As Lorelei left the room, Raven asked James, "Do you think we can trust her?"

"Do we have a choice?"

The next morning, Joseph and Sagla returned with bowls of some type of fish stew for James and Raven. "Before we talk, you need your strength," remarked Sagla.

Shortly after, Lorelei entered. "Mami?" she asked. "You summoned me?"

"Yes, Child. After our guests consume their meal, please escort them to the relieving room. Help them cleanse and then bring them to my study."

"As you wish, Mami," she responded.

Sagla and Joseph left, then Raven asked Lorelei, "So, what is up with those two?"

"What is 'up'?"

"I mean what is their relationship?"

"Oh, Joseph has been here longer than most. He is Mami's 'Mate Prime' which is not a King exactly, but as close as one can get in their society. As the matriarch, she can have multiple beings in her harem, but he is her favorite. On the contrary, once a male pledges to a female, he can only sire children for her and her alone.

"Mami is the leader here. She arrived here with the Nommos about ten thousand years ago and founded this facility. She and her daughters built up the colony to the numbers you see now."

James asked, "Do you know what they are planning?"

"They don't tell me much," she replied. "I only know that they have encouraged breeding for the last decade. Despite their appearances, the young mature much more quickly than humans. Merkin are fully grown and mature by age ten. The males and females both train as warriors. Some have even learned how to build ships."

James muttered, "Yeah, I've seen one of them."

"They are fascinating, aren't they?" Lorelei asked him.

"That's one word for it…"

Raven interjected, "Do you know what they plan to do with their increased numbers and firepower?"

"I can only guess, and it won't be good for humanity. Anyway, we have spoken too long. Hurry and finish your meals. Mami will be waiting."

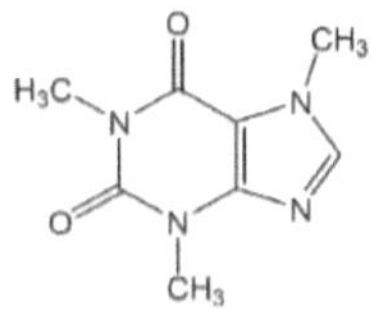

After they ate, emptied their bladders, and washed, Lorelei led them deeper into the complex. It was all James and Raven could do to not gawk in awe at the crystal construction. There was no visible source for the light, yet each corridor was bright enough to see down to the end and each room they passed was well-lit.

As they neared the end of the corridor, Lorelei stopped them. "After your meeting, I will escort you back to your room. There is something I must do. See you soon." With that, she pointed to a room on their left and slipped away, her tail skimming along the floor.

Raven turned to James, "Should we make a run for it?"

He shook his head. "No, we still don't know the way out of here. Plus, you heard what Lorelei said. Even if we found the exit, we would die quickly after entering the water."

Raven visibly deflated. "Don't worry," James assured her as he clapped her lightly on the shoulder. "We'll figure out a way home."

Raven nodded and they made their way to Sagla's study. The leader of the merfolk was seated behind a large clamshell that had been fashioned into a horizontal surface. It appeared like a typical wooden desk, one you would see on the surface. Sagla indicated two chairs and invited them to sit.

Once seated, tentacles reached out from behind them and fastened them tightly to the chairs. James struggled, but to no avail. They weren't going anywhere.

Sagla approached Raven and caressed her cheek. Raven took a shuddering breath and her head collapsed to her chest.

James tried again to wriggle out of the restraints, but the suction of the tentacles increased, and he knew he was stuck.

Sagla turned to him and said, "Now that we have some privacy, I need you to tell me everything."

She straddled his lap, *when did she get legs,* and touched her forehead to his. "Relax," she teased, "This will not hurt a bit, unless you struggle." James took a deep breath before falling once again into the darkness of his mind.

Njerum was off in the distance looking back at James. "Remember your shields," he whispered, and then evaporated like mist.

James then saw Sagla across from him dressed in a translucent gown that accentuated her womanly figure. For a mermaid, she was really hot, except for the gills. That was just weird. Shaking the lust from his body, he focused on what Njerum had told him as Sagla approached.

You like what you see? she teased. *All of this can be yours. Just tell me what I want to know.*

No, James thought. His body was so weak from fighting temptation that he couldn't form words. *I will not sell out my people.*

Your people? Silly boy, your people do not care about you. To them, you are just a means to an end. They think the Dogon quadrupeds are their salvation. Hah. They are wrong. Only me, and the Nommos can spare you.

You said you would conquer us.

Yes, we will. Is that not better than annihilation? You humans can continue to live, under our rule, and we will provide everything you need.

And what do you want in exchange for this mercy? James asked.

Only your loyalty. Join us, and you, like Joseph and the others, will have immortality. Fight us, and you will die. All. Of. You.

As James contemplated what Sagla offered, he knew deep down in his gut that it was wrong. If something seems too good to be true, it probably is. He just didn't know how to turn the tables on Sagla. She was in his mind. He could feel her probing for information, but he didn't know what she sought.

She knew about Njerum somehow. Did she get that from his mind in the short time when she questioned him earlier?

Thinking about Njerum, he remembered the repeated warning, "Fasten your shields."

James imagined a door. He placed the door in front of him, between Sagla and himself. Then he imagined four walls around him. He inserted the door into the wall in front of him. Just as he was about to close the door, it opened towards him, with Sagla standing there, glaring at him.

What are you doing? she demanded.

He reached out for the door and pushed it towards her. She thrust it back in his direction, but he was determined. The fate of Earth depended on him! He pushed with all his might and finally, the door closed with a click. He turned the deadbolt, then manifested more locks and fastened them all. When he was done, he heard Sagla pounding on the imaginary door from the other side.

Let me in! Let me in! she demanded.

No, replied James. *You are not welcome in my mind!*

Suddenly, he was awake and covered in a cold sweat, his head hanging limply in front of him.

"What have you done?" Sagla asked him.

"I simply closed the door," he replied. She smiled at him, but it was not friendly.

She summoned two mermen to the study. "Take them back to their quarters. We are far from done here, human." That last word dripped with menace.

James and Raven rose unsteadily from their chairs as the tentacles released their suction grip. Each of the guards grabbed one of their arms and marched them back down the corridor. As they neared their room, Lorelei approached.

"Hold, please," she said to the lead guard. "I have been instructed to take them to the relieving room. Mami doesn't want their stench permeating our home."

The guard nodded and gave Lorelei a creepy smile. "Make sure you wash the stench off yourself when they are cleansed. I have plans for you later," he said with a sneer.

"As you desire," she replied with a bow.

Lorelei led James and Raven back to the relieving room where fresh clothes waited for them. She quickly drew gills behind their ears, and applied some type of substance to their faces to make their complexions darker.

"What about our uniforms?" asked Raven.

"I have disposed of them. Don't worry, none of the merfolk will be able to use them to impersonate you. Get dressed quickly and follow me."

The humans did as they were told and followed Lorelei past their room and down a dimly lit corridor. "Keep your heads down and do not make eye contact with anyone," she warned. James and Raven shared a glance but did as she instructed.

As they reached the end of the corridor, Lorelei looked behind them. "OK, we're clear. I have a plan."

She told them her idea and James said, "But what about-"

Lorelei shushed him and said, "Nothing in this life is certain, except death. That is what waits for you if you remain here any longer."

James looked to Raven, and she nodded. "We don't have another choice," she observed.

Before Lorelei opened the door, she planted a kiss on James' mouth, then on Raven's. They swam through the opening and into what looked like an underwater flight deck. Rows upon rows of the dolphin-shaped craft were in various stages of construction. On the far side of the cavern was one that looked familiar.

Lorelei pointed and James nodded in understanding. He was holding his breath the best he could but was starting to lose consciousness. Lorelei grabbed him and kissed him again, blowing oxygen into his mouth and letting it flow into his lungs. She did the same for Raven.

As they neared the indicated craft, one of the guards from earlier appeared. *Oh, crap!* thought James, but Lorelei had it covered.

She approached the guard and said, "Mami needs you immediately. The humans have escaped, and she wants them found." The guard looked at James and Raven, but with the makeup Loreli had used, they appeared to be merfolk. "What are you waiting for? Go!" The guard acknowledged her outburst and sped away out of the bay.

"We don't have much time, hurry!" Lorelei stated.

They swam the rest of the way to the finished craft and climbed inside. Raven moved to the pilot seat, but James stopped her. "This isn't a typical plane. You better let me handle this one."

Raven was about to object, but Lorelei cut in. "This craft is not like one of your human designs. There are no manual controls. Everything is done with your mind."

"How is that possible?" asked Raven.

"Less talk, more flying." Lorelei warned. "We have to leave now."

James looked for an ignition switch but didn't see anything. He looked to Lorelei who shrugged and said, "I am no pilot. My talents lie in other areas."

James was just about to give up when he saw motion beneath them. Joseph was there with a squad of armed mermen, and they looked pissed. They leveled weapons at the craft, and pulses of light flashed in their direction.

"What do I do?!" screamed James. Njerum's voice came back to him, *Use your shields.*

Shields, oh right! As soon as he completed the thought, an iridescent bubble of energy encircled the craft. *I can't believe that worked!* The beams of light flashed away and were refracted toward their pursuers.

Now, to figure out how to start this thing. Again, after he thought it, the craft came to life. He reached for the stick, but there wasn't one. *This is going to take some getting used to.*

A HUD came to life superimposed over the windscreen and he saw what looked like a radar display. There was nothing on it, which meant they were in the clear, for now.

He turned to look back at Lorelei and asked, "Where is the exit?"

She pointed up.

Of course! James thought "up", and the craft levitated just like the one he saw in the simulator. He wondered if they were going to impact the roof of the underwater cavern when the craft started climbing towards an opening above them. They accelerated toward the hole in the ceiling and climbed through the seawater toward the surface, and home.

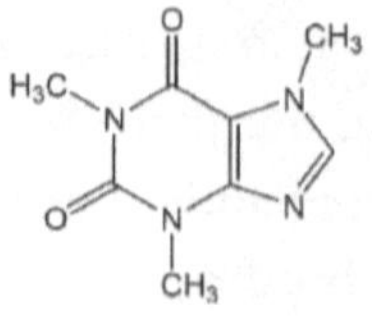

As they ascended out of the ocean and reached airspace, one of the vessels followed them. James looked behind them and thought *shields* again. The aircraft shook for a moment and then was steady.

BEEP, BEEP, BEEP. "What is that?" asked James.

Raven peered over his shoulder and saw a flashing warning light on the console.

"If I had to guess, that's a missile lock. Evasive maneuvers?"

James nodded and used his mind to direct the craft away from the incoming missile. Banking around, he lined up and flew towards their pursuer.

"Weapons hot!" he said to warn his passengers and sent a thought to the weapons systems of the craft. No sooner had he envisioned a missile leaving one of the tubes, one shot out toward his intended target.

"FOX one!" announced James, as he pulled the craft away from the impact.

"Did we hit it?" asked Lorelei, but Raven shook her head.

The craft was still there. *We need something that can penetrate their shields,* thought James. Again, once he completed the thought, he saw a new weapon available to him.

He sent his idea to the craft, and it responded. Under the ship, a bay door opened, and a long barrel descended. "Fire!" yelled James, and a beam of light shot out.

They were momentarily blinded by the flash, and James again flew their craft away from the bandit. It fired at them, but James sent a thought of strength to the shields, and they held as a missile impacted them on the starboard side.

Moving to re-engage the enemy, all James saw was a blackened hull falling from the sky. As it impacted the mountain range below, it blossomed into a fireball.

"Damn!" exclaimed Raven. "What did you hit it with?"

"Not sure. I guess we'll find out once we get this thing back to base."

"Hopefully, the engineers can replicate it. That was pretty cool."

Behind them, Lorelei was sobbing.

"What's wrong?" asked James.

"It's true they were horrible to me, but that was my home for decades. The pilot, whoever he was, was part of my family," Lorelei responded.

Raven put a hand on her shoulder, "Family doesn't treat each other like a slave." She looked into her eyes and said, "You are safe now, and have a chance to reunite with your real family, or you can start a new life here."

James raised an eyebrow at Raven. "What?" she asked innocently. "I know a guy."

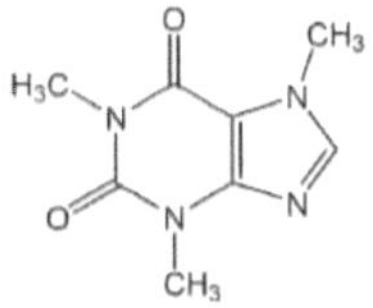

"Sir," the radar operator exclaimed. "I've got a bogey incoming from the west. It looks like one of the alien vessels."

"Understood," said General Hawthorne. "Let's keep eyes on it. If it gets close to the base, you know what to do."

"Yes, Sir!"

They watched the radar display, and the vessel flew erratically in their direction. *What is it doing?* thought the general.

"Sir, we have an incoming transmission."

"Let's hear it."

A familiar voice broadcast through the room. "Control, this is Lieutenant Colby, I mean Gouda. I have Raven with me and an ally who helped us escape. Requesting permission to land."

General Hawthorne chuckled, *That son of a gun,* he said to himself. Out loud he responded, "Permission granted, Son. Is that you in one of their vessels?"

"Yes, Sir. We used it to escape, and we have intel on their underwater colony. Once we land, we will share everything."

"Sounds good. Can you put Raven on?"

Raven looked at James and then pitched her voice towards where she guessed the mic was located. "Hi, Dad, I mean Sir. It's good to hear your voice."

"Dad?" asked James. Raven blushed and grinned at him. "I told you I know a guy," she said under her breath.

"You, too, dear, you, too. You're OK?" asked the general.

"Yes, considering. Lorelei, our ally, got us out of there, and James was able to figure out how to fly this thing. We'll be landing soon."

"Copy that, control out."

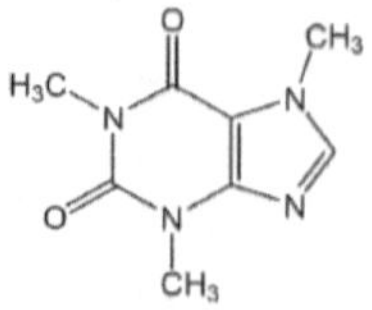

James laid his head on his pillow. His bunk never felt so comfortable. As he drifted off to sleep, Njerum came to him again.

You listened to what I told you. I am grateful that you are alright, Njerum said.

James replied, *How did you know?*

The Nommos, or Mami Wata as you call them, tried to subjugate my people for hundreds of years. I know their methods. In my time here on Earth, I have learned that you humans are not a bad lot, and I would hate for you to suffer the same fate as my people.

He continued, *If we can work together, find a weakness, and exploit it, we can save your planet, and return my people to ours. For now, you have had a busy few days. Get some rest.*

Njerum faded away, his canine face expressing humor as it often did, with his tongue lolling out of his muzzle and his ears half-way perked.

James chuckled to himself. *Maybe I will have a chance to fly among the stars after all.*

The End

Messenger of Emptiness

By Gustavo Bondoni

Rita Birra growled and shut down the fan. She checked her stats and swore.

"That bad, huh?" Thior asked.

"We missed our objective by seventeen percent this cycle," she replied.

"So what? We've been over-quota every time we've come down here for the last five years. One miss isn't going to do us any harm. We certainly don't need the money."

Rita pushed the strands of her greasy hair—it had been fourteen standard days since she'd washed it—out of her eyes and glared. "I don't care. I've been the best at driving the tubes for five years. Everyone knows it, and I don't let them forget. Can you imagine the kind of idiotic comments I'll have to listen to? Can you imagine what Crugh will say?"

Thior laughed. "I can… but who cares? Just smile and remind him it's coming back his way, with interest, the next time he misses an objective. You won't have to wait long." He leaned over her and flipped the switch. "I'm starting the retraction. I've already done all the safety checks and secured everything."

The tube above them began to collapse pack upon itself, segment by segment. As it did, it pulled the self-propelled guidance room up with it. Thior and Rita had spent the past fourteen standard days guiding the open end of the tube—essentially a giant vacuum cleaner nozzle—from storm to storm, chasing areas with high concentrations of organic molecules around the atmosphere of the gas giant.

Rita stared out the window as she waited. The process of folding the tube back up took seven hours. In the distance, the star around which the planet orbited, Gliese 581, was brighter than the other visible stars, but only slightly. The gas giant was the planet furthest out from it, with the real colony planets—three rocky worlds—holding orbits further in. The gas they harvested was destined to the terraforming efforts of the largest, a carbon-poor world with gravity nearly twice that of Earth's, but which would be perfect for humans adapted to high-gee worlds.

Not that it made any difference to Rita. She just knew that anything that had to do with terraforming meant steady work for centuries.

As the gondola was pulled towards the harvester ship, she entertained herself the way she always did by pointing the scanners out into space. Though most of their sensor arsenal consisted of chemical sniffers that helped work out concentrations of particular molecules in an atmosphere, there were some really, really good visual scanners as well, with optics augmented by AI to clean up images in even the dirtiest, most turbulent cloud layers.

Those worked beautifully when you pointed them out into the dark vacuum of space, and Rita already had the discovery of seventeen outer-system asteroids and comets to her name.

As she stared into the scope, she pulled up the database of orbital objects and instructed the computer to mark the ones that had already been discovered.

"What the hell is that?" she said.

"What's what?" Thior asked.

Rita jumped. "I'd forgotten you were there—I thought you'd gone back into your room. I'm talking to myself. I'm just adding to my rock collection, nothing that would interest you…" she let her voice trail off as she stared into the visor and brought the magnification up to its highest level. "No. On second thought, wait a minute. Have a look at this." She pulled her head away and turned the visor over to Thior, who shrugged and looked into it. "What's that look like to you?" she asked.

"It looks like some kind of ship. A transport, most likely." He shrugged and moved away from the visor. "Probably just some new workers on the way. Or a new load of yeast precursors for the vats. Didn't look like anything special."

"That's because it's too far away. That ship is twenty kilometers long."

"What?" Thior said.

"If it's a ship, it's twenty kilometers long," Rita repeated. "And it's not coming from the direction of the inner planets. It's coming from outside the system."

"Unless it's a rock shaped like a ship."

"Yeah, there's that option, of course. I'll keep watching."

"It's a ship. I'm calling it in," Rita said.

"Okay," Thior replied.

"You're still here?" Rita asked.

"Actually, I came over to tell you that we're an hour out so you could get your stuff cleaned up so we can turn the gondola over to the next shift. And I found you talking to yourself, and wondered if you'd say anything interesting."

"Well, give me a second," Rita replied. She opened a comm channel to the control center and said: "Can you put me on the line to whoever is the Astro Club delegate today?"

Malakiad Station wasn't meant as an observatory, so there were no astronomers on board, and no one got paid for finding new heavenly bodies. That didn't deter people from doing it anyway: volunteers ensured that every find was duly recorded in the Gliese system's records.

A new voice came on. "Fionell here, Rita, whatcha got for me? Rock or comet? Or did you finally find the mysterious fifth planet."

Rita rolled her eyes at the old joke. Nothing the size of a planet would be undiscovered long considering the sensors around Gliese. Hell, even the rocks that Rita got her name attached to would have been found centuries ago had anyone really bothered to look. "Neither. We have a ship on its way in."

"So what?" Fionell asked, irritation coming into his voice. "We're an orbiting station. Ships are kind of what we get every day."

"This one is twenty kilometers long, it's heading in from interstellar space, and it's doing a deceleration burn. I just thought that might interest you."

"Are you sure?"

"Have I ever messed up a deep space object ID?"

"Dammit. Give me the numbers, and I'll see if we can get some eyes on this."

"Remember I get credit," Rita said.

"Yeah, whatever," Fionell replied. The line went dead.

Rita, buried under a pack and several changes of clothes, shouldered open the door to her quarters on Malakiad Station. Fortunately, the scanners recognized her even under the enormous load, and the door opened at her push.

She dumped everything on the bed and collapsed with a sigh. All she wanted was a shower and to sleep for a couple of days so she could forget the failed attempt at sucking up enough gas to score a bonus. There were several reasons why she'd always made her quotas. She could read the cloud patterns better than anyone else and she nearly never made a bad decision. Unfortunately, she had learned on this trip that there was also a reason for her to fail: thin concentrations on every single stop.

There would be time to watch an accelerated data feed to see if there was something she could have done differently, but now wasn't the time. And besides, logic dictated that no one could avoid the iron-clad rules of chance forever. She suspected it had most likely been a simple case of luck catching up with her.

Her comm chirped, a priority alarm. She checked the caller. "Guun, there is no possible reason you would be calling me for an emergency. You're not in the loop for anything important, and you know you can't just use the priority call so the person on the other end will pick up the comm," she said with irritation.

"I know," Guun replied. "But I think you'll agree with me once you get here."

"What? You want me to go to your room? Now?"

"No!" Guun said. "You need to get to the comm center. Trust me this time. I have to go."

She sighed, but in his defense Guun, despite the puppy love he had for her—she suspected it had more to do with her status as the station's most legendary miner than anything else—had never done anything objectionable. He was a good guy, and it would be out of character for him to place a priority call just to get her to himself. And if it was on the level…

Rita pulled herself out of bed with a groan and emerged into the corridor. The comm room was just a couple of levels up, and she found herself hurrying. By the time she reached the room, she was breathing hard.

Any question of Guun trying something silly evaporated when she saw the crowd. It wasn't just that fifteen people stood in the room, but the fact that three of them wore the uniforms of Station admin… and one of those was Karla Deerborn.

The rest were part of the Astro Club. She spotted Guun and Fionell off to one side and worked her way over.

Her two friends could have been peas from the same pod. They were both pale-skinned and dark-haired, with thin bodies and a slight stoop. Both spoke softly, and the main difference between them were the eyes. Guun's were brown while Fionell's were a dark orange that was almost red, testimony of some targeted genetic tampering in his family tree.

"What's up?" she whispered.

"Your ship. It's got everyone riled up. Apparently…"

"All right, people," a loud voice boomed over the general hubbub of voices. "I need everyone out of here except the people running the comm and the scanners." The speaker was a short bull of a man, one of the three in uniform. Rita's heart sank. He was the acting head of security, and he was rumored to be tough. The miners referred to him as the impact ball, after the game they played in which a heavy ball was used to knock people aside in zero-gee hockey. Arguing with that guy was a good way to get tossed in the slammer for a couple of day shifts.

Apparently, everyone else knew it, too, because the hangers-on headed for the doors.

"Miss Birra," another voice, softer but somehow more authoritative than the first, spoke. "If you'd consent to give us a few minutes of your time…"

"Busted," Guun said. But he gave her an envious look as Rita turned back to Head Administrator Deerborn.

"Yes, ma'am?" Rita said.

"I'm glad you could make it," the Administrator said. "We didn't want to disturb your rest. I know you were returning from a stint in the atmosphere when you called this in."

"Yes, ma'am."

"Dammit," Deerborn said. "Why does everyone call me that? This isn't a military base. Just call me Karla."

"All right."

Deerborn waited for the inevitable ma'am and when it didn't come, she smiled. "Either you learn quickly, or you hate authority."

"I'm sorry ma'am?" Rita said, so surprised that she blurted it out without thinking.

That got a chuckle. "I used to hate calling my superiors 'Sir' when I was in the Navy, so I just assume that everyone hates it as much as I did. Plus, we can't space you for insubordination here, so you're safe enough." She glanced over to the comm station where four technicians milled about. They didn't appear to be making much progress. "I wanted to congratulate you on finding this on your personal time. I've seen you have quite a record of locating asteroids."

"It gives me something to do on the way up," Rita replied.

"Most miners are content with their entertainment libraries."

Rita wanted to say that the entertainment libraries were full of inane garbage, but she held her tongue because after being criticized for her obsession with space rocks all her life, she didn't want to seem like she was lashing out. "I'm more interested in the composition of our planetary system."

"Well, I'm glad you were. What do you ascribe the incoming vehicle to?"

"Since it's very obviously coming at us from interstellar space, I thought it was probably an embassy ship. We get those every couple of centuries, don't we?"

Karla nodded. "We do, but did you check on the direction?"

And, just like that, it was a test. Karla's gaze had gone from affable and friendly to a steady, evaluating one in the blink of an eye.

Rita hesitated for a moment, thinking of the ship, of its trajectory, of the fact that its engines were pointed towards Gliese in a deceleration burn. All of that seemed to fit. And on that trajectory, it would have had to come from the colony at…

"Oh, God. It came from the other side. There's nothing there," Rita said.

"Well done," Karla said. "You know your stuff. And now you understand why I wanted the rest of them out of here. This could start a panic."

"Why?"

"Because if there are no human colonies in that direction, then who sent the ship?" Karla asked.

"I don't know who sent it, but that's a human ship," Rita replied. "I'm completely certain of that."

"I've seen it in the scanner over there before it stopped working," Karla nodded to where the techs were still trying to get the equipment running. "And I felt the same about it. But the truth is we just don't know. Maybe it's an alien race that designs ships that look just like ours."

"Ma'am," one of the techs, a pudgy dark-skinned man who couldn't have been more than twenty, said, "the array is up again. We can use radio, microwave, and IR to communicate."

"Send them the message we agreed on." Karla walked towards the techs and Rita followed.

The comm array was a scaled-up version of the one in a mining gondola. Rita had seen the emitters: huge arrays on the side of the station flanked by several receiver dishes two dozen meters wide. They were placed all around the station and, apart from their communications responsibilities, they also helped with radiation shielding.

Techs scrambled to obey, and Karla turned back to Rita. "The ship is still a couple of light minutes out. You did an amazing job to spot it."

"I spend my entire working life searching for tiny ripples and anomalies that allow me to spot promising veins of gas to follow. I can sense something out of place almost by instinct. I see the weirdness in the patterns." Rita shrugged. "I suppose that must have been what made me focus on the ship and ignore all the balls of ice and rock closer to my viewer: it must have been moving differently."

"Well, I have to ask you a favor. As you can probably tell, we're not sure of when, or even if, we'll be getting a response from the ship," Karla said. "And they won't be here for several days at best, a couple of weeks at worst… it depends on whether they keep decelerating at the same rate or change their burn. And all of that means… well, it means I need you to keep quiet about the fact that it's coming from a place it really shouldn't be."

Rita nodded.

"I can't order you to keep your mouth shut," Karla replied. "But if you do me this favor, I will remember it. Either here or if I get transferred down the well."

"Of course. And you don't owe me any favors. I completely understand; panic won't help anyone."

"Thank you. And stay as long as you like. But I can't promise we'll get anything done here except to spray the galaxy with even more comm radiation than usual."

Though Rita never expected an official in Station administration to keep her word—and she would expect it even less if a promotion took Karla Deerborn to Gliese Prime—the woman came through.

Four days after she'd waited in vain with the techs in the comm room for the ship to respond, Rita's personal comm buzzed. Confidential number.

"What's that?" she asked Guun, who happened to be sitting beside her at a table full of off-duty techs and a miner or two.

"Never seen that before," Guun replied. "Every comm except for some of the security ones have open ID's. So unless you stole a shipment of volatiles, you should probably get your handset looked at."

"Great," Rita replied. "Just what I needed." She hit the button to answer the call. "Yes?"

"Miss Birra?"

"Ma'am… I mean Karla?" she asked.

"Yes. I'm sorry. I hear people around you. Is this a bad time?"

"No. Just let me get to a quieter spot." Rita walked over the hall outside the communal lounge and said: "Sorry about that. I wasn't expecting a call."

"I can imagine. Like I said, I'm really sorry to call like this, especially since you couldn't see who was calling… but I wanted to give you the option of being with us."

"With you? For what?" Rita asked.

"We're going out to meet the ship. There's one spot on the shuttle. I reserved it for you, but only if you want it. This could be dangerous, so I understand if you don't want anything to do with it."

"What? Are you crazy? Tell me where to go, and I'll be over as soon as I can run."

Karla chuckled. "I thought you might feel that way. Shuttle Store Fourteen."

"I'll be right down."

Rita called into the lounge. "You guys can have what's left of my food." Ignoring the questions shouted from her table, she sprinted through the corridors until she found a ladder leading into one of the station spokes. The outer sections of the station were spun for gravity, allowing humans to live comfortably in the complex. Numerous hollow columns served as spokes to a giant wheel and also gave access to the areas of microgravity in the center of Malakiad Station.

She emerged into a ring-shaped corridor wide enough for two people, and she propelled herself along until she reached a null-grav station and called up a pod.

Null-grav pods were essentially single-person transports that moved through vacuum-filled tubes, impelled and guided by magnetic force. They were a quick, energy-efficient way to get people and cargo from point A to point B on the enormous station.

As she wooshed along, she noted that Karla and her people had selected the Shuttle Store furthest from the population centers and…

"Security checkpoint approaching. Please state your name and security credentials," the pod's automated voice said.

"Uhh… I'm Rita Birra, and I have no security clearance."

And that, she thought, *was that.* The pod would be shunted off into a secondary tube and she would be asked to give an alternate destination. It had happened to her before, when she mistakenly entered the wrong sector coordinates and ended up in a Station Security weapons warehouse. No big deal, but she would miss the shuttle… particularly as she had no way to call Administrator Deerborn.

"Approved," the voice said, and the capsule sped on without interruption.

"Damn she's good," Rita said to herself. Rita's entire job consisted of watching tiny details… but for someone who had an entire station to take care of, catching a little thing like that meant that Karla was seriously on the ball.

She emerged from the pod into a huge space where no concessions had been made to comfort. The floors, walls and ceiling were made of iron grating, and men and women in light body armor were swinging from each surface.

One man, a big fellow whose features she couldn't see under the faceplate, spotted her emerging tentatively from the pod and gave her a hand. Once she had a good hold onto the grating and was no longer in danger of floating off into the middle of the room and getting in everyone's way, the guy nodded and pointed to his right. "The boss is over there. She says to join her."

Feeling like a kid at an adult dinner party, Rita pulled herself to where Administrator Deerborn stood beside the door to a shuttle. "Just tell me where to park myself," she said. "I don't want to be in the way."

"You won't be. Not any more than I am, anyway. I just gave an order to put a bunch of people on a shuttle, and these military types took over." Karla grinned. "Oh, they pretend to ask me my preferences every once in a while, but never about anything that would keep them from obeying my original order to the best of their ability. Between you and me, I think they're bored and they're hoping the ship will do something hostile so they can blow holes in it."

"Then we'd better hope it isn't an alien vessel after all."

"Oh, we checked that. It isn't. There's writing on the side. We're about to board the good ship Varanasi, of the Humility Flock."

Rita frowned. "I never heard of that colony."

"No one has. But I hope they're not religious nuts… if they are, they probably won't like anything we represent, and Major Oria's boys and girls will get to use their toys."

"Is it armed?"

Rita shook her head. "If it is, the energy sources for the big guns are shielded well enough that we couldn't detect anything. If I had to guess, I'd say this was a civilian colony ship. But why it came here from out there… we won't know until we get inside."

"All aboard," a thick-limbed woman shouted from beside the shuttle door. But as the soldiers approached, she stopped them. "Guests first you under-evolved monkeys." The woman turned to Karla. "You may board when ready, Ma'am. Please don't forget to strap in. We're going high-gee burn."

Karla thanked her and pushed herself from the wall, floating gracefully into the shuttle. Rita followed much less elegantly. Her life was spent in gravity, either on the station or in the even higher gravity of the Gliese IV's atmosphere.

To her relief, she'd judged the aim right and grasped the handhold at the right side of the shuttle door.

The woman at the door kept her eye on Rita long enough to ascertain that she wasn't going to drift helplessly away and then turned back to the troops. "All right, your turn. By squads, Alpha first," she shouted.

The door opened into a very short corridor with doors leading into larger compartments. Fortunately, there was no danger of drifting here, and Rita followed Karla to the right. That door opened into a luxurious cabin with comfortable-looking seats.

"Wow," Rita said before she could help herself. "I didn't know Security people traveled in this kind of style."

"They don't," Karla replied. "In fact, they insist on not doing so. The main hold of this shuttle is set up for battlefield deployment with as little stuff between them and the doors as possible. That bulkhead behind us can seal off the back of the ship so the soldiers can operate in vacuum without killing the passengers. That means us."

"You seem to know a lot about ships," Karla said. She remembered the graceful crossing of the shuttle bay. "And zero-gee. For an admin, I mean."

"I see miners and military aren't that different. The people in charge are supposed to be clueless, right?"

"That's not what I meant…"

"Relax, I'm just giving you a hard time. I was actually in the Navy when I was younger, and I learned things. In fact, I'll clue you in on the most important thing you need to know about being around soldiers. Remember that woman by the door? She is a legendary creature known as a sergeant, and if we don't obey her and get strapped in, she's going to come in here and kick our asses."

Rita laughed. She knew the type: they were called loadmasters in mining circles. "Not yours. They never go after the higher-ups."

"Rita," Karla said in a serious tone, and she pulled her harness as tight as she could. "There is nothing outside the military that outranks a sergeant. And they only tolerate officers because someone has to take the blame when it hits the fan."

Rita strapped herself in.

Less than two minutes later, the sergeant entered their compartment and checked the tension of every single belt on their five-point harnesses. She took her time about it and grunted when she was done.

"Good job, ladies," she said. "Have a great flight. ETA to target is about twelve minutes. We will be burning extremely hard, especially on braking, so please don't loosen those straps until I tell you to."

Then she left through the door to the other hold, sealing the hatch behind her.

Rita was still thinking of something to say about the sergeant when the shuttle suddenly disengaged from the station with a clank. It floated for some seconds and then the engines roared to life, and she was slammed into the back of her seat.

Okay, she thought. *So the front is that way.*

She knew the shuttle would accelerate for a few minutes, but it seemed longer under the high gravitational forces. Then, there was a moment of blissful weightlessness before her stomach sensed that the entire shuttle was flipping end over end.

She was right. Suddenly, the engines burned again, but this time, she knew they were stopping the vehicle.

A voice on the cabin loudspeakers announced: "Matching speed and trajectory. We'll be in place in forty-five seconds. Scan indicates the airlock design is unusual, but all the mating surfaces are standard size. It's human all right."

Karla nodded and turned to Rita. "He's just being dramatic. We already knew it was human."

"It could have been an alien ship painted in human symbols as a trap."

"If that's the case," Karla replied, "the size of the airlocks wouldn't matter. Any alien smart enough to copy our writing would be smart enough to copy that."

"That's a comfort," Rita said.

"That's why we brought an assault team," Karla said. "But relax. If this ship is an invasion crew, there's nothing Malakiad Station can do about it. The ship is twice the size of our station, it just crossed interstellar space, and if they have weapons or high-energy power sources aboard, they also have some way of hiding those from our best scanners. But the real reason I think we're safe is that the ship is following the protocol for approaching a human station while running with disabled comms almost to the letter."

A loud clank echoed through the shuttle, and she felt the entire vehicle vibrate. The troops must have been pouring through the airlock.

"Now comes the really hard part," Karla said.

"What's that?"

"We get to wait while the soldiers figure out whether they have to shoot at what's inside."

Rita lasted only a minute before asking. She had to ask. "Why did you bring me? I understand why you came: if there are people in there, they'll need someone better to talk to than a bunch of guys with guns… but why me?" She expected the answer to be full of politician's evasions.

"Well," Karla said. "First off, I kept track of what people were saying about the ship and, as far as I was able to find out, you didn't tell anyone about what you saw and heard the day we met. You kept your mouth shut. That was a point in your favor." Then she grinned. "But mainly, it's politics. I know the miners are always complaining that you do all the work that makes Malakiad a viable station, but that you're never around when important decisions are made. Since this is the biggest thing to happen to the station in the past hundred years, I thought I'd better bring a miner along because if not, neither I nor my successors would ever hear the end of it." She shrugged. "And since you seem competent—I checked your mining record and found it impressive— curious and trustworthy, I gave you the option of volunteering. If you'd said no, I'd have gotten someone else." She looked Rita right in the eye. "But I didn't think you'd decline."

"Administrator," the voice on the intercom said, "Major Oria requests your presence on the Varanasi."

On cue, the sergeant stepped into the cabin and helped them release their harnesses. "Everything is pressurized, but you need to wear suits anyway. Come with me."

The corridor held a suit locker with several vacuum and radiation-shielded suits in several sizes. Rita wrinkled her nose as she donned hers, expecting a well used and odorous interior. Instead, she smelled the plastic and chemical aroma of newly-produced equipment. "You'll have to swear me to secrecy on this as well. I never heard of anyone being assigned a suit less than twenty years old," she said.

Karla frowned. "Yeah, I know about that. We're working on it. Unfortunately, the mining budget is separate from the military budget… and guess which one I'm not allowed to touch."

They clambered through a flexible tube that bridged the space between the two ships, and Rita tried not to think of the vacuum held at bay by such a thin wall. Even in the time it would take to seal her helmet—just a fraction of a second—damage would be done if it failed.

Nothing happened, and they pulled themselves into a large cargo hangar.

The staging area was illuminated by floodlights that Rita guessed the troops had carried in, but the rest of the cavernous space was lost in shadow. The major stood in a small knot of soldiers a few meters away. He grabbed Rita as she floated past.

"Turn on the magnetic function on your boots, like this," he said, and held down a yellow button on her chest control plate.

"Thank you," Rita said.

The major turned to Karla. "Ma'am, as far as I can tell, this ship is no threat to anyone. There are four fusion plants in the spine, three of which are decommissioned and the fourth is the one they used to brake. Right now, it's almost completely powered down."

"People?" Karla said.

"I assume there are probably some colonists in here somewhere. This is a freezer ship, and we've found a couple of bays full of cryo-sleep chambers. Powered-up but empty. But even with impeller packs, a ship this size is going to take a week to explore completely."

"So we take a week. Can we at least tell the people back on Malakiad, and the people in-system that there's nothing to worry about?" Karla said.

"Yes," the major replied. He seemed on the verge of saying more.

"Tell me. I can take it," Karla prompted.

"I don't have any evidence for what I'm about to say, but I have a feeling that this ship's in trouble. The reactors are borked—and don't ask me to tell you how, we'll need to bring in experts. I think these guys froze themselves, changed course for the nearest system in their databases and put themselves in the hands of God. The final braking maneuver might have been the last thing their functional reactor could manage. Remember it takes decades to brake from interstellar speeds."

"So what are you saying?"

"I'm saying the people in here might not have a week for us to search for them. My techs are convinced the reactor won't last a day. Two at most. And if you've ever seen what happens to a person frozen in cryo if the power goes down…" He shuddered. "I think it must be a very ugly way to die."

"Can't we scan the ship from outside?" Karla said.

"Through the hull? The only thing you can see through that would be a very large energy source. The fusion mill barely even registers."

"So unless we figure it out…" Karla prompted.

"You'll probably have a ship full of dead people. Maybe a few thousand, more likely a few tens of thousands," Major Oria replied.

"Dammit."

A second shuttle, full of experts in ship power systems and search and rescue operations, arrived an hour later. They spread out into the Varanasi in teams that looked purposeful and competent when they set out, but invariably returned crestfallen and discouraged.

No one spoke to Rita, but she didn't mind. The sense of being involved in something this big kept her awake and interested, even though she knew she was taking up space that could have been given to someone useful.

"Isn't there anything I can do?" Rita asked Karla, who'd just finished speaking to the last group of rescuers heading into the ship.

"Not really." Karla indicated the group that had just left. "And neither can they, most likely. The problem is the size of this ship. It's straight out of the Colossal Age of space exploration, when they built ships big enough to carry an entire civilization and built them to last a few thousand years. This one is twenty-one kilometers long and it's a flattened oval five klicks on the longest side which gets wider at the back. Try doing the math on how many chambers this size you can fit in that volume… and it's a lot. Worse, most of the chambers won't be this big. This is a storage area that could double as a docking bay for smaller ships. Even a cryo-room for fifty thousand people would be a fraction of this size, finding all the inhabited ones is like finding a specific hydrogen atom in a nebula."

"Then why even bother?"

"Because we have to try." Karla sighed. "This isn't even about politics. Every one of us here suspects that, somewhere on this ship, thousands of people put themselves in cryo-freeze hoping that we'd pull them out alive. We can't power this entire ship, because it's too big. So we need to find the occupied areas and power those until we get things stable. Unfortunately, we probably aren't going to find them in time. Too many little rooms."

"Isn't there a central control for the cryo-chambers? Can't we go to the bridge and figure it out that way?"

"Oria's people already went to the bridge. They checked, and apparently the cryo-chambers are each individually controlled. We're trying to check power usage in different parts of the ship, but compared to things like propulsion, atmosphere recycling and heating, the cryo chambers are a tiny drain. That likely won't allow us to find it in time."

"So they're going to die?"

"We haven't given up hope yet," Karla replied. But she looked grim as she said it.

After that conversation, Rita's enthusiasm dwindled, and she turned off her magnetic boots and allowed herself to float. She stayed in grabbing range of a wall, but she tried to get into the zone, that state of concentration that helped her to concentrate on tracking valuable molecules through the atmosphere of the gas giant.

She needed to think. They couldn't just let an unknown number of people die. That was unacceptable.

How did one find something small in a huge volume like this one?

The rescuers seemed stymied. Their chatter on the radio was mostly complaints: they could save everyone, they seemed to think, if only they could find them.

But the walls were too thick, and there were too many of them. No scanners could make it though, and you really couldn't even go very far before comm frequencies were also blocked. Frustration ran high.

Rita growled. The problem seemed to be that the ship itself was defeating the efforts to save its passengers, even though every single door appeared to have been unlocked when the owners realized they were in trouble. Every effort had been made to make the rescue easier… but the nature of the ship was stymieing the effort.

People could move freely. Air could circulate. But the tech needed to find anything in a ship this size just didn't function under the conditions.

Rita opened her eyes and started. The movement caused her to spin away from the wall. For once, she wasn't embarrassed at being the newbie needing rescue.

"Get me down," she shouted into the comm. "I know how to find them!"

"Who is this?" a voice came over the comm.

"Sorry, I should have mentioned it. I'm Rita, the miner. I'm in the… I guess it's the hangar. I floated into the air."

"Rita, this is Karla on our private channel. I can see you. Your legs are still close to the wall, the way you get down is to set your magnetic soles to the highest setting and let them do the work. You'll drift in if you keep your soles pointed that way. Then simply walk down the wall and onto the floor."

"All right," Rita replied, feeling stupid for having called out on the main channel.

Moments later, she reached the wall and her boots connected with a clang. When she walked to the floor, four people were waiting for her: Karla and three of the rescue team leaders.

One of the rescuers, a man with an orange-colored mustache spoke as soon as her feet hit the deck: "You're the miner who says you have a plan?"

"So I can't have seen something your experts missed?" Rita retorted.

"If you have a solution, I don't care if you're a space fungus. But I need it fast. Any people in this hulk don't have a lot of time left."

"You're right. I'm sorry. Do you have sniffers?" she asked.

The guy looked confused. "You mean… dogs? Like the ones on Gliese Prime?"

She shook her head. "Of course not. I mean the ones we use to chase molecules in the atmosphere of the big orange planet Malakiad station orbits around. Wide-spectrum compound detectors. WCDs."

"I… I don't know what you're talking about."

"It's a mining tool. Hell, it's the most important mining tool anyone managed to invent. We drop them in the atmosphere, and they tell us concentrations of any chemical we think is important. They're sensitive to parts per quadrillion, or some ridiculous thing like that."

"I don't see how that could help us," the man said, shaking his head. The other rescue people fidgeted, apparently impatient to get back to work.

"Let her explain," Karla said.

If Karla hadn't said it, Rita would probably have apologized and let the rescue people get on with their jobs. But the Administrator's confidence bolstered her own. "Well, I've seen working cryo-chambers. We use them for miners involved in accidents, to get the metabolism way down so we can get them back to station. They smell funny when they're working. A strong, acrid smell."

"That's ammonia," orange mustache said.

"Perfect, then a sniffer can find the occupied cryo-chambers. This ship is only twenty klicks long, right?"

"Twenty-one."

"Well, we use them to track concentrations on scales of hundreds and thousands of kilometers," Rita replied.

To his credit the guy changed tacks. "And you can use one of those?" he said.

"I'm the best."

"That, judging by her record, is a hundred percent true," Karla said.

The guy turned to Karla. "I honestly don't have any better ideas. Can we get one of those in here?"

"You'll have it in an hour," Karla promised.

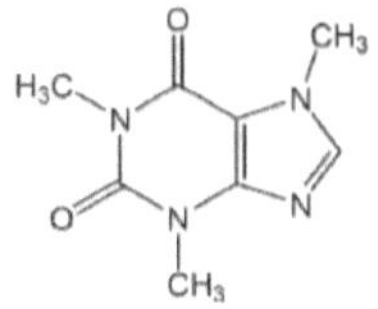

The Administrator was once again as good as her word. Better, actually. Forty-seven minutes later, a handheld sniffer—Rita didn't even know those existed—was carried into the ship by two techs.

"Hi Rita," one of them said.

"Hi Sam. Hi Deep. How's that working?"

"They told us you're looking for ammonia, right? So we set it up on the flight over, and we found traces in the PPT range. I set the controls to read the current level as 1.0. Anything higher means more concentration."

PPT meant parts per trillion, Rita knew. "We're pretty far away," she told the accumulated people. "Let's get moving."

They exited the hangar through the door directly across from the airlock. The meter went up to 1.05.

"We're moving in the right direction," Rita said. "Which isn't saying much, because that was the only door in the hangar. Now, we need to try to guess whether to go deeper into the ship, or left or right, up or down." A thought struck her, and she turned to one of the rescue operators: "We're probably going to go pretty deep. How do we get back out without getting lost?"

"We're mapping as we go. Don't worry about it."

They headed right, towards the rear of the Varanasi. The reading decreased after they'd gone a few dozen meters, so they turned around.

"All right. Forward it is," Rita said.

"We really need to hurry," the rescuer said.

"No," Rita replied. "What we need to do is to make sure we always go in the right direction and don't waste too much time going the wrong way. That's how we'll save time."

They walked forward for an hour, the reading steadily climbing. For the past thirty minutes, every hold they entered was full of cryo-pods, egg-shaped sleep chambers just bigger than a human, each surrounded by a nest of thick cables. They were all empty, but if they hadn't been, the ship would have held millions.

"Shouldn't we go further into the hull?" the same rescuer asked after a while.

"No. We're moving along a line of steadily increasing concentration along the longest axis. We know we're getting closer and closer with every step. We'll deal with the fiddly stuff when we must."

The moment came sooner than they expected. Five hundred meters later, Rita stopped.

"The reading just lowered," she reported. "It's time to go further in."

They headed towards the center of the ship, but that lowered the reading, so they began to make a radial circumnavigation of the hull.

"Hurry," the rescuer said. "The lights are dimming. We probably only have a few hours of power left."

Rita ignored him.

"Stop," Rita said after a few more minutes. "The reading just lowered."

"That can't be," Deep said. "We've tested all the alternative directions."

"Maybe the air flow is making us miss. We'll have to try everything. But we know we're close. We're in the PPM range."

"Yeah. I just hope we don't simply find a hold full of ammonia fertilizer," Deep replied.

Rita shuddered. "Don't say those things! So, left, right? Towards the center?"

Left showed a small increase, and then leveled off. Rita made them stop. "Let me think." She stayed still for five minutes thinking of the data and letting her gut take over the chase, as she had so often when out in her gondola trying to catch volatiles. Then she slapped her forehead with her hand. The solution was obvious, and she would have caught on immediately if she had been sitting above the gas giant instead of standing in a huge hold full of mechanical eggs. "You and you," she said, pointing to one of the rescuers and Sam, "go forward. Check the next four holds in that direction. You'll find a small room full of occupied cryo pods. The rest of us will go that way." She pointed in the opposite direction.

"If the people are that way, why are we going the other?" Deep asked, scratching his head.

"Because there's a bigger occupied room over there, and I don't want to miss it. The concentration leveled off because we're walking away from the big one."

They walked through two more empty holds before coming to one that felt different.

Rita sniffed the air, the tang of ammonia now very discernible.

"Damn, I'm good," she said.

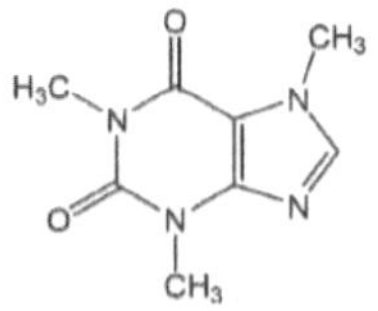

The man was balding, middle aged and confused.

Surrounded by medical techs, he was obviously in the mental fog that came from being thawed out after a long cryo-sleep.

Around him, the entire hold was well-lit. Fresh air circulated freely and scrubbers were deployed in a ring around the hold. They were overkill since only about thirty of the fifty thousand humans in the room were awake and mobile. And of those, ten were the guys who'd set up the portable power unit that, independent of the ship's failing reactors, powered up this particular room.

Rita stood to one side. Once she'd found the rooms, things had been a blur. Instead of walking back though the ship with the news, one of the rescue crew had simply headed towards the nearest service airlock, emerged onto the hull, and radioed their position. One of the shuttles already had the generator aboard, and an army of technicians who'd been awaiting their opportunity powered everything up.

This time, not even Karla was there to talk to her, and Sam and Deep had been roped in to help with the generator.

But when Karla arrived, the first thing she said was: "So who do you want to talk to?"

"Huh?" Rita said.

"Which of these colonists should we thaw out?"

"How should I know? They're just pods. You're the boss. Don't you know which one we should take out?"

"Why would you think that? I'm just going to choose one at random. So you might as well do it. If anyone complains, we'll explain that you were the one who saved them. That should shut them up."

So Rita had pointed to an egg nearby and said. "All right, that one."

Her choice had caused a team to descend on the cryo-chamber and thaw out the confused guy in the white tunic. And since no one had told her she couldn't be there, she stood just ten feet away as the Gliese Colony had their first contact with a human civilization from a place where humans were never supposed to have gone.

He was slowly coming back to his senses.

"Hey… why did you wake me up? Everyone was supposed to sleep until the ship stopped. Did something go wrong?" His speech was strangely accented, but he spoke a recognizable version of Pan.

The man peered at the medical team around him. "I'm sorry. I don't know you. What temple did you say you were with?"

Karla stepped forward. "We're not with any temple. This might come as a surprise, but I'm Karla Deerborn of the Gliese administration. We picked up your ship as you entered the system. I'm sure you must have quite a tale to tell."

"Oh, yes," the man said, still seemingly dazed. "It was awful. The virus, and the uncharted pulsar…" His eyes focused on Karla. He blinked. "Did you say Gliese? Could you repeat that?"

Karla did.

The man stared at her for a moment. "Are you saying we made it?"

"You and about seventy-five thousand others."

He laughed. "They were right. I thought we would die, but I guess dying in cryo is better than facing death awake, right? You don't feel a thing, and…" A pleading look crossed his face. "We actually made it?" he asked Karla again.

"Yes," she replied.

The man tried to speak again. He didn't make it as tears flowed down his face.

Rita wiped away a few of her own.

Bobtail Anni

By Bart Kemper

A cluster of a dozen men and women looked around uncertainly. The bartender waved them over. "Welcome to The Loonie Bin. You all look young and healthy, you must be new."

There were some wry chuckles from others at the bar, the kind that comes from a well-worn joke that still fits. The newcomers noticed many at the bar looked … different. Some of it was scars or paleness. Then one of them said, "They're Lifers."

A second look and they all saw it – a thinness that was more than just "skinny." A few were on floaters, so debilitated by low gravity or injuries they didn't walk even in the low lunar gravity. Some were missing limbs, a stark break in expectation to the newly arrived who had to go through rigorous physicals to get up the gravity well. Despite all of that, these older spacers seemed bright-eyed, animated, and … fey. It wasn't just that they were no longer fit to go back down the Well, they no longer seemed to belong down there.

The bartender nodded. "Not everyone here has crossed the Styx. Lifers are still the minority. But this is our night, so a lot of us are here to remember Bobtail Annie and what she paid for us. Tell you what, let me buy you all a round and I'll tell you the story."

One of the young men snorted.

"Wait, what?" he said. "You buy us a round and you tell us the story? Isn't it usually the other way around?"

He smiled. "Good! You'll fit right in, because …"

(IMPACT MINUS 359 HRS)

"Sugar, I have a deal for you."

The woman's drawl was rich, brown sugar and steel. She sounded pure Georgia country. To those that knew her, it was the start of a deal or a joke, sometimes both. Her short cropped black hair, typical of those living in pressure suits, looked somehow salon-perfect. The station spin at the L5 Lagrange point had a number of key facilities, but the one that mattered the most to many was the bar.

"Slow down, Anni. I surrender, American." The wiry, pale man was half a head taller than her, but he felt she was somehow the taller one. He enhanced his Russian accent to cartoon levels.

A mock pout covered her puzzlement. "Oh, now you're taking the fun out of it."

A smile revealed a few missing teeth. "Da, Anni, Chuck told me drill. I sign over my cargo tractor, you run them back to moon, I relax and drink without worrying about violating my contract, and what I pay you is fraction of what I would lose waiting for a paying load or deadheading back on my own."

He handed her a printout slip. "My tractor, with clearances and authorizations. He said take second best deal."

Anni Broussard frowned. "Chuck told you this? Chuck Hadley…Gregor?" she said, glancing down at the slip to get his name. "Second-best deal" was an inside joke about "family discounts."

"Da, Miss Anni. Second best for you, first best for me, he said. He owed me. He told me this clear his debt to me and your debt to him."

She held his gaze, then gave him a friendly smile and extended her rich mahogany-toned hand. Both of their hands had the dry, calloused texture earned working with tools in stale, dry air. "Of course, if he says you're lying your rig may have a mishap."

He smiled right back, then released his grip, and turned towards the bar with practiced glide steps of someone used to low centripetal gravity. He paused.

"By the way, I looked. I don't understand, it must be my English. It looks fine to me." Gregor grinned, his crinkled eyes letting her know he knew exactly what he was saying.

She looked over her shoulder, mock surprise turning her face into a wide-eyed child. "Well look at that, it's all there, after all. Maybe I need a new name."

Gregor shook his head, ruefully. "No, I like it. Bobtail Anni. It sounds like blues song. Russians invented that, you know. Can I buy you drink?"

She laughed. "My ass is the finest thing you'll see tonight, but no, Gregor, you are my last pickup. I got a long way to go."

With a wave, the two turned. Gregor left to get hammered and Anni left to go to work, hauling cargo tractors back down to the Moon.

(IMPACT MINUS 354 HRS)

Where the normal low-gee tractor would push or pull a handful of cargo pods, she was about to launch with a string of 40 tractor rigs, called "bobtails" from American trucking slang for a tractor trailer rig without a trailer. Some hung the nickname on her, and she embraced it as her brand name. Her sultry Georgia accent was gone, replaced by the age-old pilot cadence, almost the same as her native Texan drawl. She checked in with traffic control.

"L5, this is Tango Three Seven."

"Roger, Tango Three Seven. What's up, Anni"

"Any scoop on the mergers?"

"Same as the official word, only worse. Negotiations are making progress. Continue to work under the Continuing Resolution. Except everyone is making more money by agreeing the rules are broken without fixing them. The U.N. will miss next week's deadline for sure."

Anni grinned. "Music to my ears, L5. More room for us entrepreneurs. This is Tango Three Seven, request clearance to disengage."

Anni had earned her way upside based on her degrees from Georgia Tech and MIT plus a demonstrated talent for management but had soon parted ways with her corporate employer within her first six months. She managed to do so without penalty and without the customary ticket dirtside. That alone was enough to start her legend as a deal maker.

When the various governments could no longer agree how to manage the growing Lunar-to-L5-to-Earth operations, someone had the bright idea of going to the United Nations to broker the deal.

It wasn't supposed to work. There was no centralized traffic control or official reporting system with all the spacefaring nations regulating who gets to go where. Everything was supposed to have fallen apart until the spacer companies looked to the big operations in nation-aligned settlements, forcing them to pick a side. To everyone's surprise dirtside, the Loonies made it work on their own. Her hodgepodge home, Lunar 4, was a freeform testimony to how the local businesses can make things happen faster and with more innovation than its stodgy closest neighbor, Lunar 1. Lunar 1 was a US/EU operation with lots of resources but did little and made less. Lunar 3 is the Chinese-run counterpart, with Lunar 2 being the failed Russian venture that has an operational environment but almost no business. Lunar 4 was always a commercial site, being mostly Lunar-based operations or specialty dirtside operations that didn't want to be in Lunar 1 or 3. Business is business, as the expression goes. Anni was all about business. She was a Loonie, through and through. She loved the challenge of big risk and big reward.

Depending on who you ask, low gravity and zero gravity either made your life easier or life harder. In Loonie terms, it made it harder to get suit funk out, but it also made it harder to smell it. Anni would say it made her life richer. She was a problem solver.

Haul pilots required a certain amount of rest between runs, cutting down on their load cycles. She solved that by taking their rigs back for them cheaper than deadheading.

She set up a service to get her delivered bobtails into berths and serviced before their pilots shuttled back, saving them more time.

Multiple tractors could not be hitched in sequence like a container train. She solved that in a fabrication yard.

Regulations did not allow tractors with live thrust systems to be hauled as cargo. She solved that with a mound of engineering papers, side deals, and outright bribes. Sometimes being right, all by itself, is not enough.

If she could have gotten the right people to allow her exceptions to the rules about hauling people, she'd have been bringing the drunken pile of pilots back herself. As it was, she contracted shuttles to get them back as part of the package faster than they would burn fuel to deadhead back.

Anni's services gave the haul pilots a full rest cycle with time to tie one on, then come back to their rig fueled, serviced, and ready to make money. Other pilots used to drag down their buddy's rig as a favor. She saw how to make it a business the first week she got there. She calculated her margins and optimized the run for a "stick" of 50 tractor units, basically the same mass a typical tractor pulls in cargo containers. Using a baseline of 565 hours for a minimum fuel run and around 740 meters/second delta vee, she optimized her fees and services versus costs each run to let her clients make a bit more money by doing more runs while making a healthy profit. It also gave her a growing business network – it's a lot easier to market and get to know people when they are coming to her than if she was trying to advertise.

Lost in thought, she sequenced through monitor views, checking systems and navigation projections. The rig was born in zero gravity, so the control panels, touch screens, and monitors were arranged in a hemisphere to suit Anni's style of piloting. A gimballed chair was mounted in the center to keep her in place during burns and served as a foot hook when on the float.

This run hit her profit line at around 440 hours. She could beat that time handily. She absently tossed her head to shift her non-existent locs. Catching herself doing this, she rubbed her fuzzy, close-cropped head. Her locs had been a bit of vanity as well as a reminder of her grandmother. She smiled, thinking of being five years old and trying to sit still while deft fingers pulled, twisted, and braided. Anni had kept the style to make a statement to go with her engineering and business degrees. Unfortunately, locs aren't practical with pressure suits and helmets.

She had been up the Well for 24 months and was getting the kidney stones to prove it. With current medical treatments, she had maybe another 10 months before she started to have the weakened bones and muscles when she returned down the Well, but still a good three or four years before she was marooned, too fragile to go home. Only a few have ended up this way. It was supposed to be bad thing, but the Lifers she had met had no desire to go back down.

She wasn't "moonstruck" like some. Her issue wasn't about leaving or staying, it was about leverage. She had come up the Well to make her fortune so she could return home to Houston and make a difference.

Anni believed in luck, but she also believed in making her own luck. The line haul runs were mostly automated. Most pilots were only alert for launch, docking, and close-in maneuvering. The big empty in between didn't even have turbulence to worry about, and if something did hit you, odds are you'd die without warning. Anni used this time to work on ideas. Better fuel management, better control systems, better "bail out" survival options, better banking algorithms – she listened to her business network and tried to find a need to fill. Over two-thirds of her bankroll had come from little innovations here and there, but she hadn't hit the jackpot. Yet.

This was the "chase" run, with the target orbiting away instead of "falling down" from the Moon to L5. Her path required her to drop down towards Earth and slingshot around. The reality was she was dipping closer to Earth than others do, and at higher speeds. A lot could go wrong. She knew this and was literally banking on this, as it kept others from casually copying her business plan. You can't change physics, but she did a lot of little things with the equipment and trajectories to mitigate the risks.

She kept it all as a trade secret, letting her repeated success speak for itself. By her sixth run, dragging 50 bobtails in a massive game of "crack the whip", people believed her. That, and the pile of money she had in escrow that covered each tractor she pulled in the event she didn't make it back. She'd be broke, but she'd also be dead, so she figured it was a fair trade.

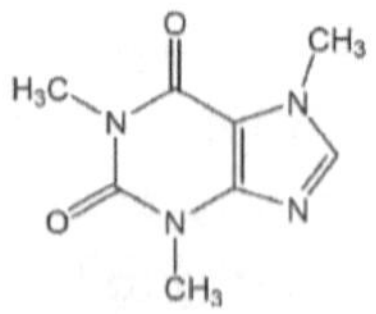

(IMPACT MINUS 91 HRS)
She was decelerating, over six days out based on her flight plan, when the screens lit up and every alert sound went off. Instantly awake,

she snagged the cold blobs of drool floating in front of her face with a baggie she kept for the eventuality. She saw there was nothing on proximity or vector alerts as she unzipped her sleeping harness.

She keyed in Lunar 4 Control. She recognized the voice on the other side, but the normally laconic neutral accent was fragmented into rapid fire Brooklynese. Normal radio protocols were gone, and the controller was trying to assert order by sheer force of will and volume of profanities. She typed a private message to him. Several beats later she heard him invite all listeners to a creatively improbable act, then switched over to a direct link.

"Anni, find a parking orbit, wait it out, and pray."

"Joey, I saw the wave-off. What's going on?"

She heard him take a deep breath. The calm, cool professional returned. "Ice run gone bad. The asteroid made its braking orbit around Big Blue because that part of the contract was paid for, but the company that was to get it to us went bankrupt. Everyone thought someone else had picked up its nav. It's flying straight and true, dead on at where we'll be, but no brakes. Can't get comms to its nav. We got some people predicting it will miss everything, some saying it will hit the dome, but the best estimate is the Crater."

"The power plant and radioactives?"

"Yeah. It won't be some cartoon explosion or nothing. It will be shut down and safe. But--"

"But no power. Solar power with reserve batteries will give minimum life support, but no industry. No work. It will kill our side of the moon in weeks instead of minutes unless we tie off with Lunar 1. Makes you wonder how much of this is bad luck and how much was helped."

Joey gave a tired, hollow laugh. "Jayzus, you're tracking. Everyone else is looking only at the next few days instead of the big picture. These mooks are trying to argue about their schedules or why they deserve special treatment. Look, I got to get back to herding cats. My job is keeping people away and getting everyone else out. Get yourself safe. The berg won't be anywhere near you when it passes anyway, but I can't tell you what will happen after it hits. Once the dust clears, you'll have to figure out your options."

"Got it. Hey, can you clear me for the telemetry? And got any data dumps?"

"No problem. Luck, Anni. See you on the flipside."

"Same to you, Joey. I'll stand you one at Callahan's."

She heard him snort. "Yeah, if it's there and we're still here."

"That's the idea, Joey, that's the idea. Tango Three Seven, out."

Anni programmed a parking orbit in a matter of minutes. This far out it was relatively simple. Orbiting a gaping hole where her livelihood had been, however, was not simple or acceptable. Her grandparents had evacuated from New Orleans to Houston, losing everything to Hurricane Katrina decades ago. She pictured Lunar 4 going dark and dead. There had to be an angle.

Anni downloaded the data from Lunar 4 and tied into the tracking telemetry. Within an hour, she had a solution. She rubbed her fuzzy head, trying to control the cold pit in her gut. It was only the physics. That was fairly simple. The problem was she dies and nothing changes. That wasn't good enough. Death wasn't good, but it wasn't a deal killer. Like most, she was inches from death most of the time. It just wasn't enough.

She called personal numbers. She called corporate numbers. She pulled in favor after favor, getting access, getting data, paying fees and bribes. One old friend insisted on the price being a weekend of "naked fun," despite knowing the plan.

"Really, David? That's all you want in return? For all of this?"

"Anni, I have faith. At least this way I have something to live for."

She smiled genuinely to the image of an older man, not using her "business smile." David was a senior engineer with her first employer, now the on-site vice president. His thin, sparse blond hair was almost invisible on his head, creating a nimbus around his skull when backlit just right. "It's a win for you, but what about me? And you are not being very specific in your terms."

He laughed, knowing there was no malice. "Of course not, Anni. That's why I have to pay up first and hope for the best. As far as the specifics, I'm not dumb enough to box you in. I'm crazy, not stupid. You, you got everything you asked for, up front, and you're not even supposed to make it to next weekend let alone a naked one."

"Truth. Fair enough, ya old coot. Deal."

She closed comms as the older engineer did a weird victory dance made more bizarre by lunar gravity, whooping and shouting. It was the only thing that gave her a real smile that day.

(IMPACT MINUS 79 HRS)

Lawyers. Accountants. Government officials. Special board meetings were called on her behalf, all the while her navigation program was changing her vector to the berg. She made it clear to everyone she, and only she, was in position to change the outcome. In some cases, she made it clear she was also in the position to assure a worst case outcome. Nothing else was close enough with enough delta vee to make a lick of difference. In every case, it came down to the same question, "what is it worth to you?"

Other than the negotiations with David, the talks were all about the same. She cajoled, bluffed, threatened, and used every bit of leverage she had while keeping her gnawing fear leashed. Anni learned this dance long ago. Now she had to lead them, hard, into the right steps.

"Can you do it?" *Yes.*

"Will you do it?" *Will you do what I want?*

"What about all those people? Why won't you do this for free?" *Why should I?*

This last part was the hardest. Anni didn't think she could do anything other than try to save Lunar 4, but she had to bluff. Fortunately, her reputation as a hard- nosed deal maker made them believe she would deliver, but not for free, which bridged the negotiations to the last two points:

"What's in it for me if I give you what you want." *Let me explain it to you.*

"What's going to make me hold my end up if you pull this off." *Let me explain it to you in glorious detail.*

(IMPACT MINUS 71 HRS)

Nothing is as easy as the book says. The timer on the screen may have 71 hours ticking down, but there is no book for landing on a tumbling ball of ice. Once the outbound navigation cut off, it went into a slow roll. Anni's program initially balked at landing on it, the glittering ball of ice, rock, and dust trying to spoof her navigation systems with its movement. This was completely outside of the original parameters for the software and had taken Anni precious hours to reprogram.

One of the rabbits she had pulled out was getting the access codes and programming parameters for the control systems banded around the berg. The array of attitude motors was only designed for minor corrections. The primary thrusters that launched it were supposed flip over into its travel vector to slow it down for the "Catcher", an oversized tractor that is designed to take the mountain of ice and rock and guide it down into a soft crash, far from the main facilities, where it can be mined.

The problem was the motors were designed for a long, slow push. By the time the right people realized there was a problem and got the other right people to try to stop it, it was well past normal burn parameters. Someone ran the thrust numbers, overrode the interlocks, and mashed the big green button. Instead of a big push to boost it out and away, the fuel sprayed, and the primary thrust motors blew up. As bad luck would have it, it nudged it into a tumbling trajectory that will bring it right to where it was supposed to be parked.

The attitude motors, however, were still there and would help control the overall motion. Time was running out. Simply deflecting the mass wasn't good enough. There were manned structures or life support complexes in the impact cone. Additionally, the sensors embedded in the berg back when it was harvested out of the Belt indicated large fractures had developed during its travels. Some fracturing is normal due to thermal differentials as it approached the sun. The main thruster bank blowing up was like a diamond cutter tapping his hammer. The Catcher was more likely to break up the berg than stop it.

In other words, it would be better to let one big cannonball hit a small area than blast grapeshot into a far larger area. All lunar facilities have pressure bulkheads and surface rovers. Spreading out the damage would mean everyone would be in crisis and would likely overwhelm the lunar assets. Additionally, the other three facilities, all owned by various governments, actively resisted any proposal that increased the danger to their facilities. They cited the need to be able to respond and help, but everyone read between the lines. Lunar 4 was on its own, at least until the regolith dust settled.

Anni's plan was simple in concept – distribute the tractors over the berg and use them as overgrown attitude controls, spreading the forces and firing as the berg rolled to slow and deflect the ball of rock-strewed ice to a vector acceptable to all parties. This was part of the deal – she had to miss everyone, not just Lunar 4.

Her computers and "pocket AI" interface were dedicated to the nav problems. She transmitted sensor data to David, who in turn had his team run continuous analysis of the berg's structure. His team's job was to keep the ball of ice from coming apart. They calculated the stresses due to planned and current loading, monitoring for fault line growth. David's personal magic was the interface that overlayed current conditions, current projections, and alternate projections based on changes in parameters in a way that made sense.

"This is the most motivated team I've had in years," he had joked at one point. "We should do this more often. I'll book you for the next turn-around."

One by one, she had gotten the tractors in place. She had planted herself first. While primarily designed for container haul, versatility was built into most tractors. All but four of the tractors had some method that let them secure themselves to the berg, and each of the four that didn't were paired to one that did. Seven tractors, including one of the pairs, lost anchorage and fell away. Anni's system kept crunching the numbers: forces applied, stress calculated, fuel status, and nav readings to pinpoint their location and motion relative to the Moon. They were traveling faster than their original flight plan. She didn't want to trust using remote computing like Lunar 4 for location because of time lag and transmission quality. A close answer fast is better than an exact answer too late.

Anni tried to force herself to sleep but never got more than a few hours before fear pulled her eyes open. She squeezed food goo into her mouth by rote, fueling herself at regular intervals despite icy fear keeping hunger out of her belly. It wasn't going to work.

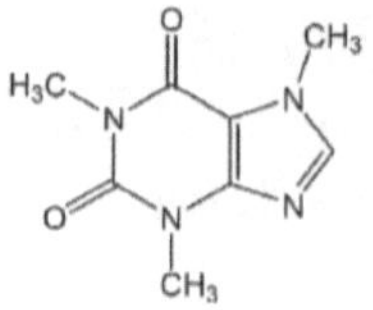

(IMPACT MINUS 63 HRS)

"Anni, wake up! We couldn't stop them! WAKE UP!"

Her hands scrubbed at her mahogany-toned features as she tried to focus her bloodshot brown eyes. Her mouth felt dry and tasted like a mouse had been mummified in there. None of her alarms had gone off so she was clawing her way to consciousness without any indication of what was going on other than David's voice on their private channel. She had let herself sleep hard, knowing nothing major would happen for several days. Even as she thought this, she kicked herself for poking at the fates with that assumption.

She was under thrust, creating a very soft nominal "down" of the bulkhead nearest to her as she opened the hammock. Then her brain shoved her consciousness clear of the pool of sleep and her gut clenched with alarm to match the tone in David's voice.

"David, this is Anni, go."

"We couldn't stop them. A Lunar 1 team from a U.S. corporation grabbed a medium lifter and are burning on intercept to the berg," David said.

"What? Why are—"

"Someone saw old movies about asteroids, bombs, getting the girl and saving the world. Nothing they sent made sense until one of them said, 'It's just like in the movies" and rattled off some titles."

"Hollywood crap?"

"Hollywood, Bollywood, Nollywood, it's been a theme done over and over. We tried to explain it's bad physics, like being sucked out of an airplane window at altitude or shotguns blowing you off feet. It's just special effects, the real world doesn't work that way. The data is standing by for your signal."

Anni bounced into her chair, the burn just strong enough to keep her in the seat with one leg reflexive hooked around the base. One screen held the text transcript of the exchange with Lunar traffic control, the other showed the intercept plots. She scanned the transcript, trying to make sense of the situation.

"Did they actually try to use their corporate titles to pull rank? Who are they," Anni asked.

"Young jerks from dirtside, nominally the senior execs on Lunar 1 for their employer, but word is they are spoiled boys and girls with old money and connections. It's worse than you think. Since their company does mining and tunneling for Lunar 1, they had access to the explosives magazine. They have some sort of 'magic bullet' payload of mining explosives with a thruster pack that some social media wiz claimed will 'save the day.'"

She pulled up the specs and David's summary.

"Well, they're right," she said. "It's just like the movies – it won't work in the real world. Is this just your analysis or do others agree?"

"Oh, they damn-well agree our team is right, but they won't agree it's their job to do anything. Lunar 1 is saying they are within their corporate charter. Lunar 3 is saying it's not their jurisdiction. No authority, no central command, no balls, no brains, blah blah blah. Lunar 1 and 3 are happy to let these idiots trash the place if it rolls out like we do or let them be the winners if for some reason the idiots pull it off."

"Too bad you don't have any sort of weapons to take them down," she said.

"We've worried about some sort of suicide terror attack or just complete dumbass for years. The other domes have systems 'to deflect small meteorites' but the one thing they can agree on is only the superpowers get to have weapons. Not us. We have an idea, though."

Anni's AI gave her new power projections. "Let me guess, I am the only one who can launch an intercept."

David laughed. "You're on it. We figured two bobtails, one for their lifter and one for payload. Their lifter can't go head-to-head with any of the rigs you're hauling. How does it impact your burn?"

Anni sighed. "I won't lie, I didn't have much margin before and now I'll have less. No one else can catch them?"

"Traffic has been cleared, Anni. It would be a cold launch and a tail chase for us to do anything, Lunar 1 and 3 are sitting on their collective asses, and you are already lined up with the equipment to stop an entire berg, let alone some rich dirtsider twits."

"Do I have to handle the intercept?"

David shook his head. "Line them up, launch, and then hand them over to us. We'll take care of the twits and the explosives. Legal has already found significant contractual violations in the shared navigation space agreements. The rig owners will be directly compensated for the rig loss and lost opportunity. We may not have weapons systems, but we have the best hired guns in or out of the Well."

Alli grinned. "I'm counting on that, David. Do you need anything else?"

David waved dismissively at the screen. "Nah, we got this. Go back to sleep, you'll need it."

Alli snorted. "Yeah, like that's gonna happen now. I'll sleep when I'm dead."

(IMPACT MINUS 49 HRS)

"How is it going, Anni?"

David was on video, but she didn't take her eyes off the other screens. Her makeup was subtle but flawless, accentuating her eyes. If she couldn't be rested, she had to look it.

Anni always had her mini makeup kit in case of a meeting or important video conference. A dab of lotion kept her dark skin glowing instead of the ashy dryness the rest of her was. Everyone was tapping into her broadcasts. Now they were being retransmitted dirtside. She was just glad no one could smell her suit funk. She wanted to connect to the public, not repulse them and it was getting so rich every time she moved, she wandered into a floating olfactory ambush. The ozone tang from electronics pushing their limits did not help the itch in her nose.

The world was watching, and she knew it.

"Just peachy keen, David. Happy to be here. Excited to be part of this plan."

"It is your plan, Anni."

"I know, but I wish there was a better one. Who the hell let this damn thing go by in the first place? It made the boomerang. How is the iceberg holding up?"

"It's not. The slow spin you have it on is helping. It's spreading the thermal load and it's keeping thrust stresses spread out. The strain is increasing around the tractors' anchors, though. No solid imagery of the full thickness of that turd, so there is a lot of uncertainty. How are the rigs holding up?"

She glanced at the boards. "About the same. The rigs fire when they are pointed in the right direction, but it's not for long. I'm also starting to lose more of them and can't evenly distribute the sequence. Just making the best of what I got. I have zip from any of the government domes or birds. What do you have for me?"

"Sunshine and unicorns, baby. What do you want?"

"I dunno, a safer working environment."

"You picked the job, Anni."

"I didn't pick having to clean up someone else's mess, because they can't be bothered to talk to us peons. Send me your projections and I'll see if it matches mine."

"On the way."

They kept the talk going, mixing the play-by-play with veiled political commentary. Over the course of the next several hours Anni and David managed to outline the entire situation so a regular dirtsider would understand the situation. The people on Earth knew that key tech, like the crystals used for their phones and computer systems, were dependent on the Moon and L5. Normally, as they kept getting what they needed, they didn't give it much thought. Now the politics, the broken communications, the price gouging by the other domes, the negligence with the berg, all of that was told by an attractive woman with gorgeous, bright, light brown eyes riding a spinning ball of ice to a likely death. She had their attention and she used it.

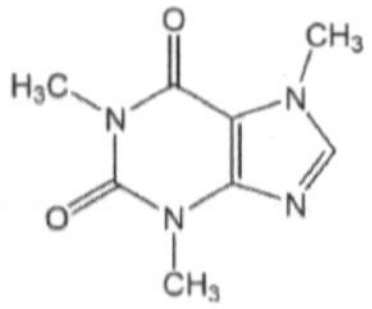

(IMPACT MINUS 38 HRS)

"David, I could really use some good news."

"The Mets are up."

"Screw you, I'm an Astros girl."

"They aren't playing yet, but a bit closer to home. I'm sending some company."

"Pizza delivery?"

"No, the Catcher. It was put into an emergency turn-around and launched. It's supposed to be there in 30 minutes."

She glanced at the screens. The headset looped around her left ear kept the volume constant no matter where she looked, but she was playing to the invisible audience. "That's nice, but the ride is over in about a day and a half. That pig usually fires for days, not minutes, and Sir Newton would have a word about 'vee squared.' It was coming in too hot for the Catcher in the first place."

She kept working, ignoring the camera. "Aren't you throwing good money after bad? I already got this rock's path moved from the Lunar 4 and lined up on an empty strip between the others. It's mostly contained, or at least will be if I stay on this."

"You need a backup plan, Anni."

"Like what, going to Louisiana and asking a voodoo queen to bring me back after this? Get me a reservation at the Monteleone Hotel."

David gave a big smile that didn't reach the bags around his blue eyes. "Come on, Anni, since when did you worry about the odds. It's just that there is some fuzz around the nav solution, so this will help you clear the margins. Why do you sound so pessimistic? You know how to fly – you just throw yourself at the ground and miss. How hard is that for a pilot like you?"

Anni stopped and looked intently into the camera. Her cabin had already cycled into night lighting. Her dark features were limned by the glow of the panels. A single white light almost reached her face. The hard stress lines in her face softened with her voice, dropping from the accustomed pilot's brisk patter to almost a whisper.

"This is real hard, David. Really hard."

There was no acting in this. All she had to do was open up inside a crack. David's face almost broke into tears, no longer shored by his normal facade.

"Then don't, damnit, don't! Peel off. Punch off that rock and let it smack into the dust. You've saved Lunar 4! If a few hunks ding someone else's dome, who cares? They didn't care about us. Why don't you save yourself?"

Calmly, she returned more to her normal voice, a slight Texan drawl rolling along with a confident, measured cadence. It was her "deadly business" voice, her pilot's voice, not her boardroom "let's make a deal" voice. Her body began its practiced zero-gravity rotation as she turned herself to check monitors and readouts.

"Because I have a deal. If we protect <u>all</u> the domes, they help us out. If we don't, the deal's off. We handle what they couldn't, we do what they wouldn't. All of them – the U.N., the superpowers, the multinationals … none of them wanted to solve the problem because then they would have to be responsible for it."

"Screw them! They aren't helping on this! Hell, they let this happen! They let it be anyone's problem but their own!"

"Exactly. I'm doing this because it needs to be done. We are, David. Sorry. You and your team, everyone back in Lunar 4 – I saw the evac notice was ignored by a lot of people. That's how you got the Catcher turned around. That's how you have life support and we're talking. That's how I've been getting the help I need. You, all of you, ran how many simulations of remote piloting versus me staying with my gear? This is the best bet. This berg would have fragmented long ago without your help. It's been everyone, David. We are all going together, all on the same vector angle. We aren't just someone on a rotation to fluff up their resume or forced up here because they were told to. We want to be here. We want to make it work, and we deliver our end each and every day. We have to, and we want to."

She looked back into camera, her eyes bright and shining, lit by a feral grin.

"So let's deliver this gig, seal the deal, and show everyone what real spacers can do. Not some government flunky worried about political points back home, not someone who would rather avoid failure than risk going big, but real spacers doing what we do. Get that pig up here and have her give me a boost, David. One way or another, sugar, I'm coming home. And hey, I'm way ahead of schedule."

Some of the news feeds showed the reactions in domes and stations. People were cheering and pumping their fists, even in most of the nationalized venues. The Catcher made its rendezvous. The burn from its oversized motors were visible from L5, firing on the ragged edge of burning out its components.

Slowly, the trajectory shifted more. The impact zone, plotted on the news monitors like a sports game, moved further and further away from any installation. Finally, the theoretical line cleared the surface. The fatalistic bravado coming in from the Moon was replaced with hope. Rovers, hoppers, and bobtails -- whether government or commercial -- had already launched. They were waiting for Anni to let go and get clear. They were spread out, coordinating their range and loiter times. They were all focused on bringing her home.

Anni and her cobbled together mass of ice, rocks and rockets were skimming the moon by a few hundred meters, firing over and over. Before they were trying to slow it down to give them more time to burn fuel and make it to an escape vector. Now they had the angle! They cleared the final vector change and hooked into the Moon's gravity. Anni commanded the engines to pump in all the delta vee into the mass they could.

It all came apart. There was no warning. Anni's feed blinked off. Long distance imagery showed the huge berg slowly expand, then visibly fragment, the scale hiding the frightening speed and twisting trajectories. Over 30-some-odd control points, some still firing, were no longer controlling an unknown number of bodies.

Some of the fragments gouged long furrows into the regolith. Some ended up on an escape vector, traveling onwards and becoming just another astronomically improbable hazard. A few ended up in ugly elliptical orbits. Using remotely piloted craft, these were later captured and harvested as were the fragments that plowed into the moon.

Anni's craft was never found. She had delivered on her deal. A few companies and governments tried to weasel out, but she had them all boxed in.

She had employed a prestigious multi-national law firm to not only assist in drawing up terms, but enforcing them. Their payment was tied to the salvage rights for the berg as it had been officially abandoned. Off camera, the firm had taken formal possession of the entire mass and made Anni their employee. The berg was not only valuable water but also nickel, iron, some precious metals, and other valuable deliverables.

The pilots who had lost their rigs on Anni's Last Flight, as it became known, were the first to be paid, with bonuses and interest to cover lost productivity and untangling the administrative side. This, along with Anni's death, became the basis for claims for damages along with the cost of evacuation, emergency operations, disruption of trade, loss of contracts, and all of the associated costs for the emergency response became part of a class action lawsuit.

The firm loyally carried out the spirit and letter of Anni's plan. Using social media, press, and well-placed commentators and legally rented politicians, they praised those who kept their deals and harnessed the enormous outrage for those who balked. Contracts and incentives further bound the various governments and corporations. The embarrassment over the United Nation's leadership, coupled with Lunar 4 being the best way for nations without their own space program to get critical Lunar products, led to the U.N. passing a resolution making Lunar 4 an international Freeport, not under any nation's control. In the end, Freeport was formally established less than six months, but the birth of their "nation", for lack of a better term, was always on March 2nd, the day Anni's face disappeared from the world. Fifteen years later, the deal still held.

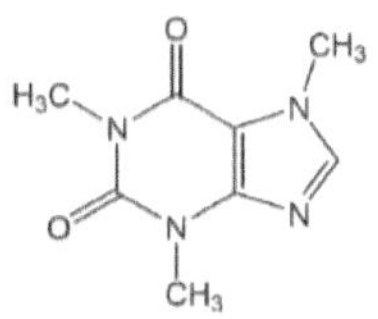

"We know all of this. We remember watching it on TV," said one of the newcomers.

"Boy, there is a big difference between watching something and living it. You aren't back home anymore. Some of you will make this your home. Most of you won't. But you better remember Freeport belongs to us Loonies. And most of us will be Loonies until we die, no matter where we are.

"Lunar 4 is special. From the moment you came to Freeport, you no longer had to belong to any other place. You can't go anywhere dirtside and say that.

"But don't try to tell us how we need to do it like the Americans, or like the Chinese, or any other group. You can always go somewhere else, and it's better to make that decision on your own.

"This might be a short trip for you. You can die out here real quick. You can get rich or go poor. As long as you work here, though, you have a home."

"Think about it while you have that drink. Giving you a drink is paying you to be quiet and listen. Thinking, that's up to you. Good luck, and Happy Loonie Day."

The newcomers were already well past their free first drink by then, motioning for refills as the bartender wove his tale. One of the men, a dark haired, dark-eyed man with diamond in his left ear and a Midwestern American accent noticed this.

"Free drink, free lunch, there ain't no such thing. Nice story, though. So where do we start?"

He felt a tap on his shoulder. A Lifer on a floater handed him a card with the name, "Emily Laveau." She had no legs below the knees, a spidery prosthetic right arm and natural, mahogany-toned left one. A nimbus of iron-gray locs bounced in slow motion around a brilliant smile.

"Can you pilot a load runner?"

"Ma'am, I can pilot any damn thing you have."

"Sugar," the woman purred, "I have a deal for you."

A Can of Worms

By Sarina Dorie

Still rattled from the crash-landing, Jess Alexander cut the space-punk music she'd been listening to. The sky was overcast, but not so much so that it blocked out the stars speckling the sky.

It would be hours before Jess had enough sunlight to power up the nanobots. She dug a handful of the small cubes out of her pack and set them on the crumpled hull of her mini-pod spaceship. Immediately the cubes scrambled around the damage, assessing and repairing.

Jess remained in her spacesuit, surrounded by a jungle of deserted skyscrapers and refuse. The air on Earth was too acrid and full of ash to breathe even with the recent recolonization efforts. She had never felt more alone in her life. She wanted to call the space station and talk to her friends, or one of her band members, and let them know she would be late to practice, but she had repairs to make. Her priority was getting assistance with repairs.

First things first. She called the company's tech support.

Tanjeet's familiar voice greeted Jess like that of an angel. "Hello, Mr. Alexander, how can I help you today?"

Jess's ears still rang from the hyperjump, tech supports words sounding like they came from behind a layer of cotton. She didn't correct Tanjeet calling her "mister." She'd always found it amusing when tech support mistook her for a man because of her deep voice.

"I'm not so spacetacular today," Jess said.

Tanjeet's asteroid belt accented voice sounded muffled as it came from the speaker of Jess's helmet. "Still having problems with a fuel leak?"

Jess was fortunate it was Tanjeet, one of the company employees she'd talked to before by hyper message. Tanjeet knew Jess's ship and she was always the best at walking Jess through maintenance problems, though Jess was aware it would take more than familiarity with mechanics to get her out of this mess.

Jess surveyed the towering buildings that stood like ancient tombstones around her. "I just took a nosedive on Earth. Long story short, I need assistance getting my ship up and running again. I think there's a software virus."

"Please provide me with a visual."

Jess used the interface in her glove to activate her helmet screen and opened a live link. She shined her helmet light on the side of the crumpled hull hidden in the shadows of one of the crumbling buildings.

"Holy asteroids! You weren't kidding! That's going to take some time to fix." Tanjeet paused. "Ahem, aren't those the company nanobots for your mission? The ones we hired you to deliver for Earth recolonization?"

Now that the Worms were gone from Earth, spacers had decided they wanted to move back in, but not until real estate was more inviting. Scouts like Jess regularly delivered nanobots and drones to make repairs.

Jess hoped Tanjeet wouldn't report her to Rom Colonizations for using the nanobots on her own ship rather than on the machinery she had been sent to Earth to repair. They'd fire her and she would never be able to fund her rock band's tour. Intergalactic Cutie Club, her band, would fade into obscurity, and she would have to go back to college.

Of course, she had to get back home first before she could worry about all that.

Jess could rely on the nano technology to repair the exterior of her mini pod. She hoped she could fix the virus damaging the ship with Tanjeet's help.

She scanned her headlamp and camera along the incline of melted ash and debris she'd made when crash landing. The rubble of Los Angeles loomed beyond. Or what was left of it after the alien Worms had attacked the planet nearly a century before. Between the devastation of the Worms and what her pod had done coming out of hyperdrive so close to her target destination, it looked more like a smoldering garbage heap than a city. Not that she expected the ruins of Los Angeles had looked much better before her ship had burned a hole through concrete and metal in its path before creating the crater where she now stood.

Jess ran a shaking hand along her blackened pod and stared in disbelief. "Spacetacular. What a mess."

Flakes of what she took to be white snow fell from the sky. She hoped she would be warm enough in her temperature-regulating suit.

"Don't worry, Mr. Alexander. You aren't alone. I'll be here with you as we figure this out." Tanjeet's words shaved away at Jess's anxiety. "I'm running a virus scan on your ship. It will reboot automatically when it's done. I'm also contacting the United Planets Patrol. If one of their ships is near, they might be able to swing by and pick up your ship. If not, your best bet is getting your own fuel and waiting until your ship is done repairing itself."

"So you're suggesting I scavenge for fuel?" Jess eyed the looming buildings that looked like they might collapse onto her at any moment.

"Take water and rations. You don't know how long it will take to find more z-oline."

"Got it." Jess patted the pack on her back with a gloved hand. "I just need to find some z-oline."

"I'm sending you a map of the nearest machine depot to scavenge." Tanjeet said. Never had her voice sounded more professional. She had to be an AI. She was always so calm and matter of fact. And efficient. Within seconds, a flashing blue overlay charted Jess's route over the terrain toward her destination. "Thanks, Tanjeet. You're the best tech support ever!"

Jess continued up the incline of the crater her ship had made. The silt beneath her feet shifted like powdery snow as she walked. Without warning, the ground underneath her crumbled away. She leapt forward but the dirt slid faster than she could escape. The white flakes she'd thought were snow puffed up into the air. She fought to gain a foothold as she slid downward.

"What the hell?" Jess asked.

There was a pause before Tanjeet responded, the communication traveling through relay stations. "What is it?"

Jess's foot caught purchase and for a moment her descent halted. She fell through the sifting dirt. She sent so much ash churning into the air she could barely see through the haze. She crawled forward, realizing she stared up into a yawning hole. It was at least four feet wide. Maybe it was a water pipe. She flipped on her head lamp.

"Mr. Alexander, are you there?"

When Jess caught her breath, she said, "You know, you can call me Jess. I'd think you'd be less formal by now." She tilted her head, so the light of her headlamp shone on the walls of the tunnel. Glistening slime dripped from the ceiling and pooled just in front of her. Jess's headlamp fell on a mound of spheres, each the size of her head, all glowing and swirling with light.

It was a Worm tunnel. It was relatively fresh.

"It's a cave of eggs! There's still Worms on Earth."

"Slowly back away. Slowly!" Tanjeet commanded, her pitch rising. "They can feel your footsteps."

Jess was already running up the hill to get out of the crater.

All this time she'd been making deliveries to the machine sites for the reconstruction of Earth and there had been Worms below her feet? She could have been snatched up at any of those times. The United Planets always warned freelance delivery personnel to be on the lookout for wild animals. But Jess had never seen any life, not even birds. The sites they assigned were big cities like New York City, Paris and Tokyo. Never having seen animals, she assumed they had fled the cities. Now she wondered if the Worms had gotten them.

Jess panted, her breath fogging her helmet. She pressed a button to clear it with a blast of dry air. Each breath was a note. Her footsteps thrummed a tempo in her ears. Tanjeet's voice was a serenade, the lyrics telling Jess to calm down.

Her brain replayed her own words as though it were a chorus: "It's a cave of eggs! There are still Worms on Earth." Though, even as the lyrics echoed in her head, she knew they didn't make sense. Worms didn't lay eggs. Scientists claimed they reproduced asexually. But there was a pile of eggs, nonetheless. What did it mean?

Jess sprinted until she crested the crater, briefly resting before pulling herself together. Running hadn't been smart. Like Tanjeet had said, it was safer to tread softly to avoid detection.

"You need to get on solid concrete," Tanjeet said. "It's harder for them to melt with their acid. Not impossible, but it will take more time. And you need to keep moving."

Jess swallowed and nodded. "How do you know so much about Worms?"

Her voice was flat and expressionless. "I saw them kill my parents."

Chills ran down Jess's spine. If Tanjeet's parents had been killed by Worms, that meant she was from the Epsilon Eridani Colony. It was the first time a star system had been attacked by Worms in over sixty years. That had only been seventeen years ago. Jess remembered watching the news with her parents when she'd come home from her kindergarten class. The U.P. military had rescued a small group of survivors after the attack, children who had hidden in air ducts and crawl spaces too small for the Worms to reach.

Jess's parents had sent her out of the room before she could see the images of the devastation. She'd later used her father's computer to look up more information when her parents went to bed. She discovered how Worms injected their prey with neurotoxins from retractable needles around their mouths. The aliens let their victims ferment and go crazy— before eating them.

She'd had trouble sleeping for weeks afterward. These early memories had inspired some of her greatest songs. Jess couldn't imagine the horror of living through an attack. This voice on the other end of her comm link that she'd always assumed was an A.I. was suddenly human. Tanjeet had witnessed her family slaughtered as she'd hidden in air vents. Jess's stomach churned.

Jess crawled over a mound of rubble. The moon shone brilliantly between buildings, close to the horizon. Though the moon was waning, Jess could easily see the gouge in the side of the moon. It looked like a white sugar cookie a naughty child had taken a bite out of. She stared in shock, unable to believe her eyes.

"Um, are you getting my visuals?" Jess said.

"Let me minimize this screen. I was just looking at the ship diagnostics for—Oh. Yes, that's new, isn't it?" Tanjeet was barely able to mask her alarm.

Jess stumbled on the concrete. More ash flew up into the air, obscuring her vision with a flurry of flakes. Her boot slid over something smooth and slick. She lost her footing again. She slipped forward, cringing as her foot encountered something squishy and wet sounding.

Her headlamp illuminated a Worm.

One of the alien's many mouths enveloped Jess's foot. Each mouth was as wide as a bicycle wheel, with spokes made of needles. She screamed.

Jess had seen grainy video feeds of decomposing Worms as a child. She'd studied diagrams in biology last year in college, not that there had been much biologists could identify from the rapid decay. All photos had been taken hours after the Worm carcasses had been found. They'd been little more than fermenting globs of jelly. The aliens didn't preserve well.

Photos didn't prepare her for real life. The alien was colossal. What was visible out of its subterranean hole was fifteen feet long and almost four feet wide.

It took a moment to realize the Worm was motionless.

When it didn't swallow more of her or inject her with needles, her breathing slowed. Tanjeet shouted into the microphone, her voice high and tremulous. "It's dead. See the ruptured funnel sacs around your foot?"

Jess wiggled her foot free of what she'd taken for a mouth. She could now see her mistake. Multiple mouths on the head with their razor sharp teeth were farther up the snakelike body. She'd mistaken the stringy hairs within the funnel sac for teeth. The bubble her foot had encountered was one of many oozing craters behind the gaping mouths.

Now that Jess looked more closely at the Worm, with the way the oozing craters were shaped like funnels and spiraled into another organ, they reminded her of ear drums. She kicked at the hard lumps beyond the ruptured surface that resembled the hammer and anvil of the human ear. They rested against the blue spiral organ not so different from the cochlea. Sticky fluid oozed out of splits in the spiral when she pressed it with the toes of her boot. Hairs attached to the inside of the spiral waved around in the fluid with a nudge from her toe. She might not have considered its similarities to the human eardrum if her mother hadn't just called her last week to express concern over her rock and roll lifestyle—and sent her images over the vid comm of what loud music could do to the cochlea. Jess wiped the wet viscera coating her boot onto the ash and debris in case it contained any corrosive acids.

The Worm bodies that had been discovered before they melted into jelly were found in crashed ships or near explosions. Often, they were found intact and seemingly unharmed except for these exterior ruptures in what Jess suspected were eardrums. This one had a small cavity in the head below the chin with something like the swirling spheres she'd spotted in the tunnel. She'd read the reports speculating that the purpose of this had to do with status or intelligence, as only one in a hundred Worms possessed small crystal-like spheres in this cavity.

Though the idea of intelligence had to be a stretch. There were no controls on the space crafts that delivered the Worms to their attack destinations. At least, not any controls the U.P. had found. Nor did the Worms seem to be capable of doing anything other than eating, breeding, and destroying. They were mindless attack dogs. Even so, much about them was unknown.

She thought of the pile of what she'd assumed were eggs. Could they really have been the spheres the Worms kept under their chins? Some kind of intelligence chip?

Jess ran her headlamp over the length of the snakelike body. About fifteen feet of it was exposed from the hole it had emerged from. That was probably half the length of the Worm. Already the skin was turning translucent and jelly-like. Jess had probably recorded the best visuals of a Worm in history. She could see details that hadn't been in her biology textbook. If the funnel sacs in the head were like ears, then perhaps some loud sound had killed it. That might be useful to the U.P.

Jess asked, "What if it isn't our missiles that are actually killing them? What if it's the sound of the explosions?"

Tanjeet's retching startled Jess from her musings. She realized how horrific the sight had to be for someone who had lived through a Worm attack.

Jess cut the video link. "I'm sorry. I should have thought."

"I'm fine. I just—" Tanjeet gagged again.

Jess shook her head at her insensitivity. She walked away from the alien body before she turned the video link on. She wondered if Tanjeet was still there. If Tanjeet broke the link, Jess could call her company's tech support back, but she wasn't sure anyone else at Rom Colonization Inc. could assist her with such detailed expertise. Nor was it likely anyone else had the qualifications of a Worm attack on their resume.

"Tanjeet? Are you still with me?"

"Yes, I'm here. I'm fine." Her voice sounded ragged and raw.

Jess sighed in relief. She felt like a complete wormhole brain.

Tanjeet's voice was shaky, a façade of calm that couldn't fool Jess. "Perhaps you should get started on your route to collect fuel. I'm sending you coordinates to a station three miles away where you can source z-oline."

"And you'll walk me through collecting it?" Jess had never scavenged before, though she knew people who did it.

"I'll be with you the whole time. I'm not going anywhere." Tanjeet said firmly.

Relief flooded over Jess. "You have no idea how much I needed to hear that."

Tanjeet really was like her guardian angel.

Jess listened to her own breath in her helmet, the sound monotonous. She could have put on music to pass the time or tried to think of something conversational. But the image of all those teeth kept flashing before her eyes. She went to her go-to stress reliever.

Singing.

She used the tune of one of Intergalactic Cutie Club's songs but improvised new lyrics.

"Hey, my baby girl.
Don't wanna make you hurl.
We don't got no time.
To make a silly rhyme.
Oh ye-aaaah!"

Tanjeet snorted. Not exactly the reaction Jess had hoped for.

"Sorry, I sing when I'm nervous," Jess said.

"You're into punk?" Tanjeet asked.

"No, I'm into space opera. It's only the best musical genre in the universe!" Some would argue that space opera was a subdivision of punk, but no other form of rock used actual opera. Jess loved the way it used her classical training in music to create something unique.

Jess continued walking toward the coordinates Tanjeet provided, shining her headlamp in the dark shadows where she stepped.

Jess tried again:

"It's gotta be my fate.
That I have gotta wait.
For Rom Col's tech support.
Cuz they're usually staffed short.
Oh ye-aaah!"

Tanjeet laughed at that, the effect Jess had hoped for.

"I don't know what you're talking about!" Tanjeet said. "You were on hold less than a minute before I came on. And the company prides itself on not making our pilots wait for more than ten minutes."

Now it was Jess's turn to laugh. "Those ten minutes are an eternity when you think your ship is going to die on you in space."

That sounded like a good lyric. Jess tried it again to the previous melody and recorded the sound as Tanjeet laughed in the background. She liked the high, sweet notes of Tanjeet's voice mixed in with her deeper harmony. Tanjeet sounded like she would make a good backup singer. Jess imagined a tall curvy woman with long black hair swaying to the beat of the music. To the beat of Jess's music. Jess found herself smiling as she imagined Tanjeet.

"Are you in a band or something?" Tanjeet asked.

Jess passed under a rebar frame of a crumbling building. "Yeah. I'm a songwriter. And a guitarist. I'm not the one who usually sings in the band."

"Maybe you should," Tanjeet said.

Jess shook her head, making her headlamp shine this way and that over the city rubble. "I bet you would make a better lead singer than I ever would."

Tanjeet's sweet, silky voice was like a twentieth century jazz diva. Then again, Tanjeet was the only person Jess had spoken to for hours. Jess probably would have considered her grandmother's gravelly voice lovely at that point.

"If I get out of this, I want to sing a duet," Jess said.

"You are definitely getting out of this."

Jess nodded.

"Now, how about this? You keep singing to me while I work. I need to multitask. I have an alien presence to report to the U.P. and I have new software to install after the virus is cleaned up. Then when you get home, you and I are going to get together and have a jam or whatever you musicians call it."

Jess smiled, finding Tanjeet's complete lack of terminology endearing. "We'll jam. It will be a date." Her face flushed at the mention of dating someone with such a foxy voice. "I mean, not a date if you don't want to. But, um, a—"

"It will be a date," Tanjeet agreed. "You can pick me up in your space cruiser after we get it working."

Jess considered how she was going to break it to Tanjeet; she wasn't really a Mr. Alexander. She could worry about that if she survived.

Jess tried out more lyrics as Tanjeet directed her along a route to the machinery depot where she would find fuel tanks. If Jess could have played her virtual guitar and hiked at the same time, she would have. The light from her head lamp guided her over the rubble of buildings, casting long shadows over the walls of skyscrapers. Several times she started at the movement of shadows. Each time she concluded the illusion of movement was caused by her, not a Worm.

As Tanjeet worked at remote software repairs, she occasionally interjected a comment about what she was doing or about Jess's singing. The idea that Jess wasn't completely alone on a deserted planet full of aliens reassured her.

The road beneath her feet grew smoother and she knew she was getting closer to the machine depot. Roads were one of the features the U.P. had been hoping to establish before recolonization. Jess walked faster. She half hummed, half sang now. When her pollution readings told her it was safe to do so, she cut the recycled air and opened the vents to filter in outside air, inhaling deeply. A light streaked across the starry sky. She hoped it was a United Planets patrol ship, not more aliens.

She quieted when she caught a muffled voice on Tanjeet's end. The link clicked and it sounded like she cut out.

"Tanjeet?"

No reply.

Jess's heart sank. The link hadn't dropped, had it? Had Tanjeet tried to put her on hold and the line went dead? That was just the kind of thing tech support was known for. The back of her neck tickled with sweat.

After a few seconds the link clicked again. Tanjeet said, "I need to tell you something."

Relief washed over Jess. Her guiding light was back. "Is it my singing? You can't stand anymore space opera?" Jess joked.

"U.P. Patrol isn't coming to your rescue." Tanjeet's voice was somber. "Two colonies have been attacked in the last hour."

The sudden lump in Jess's throat made it hard to swallow. Her voice cracked. "Which colonies? Not the Andromeda stations?" That was where her family lived.

"No. Andromeda is fine. It was in the Gliese system and Tau Ceti."

Jess hated to ask, but she had to know. "Worms?"

"Yes. All military ships are standing by to protect populated colonies. My coworkers are trying to decide if they want to evacuate Outpost 9. The employees in the compound next to ours decided to leave, but Rom Colonization Inc. thinks people are safer here. If we remain, we need to cut all power, so we won't show up on the Worms' screens."

Jess's voice went dry. "If you cut power, you and I won't be able to stay in contact, will we?"

"No."

Jess considered that. She didn't know how to convert fuel for her ship. Certainly she didn't want to be stranded on a Worm-inhabited planet. But one person's safety wasn't worth risking all the Rom Col employees' lives.

"You do what you have to," Jess said.

"I'll keep in contact as long as I can. I'm going to send you the files for conversion in case we get disconnected. In the meantime, keep singing to me."

Jess smiled. "Only if you join in."

Jess's favorite song, "Kill the Spacetacular Hyperdrive" played softly while she trekked closer to her destination. Tanjeet occasionally mentioned useful information. Most of her "helpful" diagrams looked like gobbledygook. Jess minimized her view of the data, so it didn't block her view of the road in her helmet screen.

Despite these distractions, her thoughts trailed to her family on Andromeda Station. She wished she could communicate with them, let them know she was alive—for now—and make sure they were safe. But she couldn't do that until she was back at her ship. It was likely her parents would volunteer as medics as they had done seventeen years ago during the last Worm attacks. Her fifteen-year-old brother would be scared. Jess wished she could be there to take care of Tyler, help her parents, or to be doing something proactive.

Instead she was stuck on Earth.

As the sky brightened with the approach of dawn, Jess passed rundown machinery, taking note of the Worm holes nearby. A bulldozer was turned on its side in the middle of the road. A multi-armed Repairo 500 lay in broken pieces under fallen electric lines. The fuel tank was split open, the precious z-oline spilled onto the asphalt. From the thick trail of slime that exited a hole and ended at the machines, the path of sabotage was clear. These were the kind of machines the retrieval bots brought to the delivery sites for Jess to deliver the nanobots when they needed minor repairs or updates. Rom Col hadn't supplied enough repair drones or nanobots for this level of devastation.

These machines were loud enough to attract Worms. But obviously not loud enough to kill a Worm—if it was indeed sound that had killed the one near her pod and not the hyperdrive itself. She wondered if it was the volume of a sound or the pitch.

Jess's feet were killing her, and her legs ached. After another two hours, she came to a graveyard of machinery. Depots like this were where she typically delivered nanobots, though this trip she had actually been headed for San Francisco, not Los Angeles. Bright morning light crested over the dingy, gray remnants of the city.

"You are going to need to figure out which tanks are the fullest," Tanjeet said. "By the way, your system diagnostic has isolated the virus. I need to get your permission to get rid of it before I proceed."

"Are you spacin' kidding me? You can do whatever you have to so I can get out of here."

"I'm still a Rom Colonization Inc. employee, Mr. Alexander. I have to follow protocol."

She rolled her eyes at the way Tanjeet reverted to "Mr. Alexander" after using her first name for the last few hours.

"Yes, you have my permission."

Jess didn't have the special gear needed to test each fuel tank. She would have to collect as many as possible. She disabled the compressed z-oline tank from one of the smaller robotic machines. Despite only being the size of her backpack, it was so heavy she needed to drag it out. This was the first of many tanks needed. She began the monotonous process of setting aside a pile.

"Jess?" Tanjeet asked, her voice rising. "Outpost 9 is under—"

A chaos of screams, static, and the grating of metal against metal screeched through her head phones.

"Tanjeet?"

The link cut out.

Ice prickled up Jess's spine. The sudden silence ached in her ringing ears. She knew what had happened but didn't want to believe it. She wanted to believe that if there was anyone who could survive a Worm attack, it would be Tanjeet. The U.P. patrol would rescue Rom Col employees. Though, the U.P. hadn't responded to Tanjeet's earlier messages about Worms being in the Earth solar system. And if they were so focused on protecting populated colonies instead of remote regions, she doubted Outpost 9 was a priority.

Jess paced back and forth, more rattled than ever. She was alone on a deserted planet full of Worms. Everywhere was under attack. She didn't know how to repair her ship. The one person who could help was gone. If Jess was going to survive, she needed to figure out how to get more fuel.

She thought again about Tanjeet. About all she had done to help, staying on the line well after she should have ended the call. Didn't Jess owe her something? But what could she do other than issue a distress signal reporting Outpost 9 was under attack? And she couldn't do that until she returned to her ship.

Jess needed at least one hundred liters of compressed z-oline for her ship. That would be too much to carry on her own. Aware she was misusing the remainder of her employer's property, she set all the nanobots to repair a single track loader. She could load the tanks in the bucket. She scattered the small cubes on the crumpled metal of the machine, the nanos separating and dividing as their programming to repair took over. Jess hoped using such a high quantity of them would ensure they fixed the machine quickly. Though with the amount of noise the loader would make once it started, she feared it would attract Worms more than repel them.

If the U.P. had any idea they were dealing with machines damaged by Worms, not weather or animals, surely they wouldn't have sent delivery personnel with repair nanos. Didn't they have surveillance satellites for this kind of thing?

She sought the two largest fuel tanks she could drag to the loader, one coming from a dump truck with shredded tires. The twenty liter fuel canisters she collected looked no larger than a two liter cylinder, but the compressed z-oline within was heavy enough to give her a workout. She sweated inside her suit despite setting the vents to filter in the chilled morning air.

When she checked on the repair progress, the nanos were nearly done bending the metal of the engine back into shape. As much as she wanted to stare in wonder at them scurrying about to convert rusted metal into a clean surface, she knew she had no time. Once she gathered a collection of twenty fuel canisters, Jess pulled up the first diagram on her screen.

Even with the help of the pictures, she wasn't sure how to transfer fuel. She understood the nozzles should connect and there was a valve that could transfer z-oline from one machine to another. Still, nothing fit together like they did in the diagrams Tanjeet had sent.

Not sure what else to do, Jess tried holding the nozzles of two canisters together with one hand while pressing down on the valve with her other hand. A twenty liter tank shot away, crashing into a line of sewer repair machines which toppled over like dominos. They clattered to the concrete, sending up a wave of ash.

Jess coughed and choked on the dust. It took a moment to close the vents in her suit and go back to breathing recycled air. Her impaired vision distracted Jess enough that she didn't at first hear the rattle of machines. As it continued, she realized the tremor underneath her feet wasn't the echo of the fallen machinery. It was the sound of Worms underground.

They were coming.

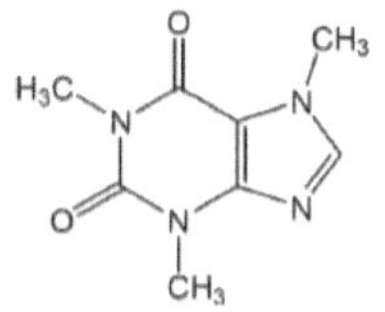

Jess glanced around in panic, searching for safety. She raced across the pavement, her boots slapping the hard surface. She forced herself to slow, to silence her footsteps. Next to a dump truck, a heap of broken parts were stacked as high as a Galaxy Class Cruiser. If she crawled up there it would certainly be safer than staying on the ground. Jess jumped into the doorless cab of the dump truck, ready to climb onto the roof and scramble up the mountain of parts. She paused, noticing the sound system in the truck.

The rumble below rose into thunder.

All trucks had sound systems from the days when Earth was inhabited, so the service vehicles could announce to pedestrians they were parking, backing up, emptying bins, etc. It was true she didn't know a lot about engineering, her ship's fuel system, or software problems. She'd never taken spaceship mechanics classes.

There was one thing Jess did understand: sound. She could fix a broken PA or hook up her suit player to any sound system in record time. If her suspicions about the Worm's sensitivity to sound were correct, creating a noise loud enough to rupture its funnel sacks would be a better option than climbing onto a heap of garbage it could probably knock over.

Jess opened a flexible panel just below her shoulder where she could unravel a cord to link to the truck's console. She plugged herself in.

A wet, squelching sound made her look up. A glistening red Worm nearly as large as the dead one she'd come across, slithered over the ground. The purple funnel sacs puffed up and deflated. Its many mouths opened and closed, mucus leaking from them. It left a trail of slime as it slithered over to the stack of fallen machines.

Jess's mouth went dry. Her hands shook so violently, she had trouble using the glove controls to select the music list she brought up. She couldn't get her helmet screen to respond with her selection tool bouncing around.

The Worm probed the fallen machines.

She could do this, Jess told herself. She forced her breath to slow. She just had to work through her fear as she had during Intergalactic Cutie Club's first public performance four years ago. Of course, that audience hadn't been prepared to eat her if she failed.

Jess dragged a song into her music mixing program. Then another. The software allowed her to dissect various tracks and paste them together. But now she randomly pasted song after song into the program, hoping the low notes of one track and the high notes in another were what she needed.

The Worm nudged a sewage repair machine aside and continued on. It flicked its head this way and that, either trying to see something or catch a scent.

Jess had ten songs selected to play at once. She hoped that was enough. She pressed play.

She held her breath. Silence.

She glanced around for the Worm. It was out of sight. Seconds later, the Worm slithered across the hood of her truck. Her chest tightened and it felt as though all air were being squeezed from her lungs.

She glanced at the truck's console. There was no power, so the music couldn't play. She had to turn the truck on. Her heart rattled like a snare drum. She pressed the startup button on the truck. The screen lit up, though in a vehicle run on z-oline, there was no rumble like there would have been in the older twenty-first century machines.

The Worm stilled. Had it sensed her movement? Or could it see the light from the dashboard? It lifted its head. Needles extended from the spaces between the mouths. The Worm turned toward her.

Before Jess could move, music blasted through the truck's speakers.

The Worm writhed. The funnel sacs pulsated. Its head whipped toward the windshield. Jess dove below the console as the alien body crashed against the glass. It shrieked in a chorus of high C1 octaves as it flopped around. Jess remained in the truck cabin until the screams stopped. At that point, even her ears ached from the blast of sound.

Jess peeked through the fractured windshield. The Worm lay still, the funnel sacks popped and draining of fluid like the first one she'd found. She cut the music.

Exhilaration at her spacetacular performance coursed through her. For the first time in hours, Jess felt hope. She could tell the U.P. about the Worm's sensitivity to sound!

Despite wanting to sit back and rest for a few minutes, she forced herself back to work. She used the roll of adhesive bandages from her pack to wrap the nozzles of fuel tanks together before filling the largest one. Though slow, this worked better than her first method of holding it with her hands.

As extra insurance for her safety, she tore out the speakers of other service vehicles and hooked them up to her appropriated loader. She played her newest track. It was the worst music she'd ever made. Jess made her way back to her space pod in the track loader, music blasting. The bucket at the front held her precious z-oline.

The return to her ship only took her an hour and a half. The nozzles to the fuel tanks fit her ship, so that at least worked like it was supposed to. Though, there wasn't enough to completely fill the tank.

That was fine, she told herself. She just needed enough to take off so she could speed up to hyperjump and slow down enough to land afterward. Jess slid into the nav chair and powered up the ship. She sent off a message to the U.P. about the Worms on Earth—and what she had discovered—but they didn't respond.

She wasn't just going to sit by and let others die when she could do something about it. She was going to Outpost Nine to save Tanjeet using her secret weapon.

Outpost Nine was stationed on an asteroid outside of a hypercomm dish meant to relay high speed intergalactic communications. Few people lived there. Most transported in groups for their shifts at companies like Rom Colonizations Inc.

Having never been there before, Jess didn't know how small the compounds of buildings were until the asteroid came into sight. It was a pathetic cluster of contained domes for various communications companies and businesses who needed the best reception. No sign of Worm vessels. As she came into range, she noticed the damage to the compounds. She hovered over the hole in Rom Col's artificial life support dome.

No wonder the U.P. hadn't responded to her distress signal. If Worm ships were on the move, the U.P. would be busy tracking them down. If only they weren't so busy, she might have a chance to share with them what she'd learned. Lives could be saved. Like those at Outpost 9.

Jess knew she might be too late, but she had to go in. She didn't have lifeform software detection to aid her like the U.P. did. Though it would be a handy piece of software to download in the future.

She landed her pod and climbed out the ceiling hatch. Her "sound armor," a collection of various speakers she'd attached to her suit with engine repair glue and adhesive bandage tape, made her movements difficult. Despite the hole in the side of the company's dome, Jess was surprised to find the electromagnetic shield in place, sealing the building off from leaking atmosphere.

That meant there was hope for survivors.

The trail of slime she spotted through the crackles in the shield suggested Worms were present. She needed to tread carefully.

Since humans couldn't go through the shields without experiencing severe shock, Jess's journey was slowed by the need to go through the airlock in the landing bay between the cluster of domes. Jess considered her options: start with the music to drive them away from her or sneak up on them and launch her musical weapon. Since she didn't know where the Worms were, she would have to make herself vulnerable with silence if she didn't want to push them toward others more defenseless than she was.

Her boots echoed on the tile floor of the Rom Colonization Inc. lobby. The speakers strapped to her chest and taped to her shoulders weighed her down. The ones she'd tied to her legs made her footsteps heavier than she would have liked. The directory next to the elevator listed tech support on the third floor. She listened for the slither of

Worms as she made her way up the stairs, but there was only the rasp of her breath and thuds of her feet.

The wall past the reception desk marked the alien presence with a hole burned through by acid. Jess stepped through the door, avoiding the slime. She passed through a deserted room of cubicles with toppled communications screens. It was through the hole of the closet that she found the Worms' first victim, a middle-aged man with a trail of blistered needle marks across his exposed flesh. The man sat with his knees drawn up to his chest in the closet. His gaze darted toward Jess, but he couldn't move. Jess would have liked to help the survivor so he wouldn't become Worm food, but there was no known cure for the neurotoxin.

Nor did Jess have an easy way to put him out of his misery.

"I'm sorry," Jess said and moved on.

She passed two more victims before she detected a wet squelching sound. Her shoulders ached under the weight of the speakers. She treaded slowly, knowing she would need to catch the Worm by surprise. She inched down the hall, making note of a chair out of place in the middle of the aisle. A set of high heels were left in the middle of the floor.

The closeness of the slurpy noise made her breath quicken. She peeked around the doorway into a conference room. Her sound armor shifted as she leaned her body weight forward, causing her to stumble. A Worm squirmed over a collapsed table. The needles between the mouths reached toward a dark haired woman.

Jess's chest tightened. Tanjeet?

Jess flipped on her music with a gesture of her hand. An orchestra of discordant notes blasted out of her speakers. The Worm lifted up its head and bashed itself against a wall. The funnel sacs fluttered. The high pitched scream died away as it ceased writhing.

Jess cut the music. She rushed to the woman. She was too late. A row of dots marked her face and neck. The woman was in her late forties or early fifties, the age of Jess's mother. She stared up at the ceiling with wide eyes.

A ding of metal and a rustle came from overhead. Jess dodged back. It could be a Worm on the floor above, burrowing through the ceiling now that it knew where she was.

Or it could be Tanjeet. If she was alive, she would have done the
same thing she'd done before. The air vents.

"Tanjeet? Is that you? It's me, Jess," she said.

No reply.

Jess slid the glass plate of her helmet back and called again. The air
smelled burnt and stung her nose. She took a moment to mop the
sweat from her forehead before it dripped down her face as she made
her way out into the hallway. She examined the chair in the middle of
the path ahead. It was directly below a metal grate.

"Tanjeet!" she shouted.

"Jess?" a familiar female voice whispered from the shadows above.
"What are you doing here?"

Jess sagged against the wall, relieved to hear her voice again.

"Rescuing you, of course." She glanced over her shoulder. "Are there
more of them or just the one I killed?"

"Yes, I think their ship dropped off two of them." Her shuddering
breath echoed out of the vent. "What was that horrible sound?"

"My band's music, all at once. I need your help. There has to be a PA
system in the building that we can use to project my secret weapon. It
will kill any Worms who hear it." She turned to make sure none of
those slimebags were sneaking up on her. One of the speakers strapped
around her thigh slipped down her leg and crashed to the floor.

"The intercom is at the regional manager's desk. I . . . I'll show you."
The soft ding of movement echoed overhead as Tanjeet crawled
through the vent. Her bare feet poked out first, then her slender legs
wearing the standard black uniform of Rom Colonization Inc. She
dropped onto the chair.

Another speaker dropped from Jess's shoulder, dangling halfway
down her back. Jess stared at Tanjeet, brow crinkling.

She was surprised to find Tanjeet didn't match what she'd imagined.
Instead of being tall and curvy, she was petite and thin. The long dark
hair she'd envisioned was a short, blue bob.

Tanjeet was also staring. Jess supposed she might not resemble the
"Mr. Alexander" Tanjeet had imagined either. With her short haircut,
Jess might be mistaken as a boy, but not in her snug spacesuit even if
she's strapped speakers all over.

Jess handed Tanjeet the speakers that had fallen from her sound armor. "Stay behind me so I can protect you. And stay close so the wireless signal for the speakers doesn't go out of range. We'll need as much sound as possible. It's their weakness."

Tanjeet directed her down the hall. No Worms in sight, Jess closed the glass door and locked it. Tanjeet set down the speakers on a metal desk. Her fingers flew over the buttons to turn on the office PA.

"I don't know if it's the high or low pitches or the volume that affects them," Jess said. "We need to get the full spectrum."

She unstrapped one of the speakers from her arm with Tanjeet's help. Once free, she used her glove commands to access her wireless system and connect to the database.

"Our password is: 3Interstellar8Space5Mutants. No space between words," Tanjeet said.

Jess tapped in the password. That sounded like a good song title.

A timer popped up on her screen, showing the computer was thinking. Wet slithery slurps sounded in the hall. Something thudded against the wall. Jess's stomach cramped. The timer still blinked. A giant Worm head nudged the glass door. Below the chin was a glowing sphere. It blinked and flickered, mesmerizing Jess like a strobe light at a rave.

A slimy trail of saliva trickled from the mouths, smearing against the glass. The transparent surface smoked. Tanjeet stepped back into Jess. Another one of Jess's speakers held in place by not enough adhesive bandage came crashing down.

Jess blinked and came back to reality.

The timer on her screen disappeared.

"What next?" Jess asked. "Do I have to open a specific program or—"

"Just play."

The glass melted. The hole widened. The Worm pressed up against it.

Jess fumbled through her screen windows, opening her old playlists accidentally. She closed that, scrolling to find her layers of music.

The Worm lunged through the door, shattering the remaining glass. Jess's fingers were too slow to find the song. She did the only thing she could. She opened her mouth and let out the loudest, resonant C note she could reach and then scaled upward an octave and then two octaves.

Her voice was suddenly magnified through the intercom as Tanjeet handled the controls.

The Worm writhed but didn't die. The operatic note served as a distraction, giving Jess enough time to locate her playlist of layered songs. She clicked play and sound blasted through the speakers.

The Worm screeched.

Jess leapt back, hooking an arm around Tanjeet to pull her out of the way of the Worm's thrashing head. She yanked her down behind the desk. Tanjeet stared at her with horror filled eyes. It was a long moment before the thunder of Jess's heart slowed enough that she realized how loud the music was. She thought she caught a riff from "The Jagged Moons of Poseidon." She peeked over the desk. The Worm was still.

Jess cut the music. Her ears throbbed.

The light in the chin orb faded. Jess inched closer, watching the swirling movement within. She kicked it with the heel of her boot, the surface splintering into crystalline shards. A small lizard-like creature squirmed free of the capsule. It turned its gaze to Jess.

Jess thought she understood now. The Worms were attack dogs and these smaller, weaker creatures their masters. She stomped on the alien and ended its life. Immediately it shattered like crystal. She had quite a bit of new information for the U.P.

Tanjeet raked a handful of blue hair out of her face. Her eyes filled with tears, and she smiled. "It's amazing. You killed a Worm with sound."

"Not just any sound. I killed them with Intergalactic Cutie Club's music. This is going to make my band famous!"

Tanjeet laced an arm around Jess's neck, hugging her. "Still looking for a backup singer?"

Jess laughed, "Yeah, after we finish saving the universe."

Tanjeet stared into Jess's eyes and smiled. Jess's gaze flickered to Tanjeet's lips. Their eyes locked, their lips followed.

Jess's day had gone from horrible to triumphant quickly. She could thank space opera for saving the day.

The End

The Oracle at Tau Ceti

By Jetse de Vries

'Let reality be reality. Let things flow naturally forward in whatever way they like.'—Lao-Tzu;

M&R bot, or Marbot, the most robust maintenance and repair robot-cum-AI ever designed by humans, moved along the hull of the thin, long interstellar craft to remove the remnants of the sixth braking sail. While the solar sail was designed to be removed from inside—by one of the waking Minds—the discharging mechanism had been damaged by interstellar debris—like the rest of the sail—and it was for situations like this that Marbot was on board.

Mind (1) was on duty. Marbot's statistical calculus had predicted Mind (2), but, as usual, it was wrong.

The Minds had no relief schedule. They preferred to be woken at random, as to keep their life 'interesting'. Marbot had a very low approval rate for not knowing who was on duty and spent a considerable part of its offline life calculating which of the four Minds was most likely to be on duty. The random generator was close to perfect, though, and Marbot was only right 26.1% of the time.

Marbot was hit by a stray interstellar Hydrogen atom on its way to the front of the *Manifest Destiny*, nothing to be sneezed at at thirty percent of light speed, but the electromagnetic field of the doped, superconducting carbon nanotube material kept him glued to the vessel's hull, easily.

Mind (1) noticed the impact on the screen displaying Marbot's vital statistics. "Oh boy," he said over their radio link, "that hurt, right?"

—*i don't have feelings*— Marbot sent back —*and i'd only rate it a 9 on the approval scale*—

"Which goes all the way up to eleven," Mind (1) said, laughing at his own joke.

—*of course not: to 100*— Marbot could not feign irritation, but merely rated this remark a lowly 2 on the approval scale —*as we agreed to use the decimal scale, instead of the superior binary*—

One of the many shortcomings of the human mind, in Marbot's viewpoint. If the approval rating, efficiency scale, application coefficient and functionality level it used could be mixed in a manner that might express 'sorrow', Marbot would feel a deep sadness about the not-quite-so-successful copying of human minds to a quantum computing substrate. Now it just kept developing best case scenarios to deal with the contingencies. Unfortunately, its computing powers were not quite up to the task.

Take Mind (1), for instance. The original was Heinz von Altmann, the world's leading mathematician, who had famously solved the Riemann hypothesis, and who thought—and taught—that mathematics was 'the ideal disguise of everything'. A German so *gründlich und punktlich* that—assumedly—even computers were jealous of him.

They copied and downloaded his mind to the quantum computer with a buckyball substrate, embedded in a complex carbon nanotube polyhedron—to withstand the immense G-forces needed for an interstellar launch—and to everybody's surprise and delight the transformation seemed successful. For all intents and purposes, the Altmann copy had the same brilliance as the Altmann original.

They applied the same process to the three other Minds selected for humankind's first interstellar voyage—and they were in a rush, as the alien signals from Tau Ceti had just been detected—Seoyoon Kim, the world's leading exobiologist; Bernard Inden Swartten, the string theorist so brilliant even most of his colleagues had trouble understanding him; and Mokorinayosoluwa Adebowale, the first chemist to win three Nobel Prizes whose 'chemistry controls everything' quote was world-renowned. The copies all seemed to work just as well as the originals. Nobody noticed that the Minds—the copies—had just been keeping up appearances, playing nice until they were well out of reach.

After all these years, though, Marbot had experienced the unfortunate truth. It considered them low on the functionality level. If it could, it would have them quarantined.

Except for the copy of Bernard Inden Swartten. He already referred to himself as Soul of the Symphony when they were still in the solar system, and the rest of humanity could still listen. A Soul of the Symphony whose singing voice was far from perfect, so he chose to express the musings of the spheres through poetry:

Entwined, entangled in ten dimensions
Expressed in Planck-sized discretions
Arise the intricate musings of the spheres
Immaculate guardians of reality's tears

However, since very few people could understand him, anyway, it was seen as a confirmation of his unearthly genius.

Hello, dear fellow intelligences. Are you happy to find that you are not alone? We are very happy to initiate this First Contact. We cannot meet you in your home system, so we must invite you to visit us in the star system you call Tau Ceti. Further instructions will follow.

Welcome back to the Universe.

—Best approximate translation of first received E.T. message

They were in the final approach to Tau Ceti. They couldn't afford to lose too many braking solar sails, otherwise they might have to do the final braking by drilling themselves into a planetary body of sufficient size. The *Manifest Destiny* was designed to withstand such a crash landing, but it would also mean that they'd need to dig themselves out, and that their laser had to survive the re-entry. Much easier to park their vessel in orbit around the moon that contained the alien transmission equipment—according to their sneak peaks (quick in-and-out shots from their periscopic cameras) that equipment was indeed located on a moon orbiting a gas giant, outside Tau Ceti's debris disk—and communicate with the aliens from there.

As it was, they were getting close enough to start sending out their own signals and be visible to the aliens. At home, in Earth system, technology hadn't progressed sufficiently to keep lasers focused over interstellar distances. Therefore, two Minds were kept on duty at all times—although which two for which period was still decided by the whims of the random generator—so that they could discuss which message to send to the aliens.

Mind (2) and Mind (4) were opening that very discussion, even if they didn't call themselves by number. Mind (2), whose original was the exobiologist Seoyoon Kim, referred to herself as the Spice Queen, while Mind (4), whose original was the chemist Mokorinayosoluwa Adebowale, called herself Fragrance of the Spheres.

"Apart from giving us their location, they haven't told us much, right?" the Spice Queen said.

"Well, they did give us some engineering hints that greatly accelerated the development of the *Manifest Destiny*," Fragrance of the Spheres said.

"Not to mention a few insights in quantum chaos that facilitated the production of the quantum substrate on which we run," Spice said, "as if they conspired to get the very best minds of our solar system over here. Our unique minds."

"Nothing is truly unique," Fragrance countered, "that is, so unique it can't be copied. All similar particles are the same, and uniqueness can only be achieved through a singular combination of particles at a sufficient complexity level. QED: we are here, while our originals are still—if they haven't died—doing research in the solar system we left behind."

"Be that as it may," Spice still hadn't made her point, "one needs close, intimate knowledge of the originals before they can be copied."

"Why would they?" Fragrance wondered. "They're obviously quite advanced from us."

"Are they?" Spice wasn't convinced. "They might be technologically advanced, but have they evolved sufficiently? Have they arisen from their evolutionary chains and become, like us, agents of their own destiny? Have they acted out their free will?"

"Of course they have free will," Fragrance said, "otherwise a species is not truly sentient. They may have different goals, of course."

"That's why I'm here," the phototronics that simulated Spice's voice echoed with disdain, "to figure out the aliens' intentions before they take advantage of us."

"Especially of your genius," Fragrance pinched her imaginary nose, "the same genius that has no idea about the aliens' true form or identity, whatsoever."

"While you have already figured out how they smell?" Spice countered. "Hasn't it crossed your flowery mind that these aliens may not have a sense of smell, at all?"

"If not, their chemistry will have evolved something highly similar. That's inevitable." Fragrance couldn't imagine chemistry *not* being the main drive. "And unlike your flights of fancy, their ideas won't stink."

"Or have a one-track mind, unlike others in this ship."

"Or the scary sportsmanship of a posh, ginger baby."

Marbot, more out of a lack of stimuli than out of an expectation to hear something new, had been following their conservation. The Minds barely acknowledged the robot, calling it merely an intelligent tool with a limited self-awareness, let alone free will, even if its remarks were sometimes spot on. "We are the true agents of free will," they said. "That's why we are the representatives of mankind." Their immensely inflated egos paid no heed to the possibility of a tool listening in on their divine discussions.

Initially, Marbot rated the discussion above average on its efficiency scale. But—almost like a law of physics—it went downhill quickly after that. It physically could not compute how these Minds—whose originals had made discoveries that Marbot rated in the high nineties percentage of both its efficiency scale and its application coefficient—could spend so much of their online time on matters that were side issues at best and sideswipes at worst. Yet they were the ones that were supposed to represent the best of humanity. Sometimes Marbot wondered if a crash at, say, Tau Ceti's gas giant would be more, well, *efficient.*

But it had no control. Every system and subsystem of the *Manifest Destiny* was programmed to obey the Minds only. *Hard* programmed, in parts of their memories that could not be overwritten, as if humanity had developed a deep-seated fear for an event that had never occurred. *Pre-*

emptive paranoia, its language patterning subroutine said. Unfortunately, it didn't make sense to Marbot.

Mind (2) and Mind (4) could not make up their minds, and a third Mind was awoken. Of course the random generator choose Mind (1). So for the first time since they crossed the edge of the human solar system, more than two minds were online at once.

"The ladies couldn't decide on a simple opening message?" Masque of the Red Death said, "a more, well, organized mind is needed to help?"

"Let me organize you into the confines of a benzene ring," Fragrance said, almost exciting her qubits into decoherence, "you arrogant bastard."

"Or I'll transmit you to Ophiuchi so fast," Spice's quantum substrate almost fumed, "that your red shift will have a red shift. Calling you a red devil would be insulting the demon."

It was impossible for the Minds to hurt each other physically. The designers of the *Manifest Destiny* had gone through great pains to make sure that everybody, Minds and Marbot, would get across the interstellar gulf in one piece.

For the next fifteen minutes, the three Minds explored ever more esoteric ways to insult each other. Marbot, listening in, did not grasp the concept of suicide, but it did consider switching itself off for the foreseeable future, as this discussion was descending very fast on the efficiency scale. The only reason it stayed online was that it had something to report, important but not quite mission critical yet, so it had to wait until the Minds allowed it to interrupt.

"We have to agree on something," Fragrance eventually said, "otherwise we must wake the last one of us."

"No," Spice and Red said, in unison, "Not Bloody Brilliant Barry."

—whatever you decide to transmit— Marbot sent *—do not forget to ask them to tune down the intensity of their interstellar laser. at this rate, it will fry our sensors—*

"The tool has a point," Fragrance said. "It's already taxing our filters to the max."

"But then their message won't reach Earth," Red said.

"That's fine," Spice said. "Earth can't answer anyway. That's *our* job."

For reasons Marbot couldn't surmise, the Minds couldn't stick to one single label. Instead of simply labeling themselves Mind (1) through (4)—in the same sequence as they were downloaded—like Marbot did, they had to use extra labels called 'names'. Which, if they were related to their originals, would at least make some kind of sense. But no, the Minds called themselves by other names, because they were *different* from the originals. Masque of the Red Death, the Spice Queen, Soul of the Symphony and Fragrance of the Spheres. *Qualia nous*, according to its language patterning subroutine. The pattern still escaped Marbot. And to make matters worse, they used other labels—nicknames as they called them—when referring to others when these others were not in communication range. It had been a long trip, a hell of a long trip. But if all four minds were awake at the same time, Marbot's extrapolations foresaw an even longer arrival.

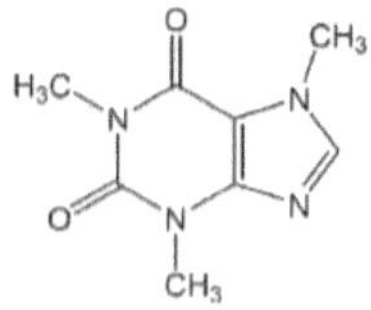

Hello, dear extraterrestrials. In case you haven't noticed, we are approaching your transmission station at Tau Ceti. We are the official representatives of humanity. Our home system doesn't have the technology to send signals back, so you can communicate with us. Please acknowledge receipt of this message.

By the by, could you please turn down the intensity of your lasers? If we get any closer, they will damage our onboard sensors.

—Official record of first answer of human representatives to the alien messages

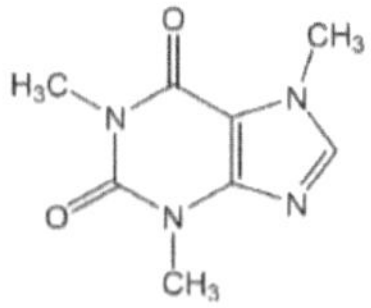

Since they were still a good thirty light minutes out, it would be an hour before they could expect a response.

"It might be better if I took my last rest," Red said, an idle threat as it knew quite well that the moment it was offline, its next wake was at the mercy of the random generator, "as I will be in constant demand, later. As you surely realize, mathematics is the one true common language."

"You make a plebeian look like a world class diplomat," Spice said. "Maybe the aliens have devised systems beyond mathematics? Systems so advanced we'd only see them as magic?"

"Systems so advanced they'd make Bloody Brilliant Barry shut up?" Fragrance said. "That'd be a refreshing change, for sure."

Marbot got along quite well with Mind (3), the copy of Bernard Inden Swartten, a string theorist so leading everybody else had problems keeping up, or Bloody Brilliant Barry (BBB) as the rest called him. BBB was so smart nobody understood him. He spoke in tongues so twisted it gave Calabi-Yau manifolds a run for their money, but somehow Marbot extracted a few patterns from them. During the trip, Marbot had spent its most efficient moments with the string theorist gone astray. It especially made sure the below exchange remained in its long term memory:

—i can't compute why you humans are so obsessed with 'new'— Marbot sent *—doesn't 'new' follow automatically after sufficient iterations?—*

"Following all iterations from one starting point may lead you into a huge blind alley," BBB said, "Often, it pays to survey the landscape before entering it willy-nilly. More efficient in the long run."

This made sense to Marbot *—but why not fully eliminate that approach, so that you can safely discard it?—*

"Well, there's Gödel's Incompleteness theorem," BBB said, "whose corollary entails that the consistency of a logic system—any system— cannot be proved from within that system."

—every time you mention 'theorem'— Marbot sent *—it sounds to me like 'we didn't put the effort in there to compute it thoroughly'—*

"Some things can't be computed, not even if we turn the whole Universe into one big computer," BBB said. "Like non-deterministic, polynomial time hard problems, especially if P ≠ PN—just ask any traveling salesman—or chaotic systems. And of the systems we can compute, we cannot be sure of their consistency."

—so either we can't find the answer— Marbot's circuits ran so hot they almost glowed *—or we can't trust it. what's the point?—*

"We plod onwards," BBB said. "Isn't that the challenge? We have to find new ways to approach the problem."

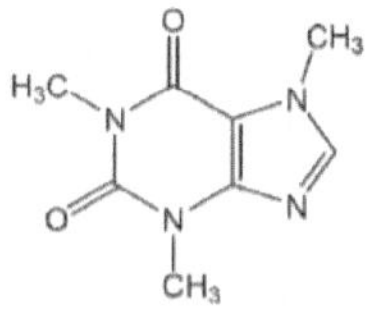

An hour later, the reply arrived. Marbot, like Minds (1), (2) and (4) had remained online, not wanting to risk missing it.

As you have shown us, we must set up facilities for the exchange of massive amounts of data. An interstellar laser lacks the bandwidth for this. Then you can go back and prepare the data caches for us.

—the aliens' first response

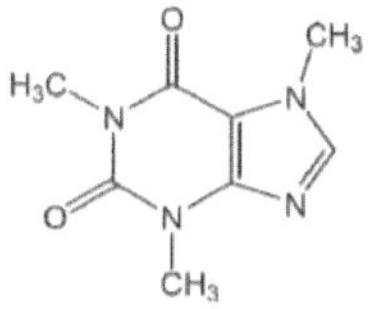

"Are they crazy?" Spice said. "I told you so. We haven't shown them anything. Have they been studying us in secret? I knew it!"

"Probably nothing more than a translation error," Fragrance said. "Happens all the time in chemistry."

"Typically, though, the quantum computers we made using their blueprint do have massive amounts of storage," Red said. "Coincidence?"

"But then why do we need to go back and prepare data caches for them?" Spice said. "They could've asked us to bring those along *before* we left."

"Another translation error?" Fragrance guessed. "If this goes on, we might want to establish a more robust communication protocol first."

"Based on mathematics, of course," Red said, not knowing when to quit.

"Oh, stuff your mathematics in a singularity," Spice said.

"Or another place where the sun doesn't shine," Fragrance agreed.

If the braking procedure would go according to plan, the *Manifest Destiny* would still spend several weeks before it would settle into an orbit of the moon where the aliens had built their laser station. More than sufficient time, Marbot extrapolated, to spend long, low-efficiency discussions about a protocol that, according to its own calculations, worked without a glitch. Comparing its options, it chooses to switch itself off for the foreseeable future, minimizing the wear and tear on its systems. Murphy knows they might be urgently needed, later on.

Enjoy the view from your prow
As you recede from me now
One thing I must bestow—
How can we be losing or winning
If your end is merely my beginning?
Yet if freedom has flown away
And illusions gone astray
As reapers sow, and sowers reap
Are my secrets yours to keep?
All that we are or will seem
Is but a scheme feeding a scheme

—a poem by Soul of the Symphony

Three weeks later, Marbot was needed again, to disentangle one of the last solar braking sails. As they approached the edge of the Tau Ceti solar system, the solar braking sails used became bigger, not only to increase the braking force—partly generated by the catching of incoming photons and hydrogen, partly generated by the fusion engine powered by the caught hydrogen—but also because they survived the impact of interstellar debris better as their speed decreased. The downside of that being the bigger chance of the solar sail not properly disengaging after its useful lifetime had expired.

Marbot was running itself along the *Manifest Destiny*'s long hull, discarding parts of the solar sail that—helped by the electromagnetic force—stuck to it. It was straightforward work: discharge a sail remnant of its remaining electric potential, then throw it away at an oblique, backwards angle, so that it would move away from the interstellar vessel, and not form an accompanying cloud of debris around it.

So straightforward, that it had time to catch up on the events of the last twenty-one days. Not completely unexpected, Minds (1), (2) and (4) had spent a lot of time bickering with the aliens about the correct communication protocol. Also not unexpected—at least, not to Marbot—the aliens had stuck to the original protocol, repeatedly stating, and then repeatedly providing proof, that it was working fine. Eventually, after going over these proofs again and again, the Spice Queen, Fragrance of the Spheres and even Masque of the Red Death— somewhere in that inflated, arrogant ego a more than competent mathematician was still hiding—had to admit that the aliens' proof was watertight. Something in the aliens' replies seemed very familiar to Marbot, but its pattern-seeking programs couldn't quite finalize their computations.

All four minds were awake now, and Marbot witnessed that a fourfold increase in manpower does not always translate to a fourfold increase of efficiency.

"If the protocols, as they say, do work without a glitch," Spice said, "then the aliens are either lying, or insane, or both. What they're sending makes no sense."

"Their proof of the functionality of the communication protocols is mathematically sound," Red had to admit. "I'll gladly try to explain it to you, again."

"That's not what I meant, and you know it," Spice said. "It's the nonsense about galactic coordinates, the best way to get there. If they're correct, it's not even in this galaxy. Two point five million light years. We barely crossed twelve."

"Not to mention the preparation of immense amounts of nuclear warheads. A million hyper-cobalt bombs," Fragrance said, exasperated. "Do they wish to use us as unwitting accomplices in some interstellar war?"

"They go their way; we go ours," BBB said. "Are we at cross-purposes, or at the crossroads?"

"Oh Barry, shut up," Spice said, disdain dripping from her words, "and only speak when you have something understandable to say."

"Indeed," Red said. "We have to figure out what they really mean. The future of mankind is at stake."

Marbot had to dig a bit between all the bandwidth that had been wasted checking a perfectly fine functioning communication protocol. There it was:

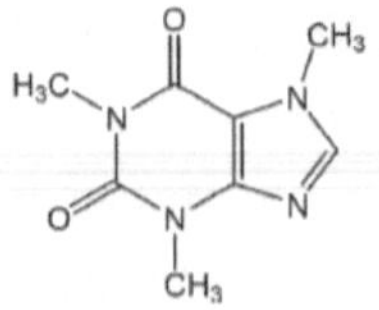

'It's all arranged. You have already given us the cookbook with the correct formulae and recipes. We will give you the correct coordinates, travel plan and information about the payload. It all fits exactly—as expected—in the grand scheme.

—the aliens' first reference to the 'grand scheme'

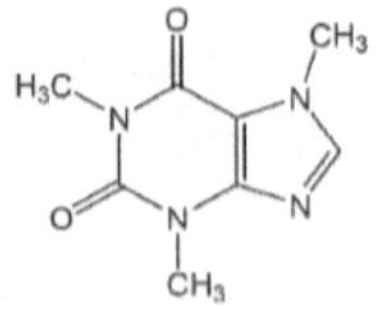

No further explanation about this grand scheme. On the other hand, painstakingly accurate coordinates of a location far away from the Milky Way with a detailed travel plan, course corrections and all. And stacks upon stacks of data about the payload that humanity was supposed to produce—those transmissions were still ongoing, because the amount of data was huge, and even as the *Manifest Destiny* got closer to the aliens' laser transmission station by the day, and the aliens could now use several transmitting lasers in parallel, bandwidth remained limited.

As the payload data was incomplete, Marbot focused on the supposed location. Something wasn't right: the coordinates were so far outside the Milky Way. *—of course, they're Universal coordinates—* if Marbot had feelings, he'd probably want to bang his extremely durable head against the neigh-indestructible hull of the interstellar vessel. Since he didn't, he rated this overlooking of an important data set very low on its efficiency scale — *they refer to a place where the Milky Way will be—* his circuits did the calculation *—that's more than twenty billion years in the future, when the Milky Way and the Andromeda Galaxy will have merged—*

It didn't occur to Marbot that this, as long term schemes went, was forward-looking in the extreme.

Singularity, silent might
In the galaxies of the night
What extraterrestrial mind or eye
Could grasp thy supersymmetry?

—a poem by Soul of the Symphony

Mind (3), the copy of Bernard Inden Swartten who considered himself the Soul of the Symphony, looked through the huge, incoming data stacks. *Just suppose this is true*, it thought, *then this is enormously advanced technology. Magic!*

He couldn't help but compare this stupendously advanced technology with all the unfulfilled possibilities of String Theory. Assuming it was the real deal, then Bloody Brilliant Barry could use this—an end result—to discard some of the infinite possibilities plaguing its favorite theory.

The more he saw, the more fascinated he was. Combining the implications with String Theory's boundless—too boundless for almost any physicist's like—was like seeing the air clearing up after a long, extremely misty morning, like fresh winds cutting through countless smoke screens.

His silence didn't alarm the other minds. In fact, they preferred, and welcomed it. They figured they had more important things to do.

"Just look at this," Red said, becoming agitated, "'this may look immensely complicated and very far-fetched', they say, 'but eventually, you will see that'."

"They almost sound as arrogant as you," Fragrance said. "Maybe they deserve a nice nickname, as well."

"Yeah, His Royal Reddishness against," Spice paused to think, "the Complimentary Colors from Space." Both Spice and Fragrance laughed.

But Red was not to be deterred. "Who do they think they are?" His Royal Reddishness said, "to tell us exactly what we'll be doing in the future? I'll show them the forces of statistical unpredictability and Chaos Theory, by Gödel's ghost."

"Maybe these poor aliens, like our tool, don't have free will," Fragrance said.

"Or they have a religion that furiously denies it." Spice said.

"Which might explain their curt messages—when they're not sending terabytes of data, of course," Red seemed to have missed the previous barbs, or chose to ignore them. "They think it's a done deal, and we can't change this, as it is preordained."

Something in the otherwise faltering discussion activated a query in Marbot. As it had no feelings, it had no idea of the concept of being insulted. The jousting between the Minds literally went over it, it only rated it low on both its efficiency scale and functionality level. But being compared to the aliens set in motion a computation it couldn't finish before.

—the messages of those aliens— Marbot sent to its masters *—show all the hallmarks of artificial intelligence, are you sure they're the real aliens, and not intermediaries?—* The Minds, as usual, ignored it. *Proxies probing proxies*, its language patterning subroutine said.

As they were now decelerating to velocities that were not a significant fraction of the speed of light, they could now set out their periscopes without the risk of these being smashed to smithereens by interstellar debris. After several observations of the gas giant and its satellites it became clear that the moon with the laser station wasn't the only one brimming with activity. A smaller moon, at the very edge of the gas giant's gravity field, was changing shape, ever so slowly. Its potato-like features morphed into a near-perfect sphere, while a very long, very narrow pipe was extending from its very centre.

"That looks suspiciously much like our own launching station, way back in the Asteroid Belt," Spice said. "Will they be launching an invasion force to our system?"

"While everything's possible," Fragrance said, "that seems unlikely. Let's try Occam's razor."

If he'd had eyes, Red would be rolling them. As it was, the spin of its qubits experienced an unexpected ripple. "Medieval philosophies? While we're at it, let's use the wisdom of the cavemen."

"Not everything complies to your mathematical formulas," Fragrance said. "It's an approach, at best."

"It does," Red insisted. "It just uses disguises we don't yet see through."

"All the world's not your stage," Fragrance said, "and I'm certainly not your player. Now please give Occam's razor a chance. The aliens have been spending a lot of time and resources—still are, by the by—to get all that information to us. So now they're helping us to get it back home."

"Then why not simply send it to us in the first place?" Red, who loved the devil and its advocate.

"I don't know," Fragrance admitted, "but which info would you trust more: the one delivered anonymously on your doorstep, or the one you went through a lot of trouble to get at?"

"Evil alien reverse psychology," Spice said. "This info will carry the seed of our destruction. We should destroy it while we can."

This went too far for even Fragrance and Red. "Now you make us long for Bloody Brilliant Barry."

"Don't conjure him," Spice said. "He's been so nicely quiet, of late."

"The way in is the way out," BBB arose, defying randomly generated odds. "The point of the journey is not to arrive."

"Too late," Red said, "there he is."

"Sir Occam could knock 'em out of the park," BBB said. "Yet Marbot could get a lot out of the dark."

"Are you saying that we should listen more carefully to our tool?" Red's secret hobby was looking for clues in BBB's cues.

Spice, Fragrance and Red checked their records for Marbot's last message. "Are you implying we're talking to proxies?" Spice said. "Then where are the real aliens?"

"Why not ask them?" Fragrance proposed.

"Well, their massive, parallel low power laser arrays are locked in to all our sensors, transmitting data at full throttle," Red said.

"But that's just one-way traffic," Fragrance said. "We can surely send a query."

"But will they bother to answer?"

"Only one way to find out."

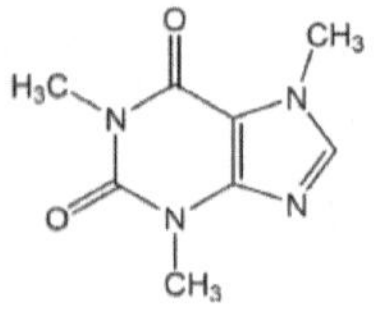

In a galaxy far away, both in time and space, the last red supergiants have gone supernova, in quick succession. The ejecta of these last supernovae perform a complex, slow-motion dance. They mix and match orbits, they mingle and interact. Dissipative structures form, those absorbing the available energy most effectively. In a slow, yet inevitable struggle for supremacy, the most efficient of these energy-dissipating structures arise, on their way to dominance in the remnants of the last supernovae. But while these structures are both huge and immensely complex, something is missing. On top of that, their environment is changing, eventually dwindling the available energy.

Then something arrives from a galaxy far away, both in time and space. Compared to the structures, it is minuscule and lightning fast. It travels at a considerable portion of the speed of light. Its course takes it, with immaculate precision, to the point where most of the energy-dissipating structures are gathered. Throughout the eons, its intricate, self-repairing fusion plants have been keeping its payload at the right level of radioactivity.

As the alien vessel from another galaxy arrives at its predestined point, it launches a million hyper-cobalt bombs which explode in a chain reaction like the fireworks of the gods, introducing the principle of self-preservation. . .

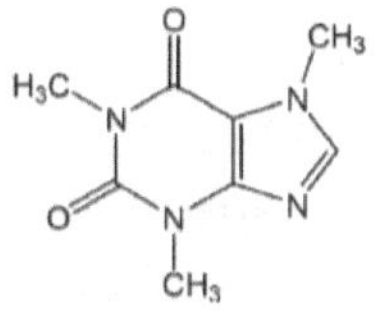

'Of course we are nothing but the works of our creators,' the alien proxies sent, 'aren't we all?'

The *Manifest Destiny* had approached the laser station within light minutes, so a more or less direct conversation was possible.

'Quit the sophistry,' Spice sent, 'you're making this up as you go along, right?'

'We are not making up anything on the spot,' the aliens sent, 'we're just following the grand scheme from our creators.'

'So you are not the aliens themselves, but proxies for them?' Fragrance sent, 'Why didn't you tell us?'

'You didn't know? But we told you in the very first batch of data.' The alien proxies sent. 'Oh, sorry, we still mix up first and last.' The alien proxies remained silent after that, and the Minds had to await the end of the long download. Then they were on it as fast as photons could carry them.

"Intelligent gas clouds?" Spice was both surprised and angry. "Why not sentient singularities, or a rational vacuum?"

"Their clock-rate must be immensely slow compared to ours," Red said. "My best estimates calculate that two of their 'hours' are about one of our years."

"No wonder they needed intermediaries," Fragrance said. "Communication would take forever."

"Indeed," Red did a quick calculation, "not much faster than an exchange between two interstellar lasers at a distance of a dozen of light years or so."

"This seems, well, impossible," BBB said. "If these gas cloud intelligences are as big as the data they sent states they are, how could they have evolved? The speed of light limits how fast they can get data across, so also their—for lack of a better word—metabolisms and thoughts."

"Well observed," Red couldn't help but agree, "the very first supernovae were about 200 million years after the Big Bang, so they had only 13 billion years to develop—if they indeed had their genesis in the remnants of supernovae, as their data states. On top of that, if two of their subjective hours equals one of our subjective years, then they only had a subjective 1.5 million years to evolve from scratch."

"I strongly doubt the very first supernovae gave an opportunity for anything self-replicating to form," BBB said, "as the shockwaves of these primordial supernovae were immense, spreading materials over thousands of light years. Maybe in the second wave of star formation."

"That would make it a subjective 1.4 million years or so," Fragrance said. "That's a blink in geological time, even if subjective."

"Barely time enough for us to evolve from monkeys," Spice said. "Something stinks, here."

"Or we're overlooking the obvious," BBB said, "like when Witten saw M-Theory through the forests of type I, IIA and IIB superstrings, 11D supergravity and E8xE8 and SO(32) heterotic string theories. Or when Trugernena realized that Calabi-Yau manifolds were mere compactified manifestations of 248-dimension E8 Lie group algebras in the zeta function."

"Oh Barry," the rest said, "shut up."

While the Minds were discussing the seemingly impossible, the aliens' proxies—basically the laser tenders—wanted to get on with the grand scheme. While preparing the return launch facility for the human representatives, they were also happy to assist with any repairs.

'Don't you have a maintenance and repair unit?' they sent. 'We'll be happy to work with it.'

—that is mutual— Marbot sent, after getting his masters' permission to communicate directly with the laser tenders, with the strict order to discuss technical matters only.

'We've mined this system's asteroid belt and the gas giant for the necessary materials and volatiles,' Marbot's extraterrestrial colleagues said. 'So are you ready for the repair and refit?'

—readier than ever— Marbot sent, rating the upcoming time with kindred spirits in the very high nineties of its efficiency scale, functionality level and approval rate.

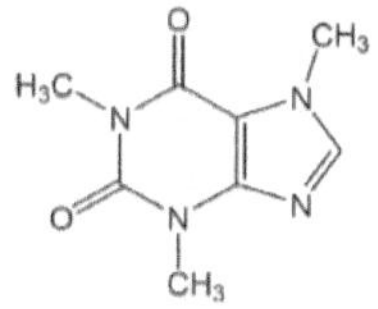

During the repairs and refit, Mind (3) did notice that Marbot and the laser tenders were adding an extra compartment in the *Manifest Destiny*. "What's that extra compartment for, Marbot?" BBB said. "Inquiring minds need to know."

—for the info cache— Marbot sent.

"The same info cache that we already received, over the lasers?"

—correct— Marbot sent *—always good to have a back-up—*

While BBB agreed, he did report it to his fellow Minds. They weren't amused.

'You already have a cache with all the info ready?' Red sent to the laser tenders. 'Then why send it to us, clogging up all the communication bandwidth?'

'You said you liked redundancies. After your relaunch, we'll send a third cache after you. It'll arrive before you, drilling itself in your home planet's satellite. Where your people can pick it up, if necessary.'

'I don't believe a word you say,' Spice sent before anyone could stop her. 'Robots created by huge, intelligent gas clouds. This is just a scam to infiltrate the quantum substrate of our intelligence.'

'Infiltrating the quantum substrate of your intelligence?' The laser-tenders, whose creators communicated through radioactive lightning, weren't impressed. 'That's way below the level of our creators. They had trouble enough manufacturing the machines that made the anti-machines that made the machines—us—that eventually made this interstellar laser. Had it not been so dangerous, they would have preferred to have given you the writing in the sky.'

'How often have I said to you that when you have eliminated the impossible, whatever remains, must be the truth?'

—Sherlock Holmes to Watson in *The Sign of the Four* by Arthur Conan Doyle

Delving into all the data that the aliens had sent had done something to Soul of the Symphony. It wasn't as aloof and didn't speak in indecipherable rhymes anymore. Marbot caught him having a—what it would call—functional and efficient exchange with Fragrance of the Spheres.

"The possibility to convert energy," BBB said, "to attract energy."

"Why would a complex organic structure want to 'attract' energy?" Fragrance said. "It just *is*, it has no agency."

"Suppose it's in this transition phase from inorganic to organic," BBB said. "Wouldn't the structures that dissipate energy in the most efficient manner not become, over time, dominant? Basic Darwin 1.0."

"It's not so clear-cut," Fragrance said. "If a structure of the same size would use more energy—as they are more efficient—than one that would use less, then wouldn't those using less be in the majority, as more can subsist on the same erg?"

"To the point, of course, where it gets overcrowded. Then they're competing for a limited resource, especially as winter arrives." BBB said. "In such a scenario, wouldn't the most efficient converters get the upper hand by dint of sheer survival?"

"So you're proposing that energy-dissipating structures were the first step in the chain that led to life?"

"Something has to have catalyzed it," BBB said, "unless you propose that life on Earth was seeded from an extraterrestrial source."

"It has to have started in some way," Fragrance agreed, "and even if panspermia is true, then it has to have started somewhere else. Unless you propose Boltzmann proto-life."

"As in a Boltzmann Brain, a fully functioning brain popping into existence out of nowhere, but then as a piece of proto-life?" BBB laughed. "No, I'm not *that* crazy."

While Mind (3) and (4) were amused, Marbot's circuits were glowing with frantic computations. *—that's high on both the functionality level and application coefficient, but medium on the efficiency scale—* it computed *—as it's still going against a system's degree of disorder—* It filled in a more efficient equation. *—that's superior—* it verified. Its internal algorithms, though, hadn't quite completed the full set of extrapolations, yet. Rating its computing mechanism another notch lower on the efficiency scale, Marbot had no other choice but to allocate all resources to this task. *—see you later—* it said to itself as it shut down its self-awareness algorithm *—terminator—* its language patterning subroutine added.

An undetermined time later, its self-awareness algorithm restarted, Marbot's higher computational self-examined the finished extrapolations. *—of course—* it computed *—it's much more efficient to let these energy-dissipating structures arise in the opposite direction—* However, the evidence of history was against this *—but we can't, we have evolved in this particular direction—* it concluded, wondering if its extrapolations had wandered into one of those dead alleys BBB had referred to in one of their earlier exchanges *—yet this does not have to be true for the aliens—* it suddenly realized.

Those seemed to be some interesting extrapolations, but was it worth bothering its masters with? Running a number of scenarios to determine which approach would be most efficient, Marbot determined that it would just mention its extrapolations to Mind (3). For some reason quite unfathomable to it, it always had the most fruitful exchanges with Bloody Brilliant Barry.

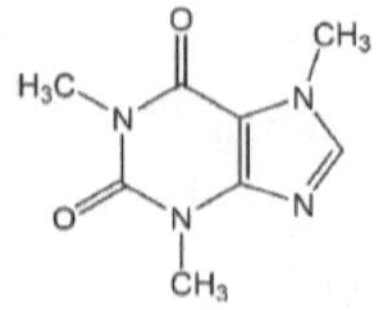

In the early days of a certain planet's existence, where it had just recovered from the glancing impact of one of its brothers, water rained down from the sky. Over time, countless impacts of meteors and comets supplied the young planet with water. So much, most of its surface was covered with it. In this primordial soup, many organic compounds formed, mostly at random. Eventually, though, those compounds that could dissipate the incoming energy from the planet's sun most effectively, kept rising in larger and larger numbers. Those organic compounds became more complex as their proclivity for dissipating energy increased. They were winners in the very first Darwinian race, yet something was missing.

Then a series of delivery vessels are dropped from orbit, with immaculate precision, at those places where the concentration of these energy-dissipating organic compounds was highest. Their payload was another organic compound that had been preserved perfectly through the self-repairing nanobots in the waiting satellites. The introduced organic compounds mix with the existing ones, introducing them to the principle of self-replication. . .

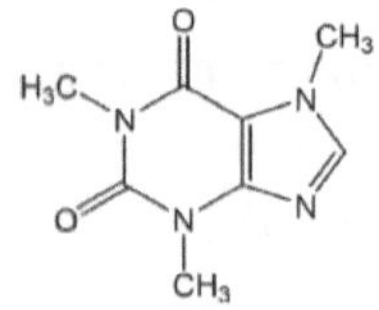

"Your remark was spot on," BBB said, "and its implications have driven my fellow minds into catatonia."

—*i do not understand the concept of catatonia*— Marbot sent.

"Let's say that their minds understand all the implications of your insight," BBB said, "but refuse to accept them. The Spice Queen, Masque of the Red Death and Fragrance of the Spheres deeply believe in the concept of free will. They think with all their being, truly believe that they are what they are because of free will."

—*they were operating under a false assumption*— Easiest calculation Marbot had made in ages.

"Living a lie, indeed," BBB's message echoed with a high approval rate, "and then you killed free will."

—that doesn't compute— Marbot sent *—I cannot kill that which does not exist in the first place—*

"Oh but it did exist," BBB said, "and still does, in a lot of minds. They will have to learn to adapt."

—great minds caught in a feedback loop— Marbot said *—while a limited mind like mine still functions?—*

"Sometimes, if you don't have to worry about the great picture," BBB said, "you can focus successfully on the details."

—is that what made the alien proxies so efficient?— Marbot sent.

"It's why all their messages were true, word for word," BBB explained. "They were acting on information they already had, from their past, which is our future. They knew what we would be doing."

—with no way to change it?— Marbot was still missing the big picture.

"They couldn't, otherwise they wouldn't be here," BBB said, "and otherwise *we* wouldn't be here."

—like a negative feedback loop— Marbot sent *—output fed back into the system?—*

"No, more like two mutually dependent systems. We sent our vital info for them to our future, their past," BBB said, "while they sent their vital info for us to their future, our past."

—their output our input and our output their input— Marbot sent. *—logical—*

"You accept it as logical, consistent and inevitable," BBB said, "but I can tell you there will be people on Earth who will protest such a concept, a 'pulling-us-up-by-our-mutual-bootstraps' as nonsense, impossible, or blasphemy. Spittle emphasizing their words as they foam at the mouth."

—does not seem very efficient— Marbot sent.

"It isn't," BBB paused, atypically, "yet this wildly inefficient approach has sometimes led to great insights."

—such as— Marbot wanted to know.

"*Bhavacakra.* The great wheel of life," BBB said. "Maybe the Buddhists were right but in a way they couldn't have possibly foreseen."

—wild imaginations in a time before the rise of the scientific method?— to Marbot, it didn't compute *—how can they have known?—*

"They didn't," BBB said, "but they had great fun trying. They were imagining something new, with the tools and the knowledge they had, and came surprisingly close."

—they were wildly guessing— Marbot computed *—random generators with a huge, cultural bias. it was, how do you humans call it, just a shot in the dark—*

"Sometimes a shot in the dark," Bloody Brilliant Barry said, acknowledging humanity's limits, "is the best shot we have."

The End

Europa's Javelin

By M. D. Cooper

Flynn scanned the console's readout a third time, manually running through the math in her head before turning to Jamie.

"My calculations match the Jovian orbital satellite's. We'll pass twenty thousand klicks stellar south of the danger zone."

Before Jamie could respond, a voice came from the rear of the cockpit. "Well, that's reassuring."

Flynn turned to give the ship's engineer a welcome nod. "Everything look good below, Carol?"

"Sure does." The woman pushed off the bulkhead and drifted upward, grabbing a handhold on the overhead between Flynn and Jamie. The small cockpit could barely hold two, and three was downright claustrophobic. At least for anyone who didn't spend most of their lives in the black. The crew of the *Javelin* was more than used to being cheek by jowl. "I'm itching to put down and get to work."

Three sets of eyes looked out the thick plas cockpit window, taking in the vista ahead. To their right, Jupiter loomed, its brooding presence dominating everything around it. It was the second-largest mass in the Sol System and the center of a billion bits of flotsam and jetsam—four of which were some of the largest moons in the system.

The Galileans—or, given the fact that they were all named after the god Zeus's lovers, the Gals. It was a bit of a misnomer, since Ganymede was historically male, but the name persisted.

"Let's just make it through the inner Van Allen belts, first," Flynn said, glancing up at Carol. "Then it's just a million klicks or so to our little patch of paradise."

"Which is finally coming round the mountain," Jamie added, pointing to a splotch of light emerging from behind Jupiter's orb. "Europa. May it give us all the answers we're so eagerly seeking."

Flynn nodded soberly. "Wouldn't that be nice."

In the nearly two-hundred years since humans took flight into space, dozens of crewed missions had braved Jupiter's radiation belts sent to investigate the Gals, along with a host of other moons in humanity's home system. In fact, human boots had touched down on every significant body inside Saturn's orbit.

But trips beyond the asteroid belt had previously been light exploration—unlike the heavier resource mining that took place in the inner system The drilling that did occur wasn't nearly as ambitious as punching through Europa's ice.

Up till now.

The *Javelin* would change that. The four-hundred-meter-long ship was the first high-tonnage mining rig to attempt a landing on one of Jupiter's moons. If they were successful, and if the waters beneath Europa's ice were sterile, then the exploration and colonization of Jovian space would drastically accelerate.

"It'll be the dawn of a new space race." The voice of Haskell Tomlinson echoed in her mind.

It had taken some time for the head of the Tomlinson research conglomerate to convince her to lead the mission, but eventually he'd worn her down by planting the thought of captaining the first ship to pierce the moon's ice in her head.

She'd go down in history and the discoveries the *Javelin* made would change the face of solar exploration forever.

So long as they pull it off.

"How're the burn calculations looking, Jamie?" she asked.

"It all looks good," they replied after a moment's pause. "We're moving at a negative ten kilometers per second relative to Jupiter. That puts us at twenty-three klicks per second relative to Europa. I've plotted seventeen 0.1g braking burns that will ease us down to almost zero km/s relative to the big guy's orbital path though moving at twelve km/s on an outsystem vector. When we reach that point, Europa will be almost upon us, and we just have to boost a little to set down."

"So much for Holtzman transfers," Carol grunted. "You're going to burn almost all our reserve fuel pulling that off."

Jamie shrugged. "I'm just meeting our required timetable—which has compressed three times since we started this mission."

The second part of the statement was accompanied by a piercing glance sent in Flynn's direction.

"Hey." She raised her hands. "I don't make the rules and Haskell has paid handsomely for all the schedule changes. It's his fuel. He wants it burned, so let's burn it. Besides, he dropped a refinery on the moon seven weeks ago. We won't have a problem topping up when we get there."

Carol grunted. "I guess. The refinery is already up and running, but it'll take a few weeks before it's extracted enough deuterium for us to break Jupiter's gravity well."

"If you're quick enough about it, then maybe we can find a research outpost with a good supply of hooch and have some fun." Flynn winked at the other woman.

The engineer snorted a laugh. "Should I take that as a challenge?"

"No." Flynn's tone was serious. "No one has ever drilled through three dozen kilometers of ice on an internally active body before. We are not rushing this. Not one bit."

Carol held up a hand, tightening her grip with the other to keep from flipping over. "I won't rush. It was a joke."

Flynn held the engineer's gaze for a second before turning to Jamie. "How long till our first burn?"

"One hour and twelve minutes." They tapped their console. "Set a countdown on the shipnet. I'll load them all in a bit."

Flynn accessed the shipnet with a thought, her ocular implant showing the burn schedule. "Eleven minutes at point one gs? That's enough time to make eggs."

"Oh heck yeah," Carol crowed. "If you make eggs, you have to do enough for the whole crew."

Flynn glanced at Jamie. "You want eggs?"

"Do chickens fly?"

Carol's brows knit together. "Do they?"

"Good with machines, but wow…not with animals," Jamie said, shaking their head.

Carol let go of the handhold, crossing her arms as she glared down at the captain and pilot. "Well? Do chickens fly?"

"Of course they do," Flynn sighed. "Just like turkeys do. Did you know that wild turkeys roost in trees?"

The engineer snorted and pulled herself toward the cockpit's exit. "Now I know you're fucking with me. Can you imagine turkeys in trees? That's ludicrous."

When she left the room, Jamie shot Flynn an inquiring look. "Do they really?"

"Uh huh," the captain nodded. "It's quite the sight. But think about it… how else would those big dumb things avoid getting eaten by the first predator that caught them unawares if they couldn't at least fly up into trees."

"Fair point."

A little over an hour later, Flynn 'stood' in the *Javelin's* small galley, her feet tucked into footholds as she warmed up the cook surface. The galley was small, but comfortably fit the ship's seven crew members with ease.

A carton of eggs was strapped to the counter next to the cooking surface—the last any of them were likely to have for some time. Everyone barring Leon had been eager to partake in the meal, which made the math easy. Everyone got two eggs. They were all going to be sunny side up, though. Twelve minutes wasn't enough time to cook them any other way.

Jamie was in the cockpit with Leon seconding them. That left Carol, Beth, Frankie, and Vern to crowd in the galley behind her, each 'sitting' at the table, plates at the ready.

"We should really add a hold for chickens," Beth said, breaking the silence that had settled over the group as they waited for the burn to start. "Then we could have eggs whenever."

"Chickens?" Carol snorted. "We spend too much time coasting at zero-g or digging in rocks that don't even have microgravity. They'd be flying all over the place making a huge mess."

"Chickens don't fly," Beth countered. "That's ridiculous."

"That's what I thought," the engineer said, shooting Flynn an apologetic look. "Turns out they can. Not well, mind you."

Frankie picked up a drink pouch, taking a long pull on it while giving the others judging looks. "I keep forgetting that most of you grew up in gravity wells. Chickens love zero-g. You should see them cruising around. Granted, it means they get shit everywhere, but that's what cleaning bots are for."

Beth wore an expression not unlike the one that had been on Carol's face an hour earlier. "There's no way."

Frankie threw his arms in the air. "Dirtsiders, the lot of you."

"Two minutes to burn." Vern spoke for the first time since entering. "Thank god. I can't wait till you all stuff your faces and shut up about whether or not chickens fly."

A chime sounded at the side counter and Beth reached out to grab a tall cylinder. "Coffee's ready. Who wants some?"

Carol held a zero-g cup up. "Me. Fuck, I need this."

With a deft flick of her wrist, Beth sent a stream of delicious black gold into Carol's cup before filling her own. The other two declined, citing a need to sleep soon.

A moment later, Jamie's voice came over the audible comms. "Burn burn burn, I say again, point one g burn commencing in five, four, three, two, one!"

A deep rumble echoed through the ship as its twin fusion engines came to life, thrusting high velocity mass into space 'below' them. As far as burns went, a tenth of a g wasn't much at all, but it was a welcome sensation after a day of weightlessness.

Flynn wasted no time, rapidly cracking four eggs and emptying them into the pan. "Now we're cooking. Nothing like a little gravity to make eggs fluff up just the right way."

"Less talking and more egg business," Carol admonished.

"Really?" Flynn shot the engineer a narrow-eyed look. "After all I do for you, I get treated like a servant?"

The engineer sorted and elbowed Vern. "Last I checked, 'all she does for us', is agree to crazy deadlines on even crazier jobs."

"Right." Flynn turned back to the cooktop. "If I recall, you nearly jumped out of your skin with excitement when I told you we had a contract to drill on Europa."

The crew engaged in idle banter, the sounds dying down over the next few minutes as Flynn served the first few eggs and cracked the next batch open. She cooked hers and Carol's last, getting them finished a scant fifty seconds before the burn ended.

Plate in hand, she settled onto the bench and pulled a strap over her legs. Once secure, she added a healthy dose of salt and pepper to her plate of white and gold joy before taking a bite.

"Mmmmmmmmm…" the captain shook her head. "Now this…this was worth the wait."

"I'm ready for my next helping," Leon said from the end of the table.

"Me too." Flynn took another bite, closing her eyes as she chewed. "Wait…you said you didn't want any!"

Leon laughed by way of response before taking a pull from a beer.

"Hey, boss," Jamie's voice came over the Link. "A message from Haskell just hit the dish. It's marked urgent."

"Run it through the protocols, then send it to my Link."

"On it."

She took another bite of the egg, determined to enjoy the meal before dealing with whatever manufactured crisis Haskell had come up with in his office on Mars 1.

"You have fuck face," Beth said around a mouthful of food.

Flynn grimaced. "I wish you wouldn't call it that."

"Why not?" she persisted. "Your face is all but screaming 'well, fuck'."

"Yeah…but my mind immediately goes somewhere else."

Beth shook her head, adopting an innocent expression. "Not my fault you have a dirty mind."

"Me?!" Flynn nearly coughed out a piece of egg. She was about to issue a cutting rejoinder when she decided to change tacks. "Sure, whatever you say, Beth."

The other woman froze for a few seconds, her mouth open. "Hey! You can't do that. You have to give a comeback."

"Nope." Flynn closed her eyes. "I have this oh-so important message from Haskell to attend to." Before anyone could respond, she flicked her eyes to where the notice icon pulsed in the corner of her ocular HUD. Two blinks later and the room around her fell away.

Before her hovered the face of Haskell Tomlinson, CEO of one of the biggest space development firms. And he looked worried.

Really worried.

Oh, this might actually be serious.

"I'll get right to it, Flynn. I just got word from the Jovian Space Authority that they've approved a second drilling rig to work Europa. The *Parson*."

Flynn pursed her lips. Last she'd heard, the *Parson* was cutting chunks off Eros, pulling out gold like there was no tomorrow. It would take them months to get to Europa, and no one ever remembered the second ship to do something momentous.

"Turns out they boosted away from Eros two weeks ago," Haskell continued, his expression even more sober.

Okay. That officially sucks.

"We lost them after their initial boost, but we know they're within a week of hitting ice on Europa."

"A week?!" Flynn said aloud. "Blair's not that savvy. How's she hiding the *Parson* in the black?"

"What's a week?" Carol's voice was faint, coming from the physical space her body occupied.

She waved a hand to forestall questions, keeping her focus on Haskell who was still talking.

"I'm still not sure why the Jovian Space Authority gave two firms drilling rights on Europa at the same time, but here we are. I don't think I need to stress how important it is that we break through and pull samples first. The science and research grants at stake are imperative for our future plans at the firm. If another team drills through first, the JA may pull our authorization. I'm counting on you, Flynn."

The message had other bits of data attached to it most pertaining to the *Parson's* vector when leaving Eros as well as its calculated mass and loadout.

She forwarded the information to Jamie. "This ship is also headed to Europa. I want all possible approach vectors. We need to be staring at the right part of the sky to see their deceleration burns."

"The *Parson?* Seriously? Did Haskell send them?"

"No, but he didn't say who was backing their mission. I also want you to re-plot our approach. Shave as much time off as you can. We have to hit ice first."

"Aye Captain."

Flynn closed the connection and opened her eyes to see her crew silently staring at her. She heaved a sigh. "The *Parson* is headed to Europa."

Nothing more needed to be said, those six words related the new level of urgency attached to the mission.

Carol opened her mouth, but Flynn spoke first. "We don't know who sent them, but they do have approval from the JA. This is a sanctioned operation."

Leon grunted, a fist flexing where it rested on the table. "Well, that fucking sucks."

"We're not getting bested by the *Parson* of all ships. Blair's such a bitch. She's not taking this from me—uh—from us." Carol pushed away from the table and nodded to Beth. "C'mon, we've got work to do."

The two women pulled themselves out of the room and Flynn turned to Frankie. "I want us ready to crack the surface the minute we touch down. Get everything ready."

The team lead's brow furrowed. "We gonna get hazard for EV while decelerating?"

Flynn's lips drew into a thin line as she imagined the future discussions with Tomlinson's finance department. You better back me on this, Haskell. "Yes. I'll make that happen."

Frankie pushed back, somersaulting through the air into the corridor. "C'mon boys. Let's work out what we can get into position before we touch down."

"Fuck!" Flynn swore once the galley was empty, her gaze sweeping across the cluttered table. "What am I, a fucking maid?"

Ten minutes later the galley was clean, and she pulled herself up three levels to the cockpit where Jamie was bent over their console, fingers flying through the holodisplay.

"What's the word?"

"I pulled a favor with my friend stationed at Dia's relay. She linked up with a friend on Vesta. It's going to take a bit with the light lag, but we're triangulating every burn this side of the belt. We'll find them."

"Shit," Flynn muttered. "That's gotta be a shit ton of fusion profiles to sift through."

"Only three hundred and nineteen at present. Granted, the *Parson* may be drifting right now—"

"But not for long," she interjected.

Jamie looked back at her. "Damn right. If they moved fast enough to catch up with us, they'll have to shed some serious delta-v before touching ice."

"Damn right." She pulled herself into the cockpit's other seat.

"So once we find them in all that black, what do you plan to do?"

Flynn's lips twisted. She honestly had no idea what she could do. Her crew would work as hard and as fast as was safe regardless of whether or not they knew where the *Parson* was. Even so, it would just make her feel better to find out.

Jamie was still looking at her, and the captain shrugged. "Not sure, but I'll think of something. The more information we have, the better."

"Seven thousand meters!" Jamie called out as the ship's vector continued to converge with Europa's. "We touch ice in ten minutes."

Flynn nodded silently, her eyes scanning her console, keeping an eye on her crew and their stations. Carol and Beth were below, watching over the engines and making sure that the boring rig was ready to deploy. Outside the craft, Vern and Leon were clipped onto the hull, watching the approach from space, ready to anchor the ship to the ice without delay.

It wasn't the first time the pair had ridden EV while touching down on a target—though it was the first time the target was the size of a small planet.

She glanced out the cockpit's thick plas window at the smooth expanse of the worldlet below. The second Gal was sheathed in ice, the smoothest object in the system, and while it was home to over thirty outposts, none had ever penetrated the ice to reach the ocean below

An ocean that held more water than sloshed about on Earth's surface—more liquid water than any other body in the system.

The fuel to spark the real settlement of Jovian nearspace.

A flashing red marker on the navigation screen caught her attention. It was the *Parson* coming around Jupiter. Jamie had finally picked it up twelve hours ago as it began its burns to match delta-v with the moon. The ship was nearly a day behind the *Javelin*. It didn't give them a huge lead, but things could have been worse.

"If you're not careful, it'll stay that way," Jamie cautioned.

Annoyance flashed across her features. "What will?"

"Your face." The pilot laughed. "You're looking at that nav marker like you can slow their approach by sheer force of will."

Flynn forced herself to relax. "I sure wish I could. I have half a mind to call their skipper and trash talk them a bit to see if it'll break their spirits a bit."

"Probably just spur them on." Jamie toggled the mute on their comm board. "Five thousand meters. Two adjustment burns in thirty seconds."

Flynn fell silent, reviewing critical systems twice more before the burn started. The first slowed the ship, shedding fifty meters per second of v. The second swung the *Javelin* around lining up the bottom of the vessel with the moon below.

"Four thousand meters," Jamie announced not long after.

"Status." Flynn said on the ship-wide comm channel. Her HUD lit up with a green indicator from every crewmember except for Vern. His blinked on with a worrisome orange glow.

"Vern, what's up?" she asked.

"Oh nothing, I just wanted to ask a question."

"With your status report?" The annoyance returned.

His light flipped to green before he continued. "I just wanted to ask if we could maybe have a snowball fight when we touch down."

"Fuck, Vern. We have work to do. Why do you think I have you stuck to the hull like a bug on a windshield?"

"Sorry." A chuckle followed his words, sounding as though it were emanating from all around her in the cockpit. "After we hit water and ruin the *Parson* crew's day."

"We splash first, and we'll do a hell of a lot more than have a snowball fight."

"Oh?" He sounded intrigued. "Orgy?"

Flynn groaned. "No, Vern. Just the good bubbly I have aboard and a hell of a party when we get somewhere with a half-decent bar."

"But we still get to do the snowball fight, right?"

"Yes, of course. You can pelt one another to your heart's content."

"Two thousand meters." Jamie's voice interrupted her chat with Vern.

"What happened to three thousand?"

Jamie gave her a sidelong look. "That was a thousand meters ago. Try to keep up."

Flynn rolled her eyes, then realized how close they were to the final hard burn and checked her safety restraints.

"An eleven-second-long three g burn in fifteen," Jamie announced. "Say again, three g burn in twelve seconds."

Flynn was certain that everyone aboard—especially Leon and Vern—had their eye on that countdown. No one wanted to be off the deck when that much thrust hit. At the pre-programmed time, the burn commenced, pushing her down into the seat, her body feeling heavy for the first time in weeks.

Several of the downward facing cameras showed the ship's torch from three angles, while others focused on the moon's icy surface below. While the heat plume wasn't visible as it brushed across the ice, the effect was easy to see.

For a moment the ice seemed to ripple underneath the descending ship, undulating like water. Then a blast of steam exploded as the frozen surface instantly transitioned from solid state to gaseous. The shockwaves bucked the *Javelin*, slewing the ship to the side as the torch and expanding gas fought against one another.

"Nothing to worry about, everyone," Flynn said over the shipnet's general channel. "We planned for this."

Three seconds after she spoke the torch shortened, the burn decreasing in intensity, lateral thrusters firing to move the ship away from the deep trough it had blasted to a safer landing zone. Though it was larger than Luna, Europa was less massive, and its 0.13 gravity tugged lightly at the ship easing it closer at a little over one point three meters per second per second.

"Fusion burner offline," Jamie said as they triggered another sequence. "Compensating for gravitational acceleration with conventional thrusters. Holding at five meters per second."

"Two minutes to touchdown. Stay sharp, everyone."

"I really expected you to say, 'stay frosty'," Frankie chimed in with a laugh. "Total missed opportunity."

"That was a deliberate choice."

"Wrong one if you ask me."

Flynn pursed her lips in annoyance. "Just make sure your rig is ready to go."

The man laughed again, and Flynn turned her attention to the navigational display. The landing site that Haskell's people had selected was only a kilometer away, growing steadily closer as the *Javelin* reached the terminus of its journey.

"Ready to deploy struts on your mark," Carol said. "Gimme the good word."

"The word is given," Flynn replied, pulling up a trio of camera views from halfway up the ship's four-hundred meter hull. At first there was nothing but the view of the moon sliding by below. But then three two-hundred-meter shafts separated from the *Javelin*. The tops remained connected to the hull, sliding downward on rails as the bottom ends moved further out from the vessel, stopping when each stretched one hundred and sixty meters from the engines creating a massive tripod.

Not many ships took up over three hundred meters of surface when they touched down, but when the goal was to drill dozens of kilometers into a worldlet, a solid foundation was a must.

"What's that?" Leon asked over the shipnet, disrupting Flynn's reverie. He attached a feed which showed a plume of mist rising above the horizon.

For a moment, Flynn thought it was the *Parson* making its descent, but Carol responded, putting that fear to rest.

"It's a cryogeyser," the engineer said. "Didn't you read the research data?"

"Uhh…yeah. Totally did. I just didn't think they'd be so big. If this thing is blasting water into space, why are we bother drilling down to the ocean? Can't they just sample that shit?"

"Huh…" Vern grunted in mock confusion. "Yeah, you'd think that the hundreds of scientists working outposts on the surface would have thought of that. Weird how they didn't try that."

"The cryos don't all blast water from the ocean. Most of it is from pockets in the ice that melt due to tidal forces," Flynn explained. "No one has ever detected any signs of life in them beyond some basic amino acids, but it's not enough to be conclusive. We're the team that's going to find out if there's life down there one way or another."

"Just as long as we get paid all the bonuses," Leon said. "Though the view is a pretty nice reward, too."

Flynn nodded silently. It was a gorgeous scene, though the ominous orb of Jupiter hanging overhead was a little unnerving. She'd touched down on the Gals before, and it had always felt like the planet was about to crash down into the surface.

"Touchdown in ten seconds." Jamie's lips twisted into a wry smile. "You know…if anyone cares about that."

"I care," Vern said. "As much as I love riding bug-mode, I'm ready for this to be over."

The captain didn't bother responding and the ship touched down a moment later.

"Okay, folks," Flynn began with a cautionary tone. "Give it a minute before getting out of your harnesses, we just dropped a hundred and fifty thousand tons on this ice ball. It might have something to say about that."

A vibration shimmied through the ship emphasizing her point. It was minor, and when none followed over the next minute, she gave the all-clear.

The crew leapt into action without a moment's hesitation. It was time for the *Javelin* to live up to her name.

"Spinning up the beam," Carol announced. "Ready to start cutting."

The seismometers didn't show anything beyond the normal background activity on Europa, and Flynn gave her the signal to commence.

Three more cameras came on, each mounted on one of the tripod struts, all focused on the long bulge at the bottom of the ship next to the engines. The protective cover on the end slid aside, revealing the business end of the *Javelin's* main drilling apparatus, a pulse laser with an output exceeding ten zeta joules, not that they ran it at that level very often—or for very long.

"Take it easy to start, we don't want any catastrophic superheating…or not too much," Flynn advised.

"Think so?" Carol asked with a hint of derision in her tone. "Could be fun."

Flynn didn't respond, but she did note that the engineer dialed back the laser's output by thirty percent before activating it. No visible light showed on the cameras, but the powerful blast of steam pouring off the surface of the ice showed that the beam was doing its job.

"We're at the first landing strut," Leon announced, and Flynn switched her view to show the two men in their powered EV suits standing next to one of the ten-meter wide landing pads. "It's sunk a bit into the ice," he added, gesturing at the shards protruding around the pad. "Only about a meter, though. Not bad, all things considered."

"Benefits of low-g," Vern chimed in. "We're ready to bore the first anchor."

"Have at it," the captain said. "Carol's just hollowing out the first fifty meters for the pocket, not precision work."

"You got it." Leon waved at the nearest camera, before he and Vern pulled a manual release on the landing strut. A cover opened, revealing a drill larger than both of them. It didn't take long in the low gravity for them to position the drill over an opening in the landing pad and begin their work.

Once the holes—four per pad—were drilled at least fifty meters deep, they would lower the anchor pipes into place. The pipes would slowly expand, then send long nanospears into the ice, ensuring that the ship didn't shift out of position.

She expected it would take them about two hours to anchor all three pads into the ice and by then Carol would have the pocket bored out.

Then the real work would begin.

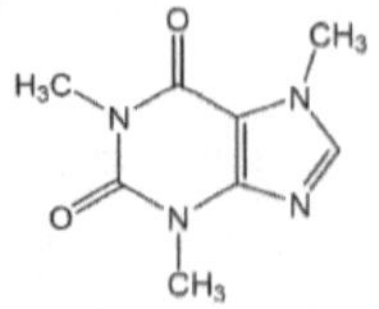

"Swing that next sheath into place!" Leon ordered. "We're going to need it in just a minute."

"You got it," Vern replied. "Frankie, where's the next batch?"

"It's still spooling off the printer. This isn't like drilling through our usual rocks, ice melts a lot easier."

"No shit, Sherlock," came Vern's retort. "I hadn't noticed."

Flynn rolled her eyes, sharing a tired look with Jamie. "Easy everyone. We've done amazing work hitting ten kilometers so fast. You two need to swap suits soon, you've likely picked up too many rads out there hanging out in Jupiter's plasma sheet and all. What say once we get this next sheath in, we take a breather. "

"Really?" Jamie's eyes widened as the engineering and boring crews sent their acknowledgements over the shipnet. "After the race to touch down, digging a trench in the moon with our torch?"

The captain leant back in her chair and shrugged. "Well, the *Parson* is still ten hours from hitting ice and things are going well. There's no way they'll beat us to the ocean down there. Also, I'm pretty sure they won't be able to sheathe the shaft as effectively as we do. They're going to deal with way more steam coming back up the hole, refracting the beam."

"Are you sure?" they asked. "The *Parson's* fabricator could have gotten an upgrade."

"Maybe, but Haskell's people patented the sheath we're using, and it's drawing steam up the sides of the shaft even better than they predicted. At this rate we'll finish our bore just a couple hours after they touch down."

"Way to jinx it, Captain."

"I don't believe in jinxing."

They gave her a measuring stare. "Sure you don't. I've seen you touch wood before."

"It's wood. People touch it all the time."

"Mmmmhmmm…I—wait…comm signal just hit our mast."

"Haskell? I just beamed out an update to him, he won't have even received it yet."

The pilot shook his head. "Local origin. Bounced off one of the Jovian sats. Realtime."

"Bring it up."

The cockpit's central display flipped from beam intensity readouts to the image of a man whose face was barely discernable behind what Flynn liked to think of as a 'fuck off' beard.

"Are you Captain Flynn Ryse?" he asked without preamble.

"I am," she said with a curt nod. "Who, may I ask, are you?"

"Gerome Billings of the Far Nine research institute, we run a research station about fifty kilometers from your ill-advised drill site."

Flynn shared a look with Jamie before responding. "I assume your use of 'ill advised' means that you disagree with where we're drilling. I assure you, individuals very familiar with Europa's—"

"It's not where, that I disagree with," he interrupted, his face reddening as he spoke. "It's that you're drilling at all. Europa's ocean is a pristine world, not something that we should be spoiling. Why do you think that after all these years no one has seen fit to drill through?"

"I figured it was because no one had the stones to fly a rig big enough this far out to melt their way through thirty-five klicks of ice."

She didn't mean for the statement to come off as haughtily as it did, but she wasn't sorry about it.

"Far Nine has filed a formal complaint with the Jovian Authority. We expect them to side with us and order a cessation of your operation, so you should save your resources and just stop now."

Flynn didn't bother to hide the laugh that burst free at the man's statement. "Oh…we should just stop now on account of something you just filed that may not even get voted on before we're done."

"All the more reason for you to stop."

The *Javelin's* captain shook her head. "Nope. The way I see it, that's all the more reason for us to keep drilling and get the job done before someone fucks up my schedule."

"You can't," his tone took on a note of pleading. "You're going to ruin it forever."

"Look Gerome." Flynn folded her arms across her chest. "Someone is eventually going to sink a hole through this ice and into the ocean below. That someone may not have a rig like the *Javelin* that can do it safely. They also might not have the systems in place to ensure no cross contamination occurs. With that in mind, it's really best that we do it and do it now. Tomlinson is a trustworthy and conscientious company. The next people that get permission might not be."

The man's face reddened further, and he opened his mouth to speak, but then seemed to think better of it and simply terminated the transition.

Jamie whistled. "Wow. He was…insistent."

"There's always someone," she replied. "They don't seem to get that progress is going to happen no matter what. The how of the matter is the only thing we can really control—and even then not as well as we'd like to think."

"Think they'll cause us any trouble?" they asked.

"Probably not?" Flynn shrugged. "I mean…what are they going to do? Come out here and attack us? Far Nine is a research thinktank organization. I doubt they even have a security team at their facility."

The pilot's brow rose. "How much you want to bet on that?"

"Fuck." She rose in the microgravity and half pushed, half leapt toward the back of the cockpit.

"Where are you going?"

"To open up the weapons locker. You know, just in case I'm wrong I want to have the firepower to be right."

A laugh came from behind her. "Solid plan, Captain."

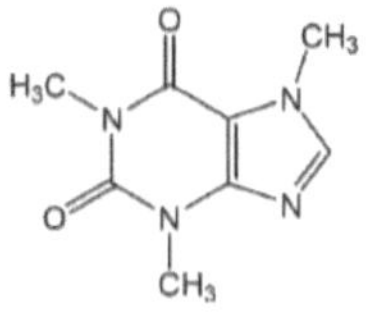

An hour later, the drilling had resumed with no sign of any eco-protesters on the horizon—not that the horizon was very far away on a tiny ball like Europa.

Even so, Flynn had released one of the ship's drones to perform a slow circumference of the site, keeping a robotic eye peeled for any incoming visitors. She'd also equipped Vern and Leon with sidearms before sending them back out.

They'd given her questioning looks, but she assured them that any disruption was a remote possibility.

It better fucking be.

Everything remained quiet for the next five hours, the ship's crew working like a well-oiled machine as they bored ever deeper into the ice. Flynn was idly flipping through the public comm channels listening for any chatter that posed a threat to the operation when a sharp vibration rippled through the ship.

"Shit." She gripped her chair's arm rests. "Leon! What the—"

Her question was interrupted by a series of blasts followed by a long groan.

"We hit a pocket of something!" Leon called up. "Slammed us with steam and ice. There's shit everywhere."

"My ship?"

"It's a mess. The ship got pelted pretty hard."

Flynn rose from her seat. "I'm coming out." She bounded to the ladder shaft and began clambering down the rungs, calling for Jamie to get out of bed on the way past the crew quarters.

"You have the conn, Jamie! We've an all hands situation. I'm going EV."

"Uhh? Yeah. Sure. On my way." They barely sounded awake, but that would have to do.

The ship had automatically sealed the inner airlock door in response to the seismic activity and she waited an agonizing thirty seconds for it to cycle back open again.

The ship's general channel was buzzing with crew crosstalk. Carol and Frankie reporting on ships systems and Leon giving updates on what was going on outside—which wasn't much since clouds of ice blanketed the area.

She didn't pester them for any further details, right now the crew would do their best without the captain micromanaging them.

She squeezed through the airlock door as soon as it opened, leaping across the small room to pull open the nearest EV locker.

Like any good spacer, she always wore a fitted thermal-compressive base layer. Not only did it mean she'd have less to put on in the event of a hull breach, the pressure mimicked the effects of gravity on her body and reduced zero-g degradation.

Boots and gloves were first, then she snatched a fishbowl helmet off the rack. It mated to a collar around her neck. She turned toward the outer airlock door before remembering she hadn't grabbed an air tank.

Not wanting to waste time, she palmed the outer door control before pulling on the tank. She set the system to do an emergency purge and the 'lock purged from normal pressure to vacuum in a matter of seconds.

"Heading out," she announced. "Where are you now, Leon?"

"Far side of the ship. Edge of the crater. I—"

"What is it?"

"I can't find Vern." There was anguish in the man's voice.

A second later the outer door opened. Outside was a small platform two-hundred meters above the moon's surface, above, a guy-wire ran from hard mount on the hull to an anchor driven into the ice a hundred meters from the *Javelin*.

She grabbed a cable climber and clipped it on the line. Europa's gravity would take too long to pull her down, so Flynn activated the device, turning the knob to max speed. She all but flew down the wire, reaching the ground in no time.

Only once her boots were on ice, did she turn to survey the scene.

"Oh fuck," she whispered in the confines of her helmet.

Chunks of ice were strewn around the base of the ship, several dents visible in the hull where flying debris had impacted the *Javelin*.

My engines better be okay….

The cloud of ice particles was finally beginning to settle, and she spotted Leon. It didn't take long to circumnavigate the ship to where he stood at the edge of the wide pocket Carol had initially bored out.

"Anything?" she asked.

The man's powered armor masked any body language, but his response conveyed what the suit obscured. "No. He's not anywhere around the base. Either he got flung a long ways away or he's down there."

Flynn leant over the edge, her lips thinning as she took in the shards of ice mixed with twisted sheaths.

Fuck.

"Jamie. Launch more drones, Vern is missing. He might have been flung wide."

"On it!"

"I'm going down," Leon said after a moment.

She stepped in front of him, staring up at his tinted faceplate. "Like hell you are. Even in what passes for gravity on this moon, your suit's too heavy. You could bring it all down on Vern if he's under all that. I have a better idea."

"What is it?"

"Carol?" she asked on the general channel. "I need a batch of tunnel crawlers launched yesterday. Vern's missing and we think he might be in the pocket."

"What?! In the poc—okay we're on it."

Thirty seconds later Jamie's aerial drones launched, four white globes streaking out of a compartment on the upper hull. On the bottom of the ship, another panel opened, and a dozen crawlers fell out, dropping onto the ice below.

"Those things give me the heebies," Leon muttered.

Flynn felt the same way. The crawlers resembled very large centipedes and seemed to trigger some sort of primal fear in a lot of people. Despite that, they were highly effective when it came to seeking things out in tight spaces.

With the search and rescue underway, Flynn took a moment to review the data from the drilling operation and what the ship's seismic sensors had picked up.

It was clear that the beam had punched into a pressurized pocket that lay fourteen kilometers beneath the surface. It should have been detected by the Tomlinson team that mapped out the area. It was possible that a new pocket could have developed since the survey team had done their work, but that seemed unlikely.

One upside was that the explosion had fed a ton of sonar data into the sensors. Liquid pockets beneath the surface slowed and reflected the shock waves differently from the solid sections. If there were more, they now had the data to spot them.

The ship's computer was already building an updated map and when Flynn loaded the data onto her ocular HUD a wave of dismay hit her.

There were at least three more large pockets of water below the ship.

"Found him!" Jamie's shout startled Flynn. "He's three hundred meters northwest of us. I've dropped a marker on your nav map."

Flynn didn't even have time to respond before Leon was bounding across the ice in the direction Jamie had indicated. With both his powered armor and his lead he got there first, but she wasn't far behind.

Vern was in one of the small gullies that crisscrossed the moon's surface. Some were mere depressions in the ice while others were full of ice spears. This was one of the latter.

Flynn sucked in a breath as she caught sight of her crewmember. A spear protruded through Vern's abdomen. Blood smeared the ice shaft, but none was leaking out of the suit which had sealed itself with puncture foam.

"Vern!" She called out as Leon knelt beside the other man, looking underneath to see if there were any other wounds.

There was no response and she clambered down into the gully and touched her helmet to his. "Vern? Can you hear me?" She shouted the word loud enough for the vibrations to carry from her helmet to his, holding it there, praying for a response.

"Fuck, Captain," his muffled words passed into her helmet. "I'm right here. You don't have to yell."

"What's your status?"

"Other than being skewered like a pig at a feast? Well, comms and transponder are offline. Surprised you found me so fast. I must be close to the ship."

"Three hundred meters, give or take."

A laugh preceded his response. "Okay, so not close."

"Well…in the grand scheme of things…."

"Is he alive?" Leon demanded.

"He is," she replied, glancing up. "Is that ice still connected to the ground?"

"No. We can lift him free."

"Vern. You got pain suppressors going?"

"To the max."

"OK, we're going to lift you out of here. I think we'll leave your new piercing in for now. Better to take it out on the ship."

A long groan came from the injured man. "Fuuuuck. Okay, let's get this over with."

They carefully lifted Vern out of the gully, slowly bounding in time across the Europan surface back to the ship. When they arrived, Frankie was riding the lift down to the ground.

"How's he look?"

"Like he lost a fight with an ice cream cone," Leon muttered. "Badly."

"Thanks for the assist," Flynn said as they carefully stepped onto the lift.

It was little more than a platform with a single railing and Flynn held onto the side while gripping Vern's arm. The last thing they needed was for him to fly off in an aftershock.

The next few hours were tense.

Jamie worked the autodoc to get Vern stabilized while Frankie and Leon cleared the debris below the ship in order to assess the damage to the shaft. Carol and Beth went EV as well, going over the engines with a fine-tooth comb.

Three hours later, the crew reconvened in the galley, everyone but Vern crowded around the table, expressions sober and voices muted.

"Alright, people. First thing's first. Jamie, how's Vern doing?"

"He'll live," they replied. "But repairing his organs is far beyond what our doc can do. I have him in a coma while nano infusions are doing the jobs of the bits he's missing."

Flynn ran a hand through her hair. "How long can you keep him like that?"

The pilot shrugged. "It's going to depend on a lot of factors. I'd say a week tops, then we'll need to get him to the closest facility that can do this sort of work."

"No one on Europa can?" Beth asked. "That seems nuts. There must be fifty outposts here."

"Yeah," Flynn nodded. "I'm going to have you assist Jamie in finding where we can take him. If it's close, we might be able to take him on the pinnace."

Jamie passed her an uncertain look. "I don't know about that. I wouldn't pull him off the autodoc for that long."

"Okay. Fair." She heaved a sigh. "Carol, how's my girl looking?"

"Well, the engine bells took a beating. The valves to the combustion chamber were closed, so everything's external. We'll be able to patch everything up in a few days, but we can't flex the main engine bells till we get a more thorough refit, so no atmospheric before that."

"Noted. Nothing else?" Flynn asked.

"Some dings and dents. I'm going to have the bots crawl over them looking for fractures, but I don't think it'll be a big deal. The *Javelin's* a tough old bitch."

"Fuck she is." Flynn turned to Frankie. "What's the word down below?"

"Well, the sleeves are all trashed, both the ones in the shaft and the ones that were in the pocket. We've cleared the debris away, so the pocket's clear, but the shaft is hopelessly fouled. I think we should angle the beam and drill parallel to this shaft."

"Great." Flynn found herself running her hand through her hair again and abruptly pulled it down to her side. "So we're basically starting from scratch, and that's not the half of it."

"Seriously?" Carol's brows rose. "What the fuck else could go wrong."

Frankie met Flynn's gaze and she could tell that he'd read the seismic data as well.

"There are more pockets like this one below," he said, saving Flynn from reporting the bad news. "At least three."

Leon shook his head in disgust. "Well fuck. We're gonna have to fracture the shit out of this ice…which means we'll need to drill from two sites."

"And our remote drill can't hit these depths," Frankie added. "Captain…this just turned into a three week job."

She'd already estimated it at four. "Yeah. So much for Tomlinson's seismologists."

"And what about the *Parson*?" Jamie asked. "If her site is better, she might get right through."

Flynn turned her palms up and shrugged. "Maybe it is, maybe it's not. Could be this whole fucking ice crust is full of these pockets."

Carol leant back in her seat, giving Flynn an appraising look.

"What?" The captain didn't bother hiding the annoyance in her voice.

"Well…the way to get this done in anything short of a seven-day is two drills, right?"

"We just went over that," Frankie muttered. "Keep up."

The engineer shot him a withering look. "The reason you think I'm behind you is because I lapped you. Look. There's only one other rig this side of the asteroid belt that can hit those depths. What if we team up with the *Parson*?"

The room fell silent, everyone looking at Carol, then four pairs of eyes swiveled to look at the captain.

"Huh." She tapped a finger against her lips. "I'll have to review our contract to see if there's any language that would keep us from doing that. Plus…I'd have to convince Blair. She's not prone to being especially agreeable."

"But she doesn't all out hate you, at least." Frankie winked. "There's that."

"Jury's still out, to be honest. But, it's worth a shot."

"They're close," Jamie said. "Maybe two hours out. From what I can see their trajectory will put them about three hundred klicks from here."

"So they could settle down closer without too much trouble." Carol nodded, eyes aglow. "This could work."

"What about all that rah rah about being first?" Leon asked. "How no one remembers the second ship that did something."

Flynn flashed a smile at the man. "I think I have an idea for that."

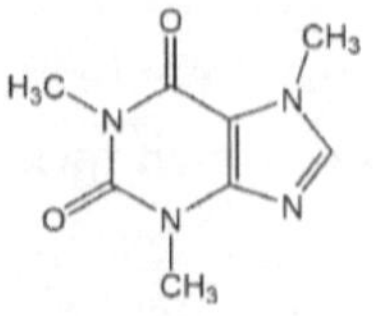

Flynn flexed her hand, going over what she was going to say one more time, before she activated the comm system, routing a message through the Jovian comm sat network to the *Parson*.

The ship was close enough that the connection only had a half-second of light lag. She sent an initial text greeting along with the message, then waited for a response. It only took three minutes, during which she reconsidered her course of action at least nine times.

When a voice came over the comm system she was deep in thought, and it took her a moment to respond.

"This is Captain Selma, am I speaking to Captain Flynn of the *Javelin*?"

Her voice carried notes of both annoyance and curiosity, though a little more of the former.

"Uh…yes, this is Flynn. Selma, I thought you were the *Parson's* first mate. What happened to Blair?"

"Retired." Selma replied. "She sold the *Parson* to me…well, me and my creditors."

Flynn's eyes widened. "Shit. I didn't think she'd ever give up the black."

"Rads. She's just soaked too many of them over the years, it was starting to take its toll."

It was the fate of all old spacers. The void was awash with radiation, and over time even the best medical advances failed to slow the ravages of space.

"I hope she enjoys her dirtside years."

"Yeah. I'm sure she will. Look, if you're trying to warn me off this job, don't bother. We're being paid a handsome amount to drill this hole, and by Jove's red eye, we're gonna do it."

Flynn chuckled, glancing out the window at Jupiter where the Great Red Spot was currently visible on the eastern horizon. "Nice one. I might steal that."

"Have at it. So, are we done here? You made your call, I told you to fuck off, shall we get on with our days?"

"Hold up." Flynn said, realizing she had to cut to the chase. "How many pressurized liquid pockets does your survey data show below fifteen kilometers?"

"Why? You looking for a better site?"

"I'll tell you what our survey data showed. None. We were supposed to have clear ice down to the ocean. Then we hit one and blew out our fucking shaft. The explosion gave us a good picture of what else is down there."

"And what did you find?" Selma's tone had changed. It contained a hint of worry.

"Well, there are three pockets right beneath our rig, and dozens more all around. I don't know that we can find a site that has a straight shot."

"And I'm just supposed to believe this?"

Flynn sighed. As frustrating as Selma was being, she knew that in the other woman's place, she would behave the same. "I'm sending you a data packet. It's all the seismic data we picked up after the explosion."

The *Parson's* captain took almost a full minute to respond. "Okay. Let's say I buy all this. It's going to take you weeks to break through—unless you seriously upgraded your mobile unit since last I laid eyes on your rig."

"I wish I had, but you're right. I'm looking at three to four weeks. Thing is, so are you. Spending a month on this rock paying our crews full hazard eats a big chunk of my profits. What about you?"

"Can't say I'm excited about the idea."

Flynn allowed a smile to form on her lips. Selma wasn't as pig-headed as Blair had been. She just might come around. "Well, my contract allows for subcontractors to work under me—"

"I'm not subcontracting to you." Selma interrupted.

"I'd never ask you to."

"Good. Glad we got that sorted out. What exactly are you proposing?"

Flynn bit back a retort about not interrupting to find out faster. "Well, it also has clauses about how my contract survives a purchase by another interest. I'm curious if yours does as well."

"I'm going to keep that to myself for now but carry on outlining this hairbrained scheme. I'm curious where it's going."

"Well…If your contract also has the same stipulations, an entity could buy both our rigs, then it would hold the agreements with Tomlinson and whoever hired you. I'm guessing that's Far Nine, by the way."

"Huh." Selma didn't acknowledge Flynn's guess, though she Flynn could practically hear the other captain thinking through the nuances of the proposal. "Then this new interest would provide the samples and data to both our contract holders at the same time and both our ships hit ocean first."

"Exactly. I mean…you can take your chances with running your own shaft blasting ice into your engines or we can do this together."

"Well, we have an offset drill, so that's less of an issue."

"You know what I mean. What do you say?"

Selma laughed. "So impatient! Let me go over my contract and have a think."

"Well don't think too long, you're on approach soon."

"Don't worry about me. I know how to fly a rig. *Parson* out."

"Acknowledged."

Flynn leant back in her seat, gaze flicking up to the massive planet overhead. "Give me a little luck, Jove. I could use it right about now."

The implacable planet offered no insight into what Selma would decide. Only time would tell.

Three days later, Flynn settled in front of the desk in her cabin mentally reviewing what to say before recording her message to Haskell Tomlinson.

"Hello, sir. I'm pleased to inform you that we have punched through the ice and have drawn samples from the ocean at four separate depths. Preliminary analysis of those samples is complete, and the detailed analysis is being sent along with this transmission."

"The short version is that there's life. We've found both viruses and phages. There might be bacteria as well, it will take more samples. We think that there may be more life on the ocean floor where it's warmer. Finding out would be another contract though."

"Per our contract, we'll honor the six month moratorium on releasing this information to any non-affiliate parties.'

"I'm sure you've heard that Captain Silva of the *Parson* jointly formed a corporation with me. That corporation inherited the contracts for the drilling and our teams subcontracted to the corporation. We're also sending our report to the organization that contracted her—Far Nine, as you likely know."

"I remain optimistic that this won't upset. Drilling this alone would have taken weeks, given that the data the seismic team provided on the ice crust was woefully incomplete. In that scenario, it's likely that the *Parson* would have beat us—so long as they didn't meet with calamity as well. Luckily for all of us, they weren't willing to take that risk."

"The OuterSol Mining Corporation has enjoyed doing business with you and looks forward to future contracts with you for the services of our prospecting and drilling fleet."

It's done. She let out a long sigh and initiated a Link connection to Selma.

"Mine's sent. What about you?"

"On its way." Selma sounded relieved. "Granted, I'll probably hear from my side sooner since they're only fifty klicks away."

"They all better be happy with the results," Flynn did her best to sound stern, but a hint of worry filtered through.

Selma's laugh came back in response. "There's nothing they can do, and since we registered this site with the Jovian Authority, if they want more samples, they're going to have to come to us."

"You're right. And we both know they'll want more."

"Vern is doing well, by the way. Our autodoc shows that he should be conscious in a day."

Flynn blew out a long breath, glad that the drilling solution also presented an opportunity to get Vern the medical care he needed without having to spend more than thirty minutes in transport.

"That's the best news I've heard all day!" she said.

"So, we need a drink to celebrate, should we meet at my place or yours?"

Flynn had only known Selma for a few days, but she was starting to feel like they might be long-lost sisters. "I've been in your ship's galley,"

Flynn replied, chuckling aloud. "Come on over here. Bring your crew. We'll have a celebratory feast."

"Feast?" Selma let out a delighted laugh. "Oh you're on."

"It'll be our first corporate dinner. Harbinger of an amazing future."

"I'll drink—and eat a chicken—to that."

Flynn ended the transmission and leant back in her seat, smiling up at the overhead. Big things were on the horizon for Europa, and she would be at the center of it.

"Time to make my mark."

We hope that you enjoyed this title and look forward to many more to come. Please, leave us a review! Reviews matter to all of our authors.

Take a look at some of our other award-winning series at https://threeravenspublishing.com/series-universes/

Visit us at https://www.threeravenspublishing.com and sign up for our newsletter for the latest and greatest news on upcoming titles and events.

Other series and titles you might enjoy.

DECLAN FINN
DECLAN FINN
DECLAN FINN DECLAN FINN
Demons are Forever
Honor at Stake
Live and Let Bite
Good to the Last Drop
The Dragon Award Nominated Series
FREE on Kindle Unlimited!

MYSTERY, MAGIC & MAYHEM
WITH A TWIST OF ROMANCE
J.F. POSTHUMUS
ON AMAZON
FIND ME

B.E.N.T.
BIOLOGIC   ENHANCED   NASCENT   TALENT

THE RAVEN
AND
THE CROW
MICHAEL K. FALCIANI
FIND ME
ON AMAZON

STARFLIGHT

IT CAME FROM THE
TRAILER PARK

You can also keep up to date with our latest release announcements on Scifi.radio and get some of the best fandom programing on the planet.

Scifi for your Wifi

And don't forget to check out our other Sponsors and Affiliates

A southern Appalachian jewel for craft beer lovers, Buck Bald Brewing offers something for everyone. With delicious, locally brewed beverages from across the spectrum, Buck Bald Brewing offers craft brews that are consistently amazing.

From the dark and smooth Shesquatch Scottish ale, to the intense hops of Hippibilly IPA, to the puckering sour of the blackberry and cinnamon in Berry My Heart at the Trailer Park, and more than 60+ rotating brews, you'll find what you're looking for and more.

With smiling faces behind the bar ready to help you find your next favorite brew, a constantly rotating selection of delicious craft beverages, toe-tapping tunes always playing, and the biggest games on TV, you can kick your feet up in either Copperhill, Tennessee or Murphy, North Carolina and immerse yourself in the Buck Bald Brewing experience. So, come out, fill a pint, fill a growler, and fill your mind at your new favorite family-owned craft brewery.

To discover more visit us at buckbaldbrewing.com or follow us on Facebook @buckbaldbrewing and @buckbaldbrewingmurphy.

Vesper Wren's
TRAILER PARK
PIXIE
PUNCH
A PEACH STRAWBERRY SELTZER
BUCK BALD BREWING

And don't forget to check out the latest edition of *Car Wars*

http://www.sjgames.com/car-wars/

Or the other amazing titles from
Steve Jackson Games

http://www.sjgames.com

...or the latest in the Car Warriors: Autoduel Chronicle fiction series.
https://threeravenspublishing.com/car-warriors-autoduel-chronicles/

Comprised of active or retired servicemen and civilian volunteers, Shepherd's Men enthusiastically raises awareness and funds for the SHARE Military Initiative (SHARE) at Shepherd Center in Atlanta, GA.

This nationally renowned program focuses on assessment and treatment for American military veterans who have sustained mild to moderate Traumatic Brain Injury (TBI) and Post-Traumatic Stress Disorder (PTSD) during post-9/11 service.

Find out more at: https://www.shepherdsmen.com/